Nelson & Leviasa.

Arise, Awake, Pray!!

THE
COALITION

THE
COALITION

A NOVEL

LTG (R) JERRY BOYKIN

AND

KAMAL SALEEM

Post Hill
PRESS

This book is dedicated to:

The men and women who have and will answer the call.

If ever the Time should come, when vain and aspiring Men shall possess the highest Seats in Government, our Country will stand in Need of its experienced Patriots to prevent its Ruin

—Samuel Adams: Letter to James Warren,
October 24, 1780

ACKNOWLEDGMENTS

KAMAL SALEEM

Life's luster is found in the presence of love, laughter, and friendship; all of which my wife has given me. To my partner who, for better or for worse, for richer or for poorer, in sickness and in health, has stood by my side and made me a better man.

Family forms a bond that makes life richer. To the members of the Koome Team, my family, who have made our ministry thrive. To each of whom have filled in the words I cannot say, guarded my steps, and held me up along the way.

Those who stand by my side, who have fought for our cause, and held strong with us against all adversity, you are some of God's greatest gifts. To our close friends, supporters, and intercessors; I wouldn't have made it without you. (Jeremiah 51:20-23).

LTG (R) JERRY BOYKIN

I could never be a complete success at anything without the love of my best friend in life, my wife, Ashley, who is the toughest warrior on the battlefield. And a special thanks goes out to the real General Sam, a ninety-one-year-old icon and mentor, but most importantly a very good friend.

We would both like to thank the great folks at Post Hill Press. Anthony Ziccardi and Michael Wilson have been encouraging and supportive since receiving our proposal and it's been a pleasure to work with them. Thanks also to Bobbie Metevier and Matthew Baugh for their valuable editorial work on the manuscript.

Are the myriad life paths traversed by mankind
ordered or beaten by every decisive step?

A LLAH, HELP ME! was Omar's desperate prayer when he heard the first shout from the gang of Armenian boys who would surely give him another thrashing. Throwing his lunch in their general direction, hoping it would appease or at least slow them down, he took off in a dead run down the sidewalk.

Over the pounding of ten pairs of feet, Omar heard the shouts of, "Get him . . . grab him . . . hurry!" They were gaining on him.

Faster . . . must run faster . . .

Omar's tremulous eyes scanned the block ahead hoping to find a safe haven into which he could duck. A shop run by an Armenian would be of no help; they'd simply turn him over to his pursuers.

He made the mistake of turning his head to see how close his tormentors were. The act slowed his pace slightly, but it also made him blind to the way ahead. He swiveled back just in time to avoid a full speed collision with a local shopkeeper. From behind, he heard, "Stop him, Farouge!"

Before he could get around the human obstacle, a hand caught him by the collar and his feet lost contact with concrete. The arresting hand kept him from violently reengaging the sidewalk. *Now what . . .*

"What has he done," asked Farouge.

The apparent alpha male of the pack, bigger and older than the others said, "He stole my umbrella."

Dangling from Omar's wrist by a strap was his father's best umbrella, one he'd pled to use, as rain threatened the day and his walk to work. He threw his head left and right casting the mournful look of a victim to his captor . . . to no avail.

After moving Omar toward the wolves, Farouge released his grip on his shirt and said, "Take it easy; don't hurt him." On that he wheeled and reentered his cobbler shop.

With a motion from the leader, two of the boys grabbed Omar by his arms and the others closed in to pat him down for anything of value.

"I have no money, but I get paid in a few days if . . . "

"Shut up you son of a whore, your whining is not going to save you." With that the Armenian teenager delivered as hard a blow to Omar's gut as he could generate. Omar's body was evacuated of all air as he crumbled to the pavement. Before he could recover enough to get a breath, a square-toed boot came in with enough force to cause his nose to spray blood in an arching pattern a foot from his face.

Through the roar of pain in his head, Omar heard the familiar click of a knife being opened. The same knife he heard the last time he'd been set upon by this gang. That time, thanks to the intervention of a neighborhood lady, he escaped with a cut on his hand. She was not at her balcony this time, so he was likely to come out far worse now.

Allah, is this how you look out for your servant? Will I die here with no hope of jannah? Will you not help me conquer these, your enemies?

. . .

So you see, my sons, even the most sinful man is able to redeem himself with one drop of an infidel's blood." The words and even the voice of his mother mingled with Omar's sight and fear as he stood on the last safe street corner between him and his workplace. He was running late, again, so this route was the only hope he had of reporting to his job on time. Going around the three contiguous neighborhoods was his normal way to work and it kept him from being pummeled.

Though only seven, he was already well schooled in Islam and aspired to the day when he would wield the sword of Jihad and destroy the enemies of Allah. This street corner seemed worlds from that dream. Here, he was small, young, and helpless against the gangs of boys, most of whom were older, patrolling the streets in the Armenian section just across the street, the Kurdish after that, and then the Shi'a enclave.

The last group troubled Omar most. He found it hard to understand how other servants of Allah could be his tormentors. His mother told him about how they were Sunnis and more favored by the Prophet than the Shiites, but his young mind couldn't quite gain purchase. What he did understand, was what would happen if he was caught in their neighborhood.

What made his situation most bleak was he could not go to his father for help. In fact, if he failed to go to work after being caught in the gauntlet he now faced, his father would likely apply another layer of welts. His early memories of his father reflected warmth and attention. Over the last year, however, he'd become surly and seemed only interested in the money Omar brought from work. His memory flashed back and became alive like it was yesterday. His father's words were running in his head: "You are not good enough, Omar, to be a boy. You are stupid. I wish you were a girl . . . I could have gotten rid of you! But I am stuck with you . . . You are good for nothing but to work." His words cut through Omar's heart worse than a million daggers or any Armenian ill will.

His mother on the other hand would be sympathetic, but unfortunately that would not come between him and his father's wrath, and she was pregnant again. As in every other part of his home life, Mother was subservient, which was another conflict his young mind had trouble parsing since she did most of the teaching from the Quran and *Hadith* in their home. As far back as he could remember, he was taught from the al-Bukhari *Hadith* about Muhammad of Islam, all women and girls in his family were created as less, as half of a man; woman has only half the brain of a man, which is why Satan so easily fooled Eve in the Garden. He was told more than once they were only created by Allah to serve men.

He remembered the recent lesson he was taught about the reward awaiting the warrior of Jihad who died while spilling the blood of Allah's enemies. Seventy-two virgins of jannah and thousands of servants tasked with the singular mission of service to the *shahid* was at once exhilarating and confusing. In his innocence he asked if his mother would be attended by seventy-two male virgins when her time came. His father's derision was as scathing as was the slap. "Insolent boy! Never talk about your mother that way!"

Allah!

. . .

A BURLY MALE VOICE boomed from just outside the circle of thugs.

"Hey! What are you boys doing? Farouge, come see the mess they make."

With the boys distracted, a feral drive to survive had Omar on his feet and running through traffic to cross the street. The cobbler shop owner emerged and prevented pursuit as he upbraided the clutch of predators for defacing the front of his business with blood.

Three blocks later, Omar slowed and checked behind to see if he was being chased again.

Nothing.

He looked down to see an expanding splay of blood soaking his white work shirt which was made for him from a flour sack. More trouble loaded his future as he considered his mother's reaction at the sight of him. He removed his dark colored vest and mopped his aching face of blood and mucus. A quick assessment listed a broken nose, one eye swollen to a slit, a gash in his mouth, and a deep ache in his gut.

At least he still had his father's umbrella.

Triage took Omar a couple more blocks toward his work, a construction site for which his uncle won the plumbing contract.

As he was about to lift his head to get his bearings, a pair of boots appeared in his path. The frostbite of dread radiated shivers out from Omar's chest when he looked up to see Iskendar, the Kurdish section's most foul bully.

"What's wrong?" The question was delivered as though by a friend.

Omar stood frozen, confused by the teen's tone.

"I asked you a question. Tell me what happened. Where's your lunch?"

The shakedown begins . . . "I threw my lunch away."

"That's too bad. Give me your vest and umbrella."

"My vest you can have, but the umbrella is my father's. He'll hurt me if I come home without it."

"That's your problem," Iskendar declared as he snatched the umbrella from Omar's hand. "I think I'll let you keep the vest since it looks like you pulled it from a toilet."

The pounding of feet grew louder behind Omar, but he was too scared to turn around. Several pairs of hands grabbed him and pushed him through a door into the foyer of a stairwell as Iskendar lead the way.

As soon as he was backed against the ascending banister, Iskendar slapped Omar across the face so hard he was at once dazed and shocked at the eruption of fresh pain from his already- battered face. He tried to cover his head with upraised arms, but a couple of the pack climbed a few stairs and started kicking and punching him over the handrail and through the balusters.

Omar dropped to the tiled floor and, instantly, hands pulled his shoes from his feet and rifled his pockets looking for hidden money. When nothing of value was found on him, the shuffling of feet, laughter, and curses moved out through the door.

Omar curled into a ball and wept.

Allah, why are you punishing me? I am your slave. How can you stand by and let these infidels have at me?

Shoeless and hurting in every part of his body, Omar pushed up from the floor and staggered to the door. He peered through the smallest crack he could make between the door and jamb, he saw and heard nothing of the gang. He pushed the door open in increments until he could stick his head out to view down the other direction of the side-walk. There was no sign of his attackers.

Now what do I do? If I go home, I run the risk of getting second portions from the Kurds and Armenians before I get there. If I keep heading to my job, I have to get through the Shi'a neighborhood and its street gangs.

Oh well, one more beating is better than two.

Omar kept close to the buildings and tried to make as small a profile as possible. At each corner, he hunched and moved as quickly across the street as his unsteady legs and bare feet could manage. His peripheral vision was diminished by his swollen eye, but he scanned the way ahead to gain some notice before encountering danger.

This was his second pair of shoes lost to street dogs since being forced to leave school and take work with his uncle. Even though the ones just lost were handed down from his older brother and had holes in the soles, they at least held some of the wet and cold from the pavement at bay.

The realization hit, he was inside Shi'a domain. Fortunately, he neither heard nor saw any sign of yet another pack of wild boys. Omar quickly ducked into the nearest apartment building foyer for respite from the chill and to plot his next move.

Maybe I should head back home; I could get lucky and avoid the gangs since they probably think I'm gone for the day. But, if I make it home, I'll have to face my father when he gets home. He'll be greatly angered to discover I not only skipped a day's wages—such as they were—but I lost his prized umbrella. I wish I was smart like other boys; I could be sitting in a classroom and have lunch and two breaks. My dad would be honored by me and tell all his friends about me.

Omar could imagine his uncle sitting in his office glancing up at the wall clock every few minutes, marking increments of his lateness. He also considered how much later he would be if the Shi'a boys caught him, not to mentioned the abuse he would receive.

I must press on . . . may Allah grant me passage.

Allah, I expect evil from the infidel Christians and Jews, but I do not understand why you have allowed such cruelty on me from the Shiites. Are we not all followers of the Prophet, peace and blessings be upon him. I remember the prayers my grandmother taught me from the Quran 7:11 "We have set a barrier before them and a barrier behind them: We have blinded them, so they cannot see anything." *I pray this again, hoping for your protection according to your words in the Quran.*

Again, Omar peered through an ever-widening opening of a door to the sidewalk, pushing his pain and shivering back in his consciousness to make room in his senses to detect threat.

He slipped through the doorway, kept his shoulder to the building fronts and paced to safety. He made a block of progress before he heard the all too familiar laughter which to Omar's ears rang like the howls of approaching wolves.

Run!

"Get after him!"

Guttural fear and flight instinct pushed so much adrenaline through Omar's heart that he was running faster than he'd ever known. He was oblivious to his injuries and bare feet. The encroaching thunder of shoes on concrete behind him pushed him even harder.

He lowered his chin and pumped his arms like the drive links on a runaway locomotive. A block more and, as he slightly raised his head to navigate the intersection, he saw salvation in the walls of a Sunni mosque. Without breaking stride, Omar dashed across the street, causing an American car to screech to a halt inches from his churning legs. The gamble worked as the boy about to grab his collar had to pull up to avoid broadsiding the cursing driver's fender.

Omar's bare feet suddenly became a blessing as they allowed him to burst through the mosque doors and through the foyer. The dog pack would have to stop and remove their shoes before following.

When he entered the main hall, he was confronted by several men with long beards and dressed in the robes of imams, all but one.

"*Allah Yakhlikum*, Help me, please help me!"

"Stop him. He's a thief. He stole from my father's store!"

The evident leader of the band of predators continued to approach as he spoke. One of the robed men stepped up and pulled Omar behind him.

"He lies! I've been in no store, and I've stolen nothing from anyone," Omar explained.

With an almost eerie calm and quiet, the imam said, "What did he steal and who is your father? "

"He grabbed something off one of the shelves."

Before the cleric could fully turn to Omar, he had the white flags of his pockets out and his hands up as if ready to be searched.

The look on the faces of the men was more than enough to convince the attacking boys it was time to go.

"Let's get out of here . . . you've got to leave here sometime, you little bastard. We'll be waiting."

The voice coming from the man in the group not clothed in religious vestments projected like an iron bar. "If we even hear you've hurt this boy, you will be visited, and you will be fortunate to hobble away with just one broken leg."

The doors to the mosque shut out the dank glow and the rabid curs of the street.

The men took Omar back into the ablution room for a cleansing and to tend to his injuries. Never before had Omar felt such kindness and compassion from men. After their ministrations, he was given clean, though slightly oversized clothes.

When he started to collect the tattered and stained remains of his outfit, the man who leveled the threat earlier stopped him and said, "I think these should be burned, this part of your life is best left without reminder."

"But, I've already lost my shoes and my father's umbrella. If I come home without my clothes, I'll get an even worse beating."

"We'll take you home and explain things to your father; I think he might listen to us. On the way, we'll stop and talk with your Armenian and Kurd persecutors. We'll take care of the Shi'a boys later. I know their families"

"My name is Abu Hamza. I see a holy warrior in you. How would you like to start a new life under our protection and guidance?"

2

{ PITTSYLVANIA COUNTY, VA – 2020 }

B LAKE KERSHAW, CLAD in camo and equipped with all he needed to spend a couple days on the land of his childhood, hunting, crept to the tree bearing his stand. It took him weeks to pick the spot, attach his stand to the tree, and clear shooting lanes around his selected spot from which he fully expected to ambush the nice eight-pointer he had seen in the area. The anticipation leading to this day accumulated for years.

He was ready to leave this home when he joined the army, but the attachment between him and this land was like a bungee cord; time and distance only increased the tension. One of the bends in his military path made it impossible to return for a while, but now he could come and go without worrying about being discovered. Blake stopped to calculate the years that had passed since he'd last stalked whitetail through these woods, but then he quickly jettisoned that pursuit. Along that road crossed too many memory paths, which he did not want to be detoured down.

His mom moved from the property a few years earlier to Richmond with her second husband, a doctor. Though Blake could have no direct contact with his mom, he was able to keep tabs on her through one-way channels and by using field craft. One of the few good things about their separation was knowing how happy she was with her new mate and life.

Her husband's financial situation meant she didn't have to part with the land on which she and Blake's father built an almost idyllic life. It could have ended better, but she held no regrets or bitterness from her losses. The wisdom forged by a life of dependence on the Sovereign left little room for gangrenous baggage. With both Blake and his father gone, she wasn't quite sure why she loathed the thought of selling the eighty acres of Virginia woodland. She only visited the old home once a year in the spring. Even that wasn't really necessary since she arranged with a neighbor to keep an eye on the place and to perform routine maintenance in exchange for the use of a few acres for farming. The outlying property needed no such attention. The insurance and survivor benefits after her husband's death allowed her to clear the refinanced mortgage and pay the yearly taxes.

The last set of stills from Blake's Moultrie game camera, covering nearly 150 degrees and a hundred feet from his stand, had a couple shots of a big eight-point buck. Along with the big boy, shots were taken of several other bucks and quite a few does and fawns. The land lying fallow for so many years nurtured an explosion in the wildlife population. He might actually have to spring for the taxidermy fee this time.

Through a third party, Blake made arrangements with the supervising neighbor to hunt on the property this season. It seemed strange to pay to hunt on what was essentially his own land, but it insured he wouldn't be disturbed and his anonymity preserved.

Blake ascended the twenty-foot stick ladder and settled into his stand. As with most hunting and fishing pursuits, silent waiting usually makes the difference between arriving home with a prize and making excuses. In Blake's case, his training to hunt humans made this kind of waiting enjoyable. Sniper training was one of the most difficult among the many courses required for the skill-set he honed to become an elite soldier. He spent hours slow-crawling to get to a vantage point from which to send a single shot within a narrow window of opportunity. In some cases it required lying prone and motionless for the better part of a day.

SITTING IN THIS NICELY padded chair, feet propped, arms on rests, Blake felt what he could only imagine some women feel at the spa.

His first order of business was to use his tactical binoculars to scan the kill zone. One of the advantages a sanctioned warrior has is access to the latest and greatest hardware. One of the best advances made to combat optics came when they figured out how to make one device switch between day and night-vision. Pre-dawn and post-dusk were now just as productive as day, and gear load was reduced to boot. The latest night vision was truly remarkable. It had advanced greatly from the beginnings of the technology when images were glowing green with little detail. What Blake used now was like HD TV, though in black and white. He expected a full color spectrum to be added before too long.

His perch was perfect. Three clearings were in the zone, and from this angle he'd be able to see movement from every direction into them.

As he expanded the scan radius, he noticed a clearing to his far right and almost at the limit of his binoculars. It was between him and the house—which he couldn't see—and it ignited a neural pathway to an obscured memory. Blake strained for details and an almost indiscernible speck made him realize what he was seeing. The speck was the last remnant of a post, one of the posts of what had once been a barn, *the* barn.

. . .

THE BARN WAS crammed floor to ceiling, wall to wall with rows of drying tobacco. The confluence of situation and circumstance finally worked in the farm's favor, yielding a bumper harvest. After struggling to keep the bills paid on their heritage land through years of cultivating the new cash crop, Blake's family knew this bounty would not only catch them up, but would pad the bank account going into next year's cycle.

Blake got home from school, ate a snack, and did his homework and chores. He now had a precious few minutes to himself before dinner. Walking from the bus stop that afternoon, he'd found an odd looking box near the road's edge. On closer inspection, he discovered it to be matches like he'd never seen before; the business ends were three or four times longer than a normal match. Now was his chance to try them out.

He figured the barn would be a safe place, especially since it was so full of tobacco and there'd be no breeze.

Pressed against the wall to avoid disturbing the massive browning leaves hanging on their poles, Blake made his way to the back of the barn. A little over from the corner, a gap between two rows gave him just enough room to sit Indian style without anything directly over head.

He pulled one of the strange looking matches from the box and dragged it across the sandpaper on the side. The sustained brilliant flash took him by surprise to the point he almost dropped it.

"Whoa! That would be bad." He blew it out just as the flare diminished. A brief shiver of fear shot through him as he considered the possible results of starting a fire inside the barn.

It was also exciting, so he quickly pulled another from the box. His excitement caused him to apply a bit more pressure this time. Fascinated by the flash, Blake failed to see a piece of the ignited tip fly off at the end of the striker. When he extinguished this one it did seem somehow shorter than the last.

"Oh well, the guys in the factory must have messed this one up."

Just as he was about to strike a third match, his mom called him to dinner. For such a small woman, she could put out some volume.

Blake tucked the box between one of the posts and the wall and noted its place so he could come back later and do it again; it would be even more fun after dark. He scrambled through the tobacco and out the front door ready to see what his mom had on the table. She was hard on him when it came to work and conduct, but he never doubted her love. One of his favorite ways she showed her affection for his dad and him was through her cooking.

After washing up, he took his place at the table in the kitchen just as Mom was putting the last of the sides out, mashed potatoes. For Blake, that was the crowning touch to perhaps the best meal from Mom's vast repertoire. Pork chops, green beans, and yeast rolls were laid out and it was all he could do to wait for the blessing, which his dad requested from the Father in his way of never sounding rote. Blake resisted the temptation to lick his plate. It helped knowing dessert was coming. When his mom rose to retrieve the cobbler from the stove, she froze mid turn and gasped at what she saw through the window. Blake and his dad bolted from their seats and barely paused before running out the door, headed to the barn.

Smoke was billowing from every crevice and flames were starting to lap from under the eaves. Dad yelled over his shoulder for Mom to call the fire department, though he probably knew even then it was too late. They could not arrive in time to save his tobacco and most likely not even the barn. There was no way the hose from the house was going to reach far enough to do any real good.

They stopped about fifty feet short and could do no more than watch. The only blessing for their day was the lack of wind spreading the fire.

By the time the volunteer fire brigade arrived, the best they could do was to be sure the heap of charcoal and ash harbored no embers. Just a few charred posts rose from the remains, like the rib bones of a long dead, beached whale. The acrid smell of smoke tinged by the sweet aroma of tobacco hung in the air.

Blake braced against the quake radiating from his gut as he stared at the conflagration and its conclusion. He awaited the evitable questions from his parents about where he'd been before supper and whether he'd seen anything related to the fire. They never came.

His father, normally a borderline stoic, was visibly shaken. In the same amount of time they usually took for supper, their barn and the year's livelihood was gone.

In the days after the fire, the insurance company's settlement projection came back well short of what it would take to rebuild the barn and replace the tobacco revenue. The fire marshal determined ignition came from the small electrical panel at the back of the barn. That news came as a huge relief to Blake, though he knew that was also where he'd been playing with the matches. He never fully bought into the fire marshal's assessment, but he was glad no one was blaming him.

His mom and dad tried to shield Blake from their stressed conversations about their options, but after going to bed and waiting a bit for their muffled voices to start reaching him from the kitchen, he crept from his room.

"If I don't find another source of income and right now, we could lose the farm," his father said.

"I know that, Sweetheart," his mother replied, "but I dread the thought of you not being here."

"You know there's no business anywhere in this area that can pay enough to cover the difference between what the insurance paid and our bills through next year. If I go back to active duty, the benefits and pay will barely get us through, but we won't lose the farm, and we won't have to go into more debt."

"Maybe we could both get work around here. I could clean houses and work part time at the farm supply store."

"You never fail to prove my great fortune in finding you. I know you would do just that and never utter a word of complaint. I also know that boy upstairs and this place already keep you busy dawn to dusk and that's enough."

"I just don't want you away from here and with what's going on in the Middle East. I'm afraid they could send you into that mess."

"Of course, I'll have to go and do whatever they say, but with my background, I'll try to get a training assignment at one of our forts. Another two-year tour and I'll get back here and get the farm working again, which won't be so hard since you and Blake will be here to keep it up."

"Let's tell Blake together over supper tomorrow, I'll make meatloaf. That boy's stomach has an amazing affect on his attitude."

Lost in thought, Blake almost missed the footfalls headed his way. He quickly rose from his crouch and snuck back to his room. *What have I done . . . ?*

Over supper the following night, Blake managed to react as though the news caught him off guard. It helped to have several questions ready to go. After a somber talk, they prayed together. Blake couldn't help feeling the prayer could mean trouble for him.

• • •

Two weeks later, the three of them stood at the open door of the Greyhound bus that would take Blake's dad to Fort Belvoir for final processing.

"Blake, I know you will take good care of your mom for me while I'm gone. You're a great young man, and I'm going to really miss you. I'm sorry I have to leave you with more work and responsibility when you should just be left to school and a few chores. I love you, Son."

"Dad, I need to tell you something, but I don't know how—"

"I know, Son, we've never had to do this before. I also know it's all hard to understand, but it boils down to our loss needing to be covered and this is the only way I can think of. Don't worry; none of this is your fault."

"Dad . . . eh, I'm sorry you have to go. I love you, too."

Wrapping his wife in a hug that almost caused them to merge, he said, "Sweetheart, I will write or call every chance I get. I spoke with Joe Guthrie and he's ready to help with anything you need. To say 'I'm gonna miss you' doesn't get it done."

With that he gave her a kiss, wheeled and mounted the bus.

All mom could get out was, "I love you." from a face overcome with sadness.

A few seconds later, the bus pulled away and they waved until it turned the corner two blocks down.

. . .

THE DIFFICULTIES OF life without Dad smoothed out over a couple of months and a new routine emerged. Their days were always brightened by a letter or phone call from him to hear how he missed them, questions, and reports. He was doing well reorienting himself to military life, and he liked his unit and commander.

So far, his pursuit of a training position was stuck and there was some talk of having to deploy. Rumors were all over the map, literally. Dad didn't really want to leave the U.S., but he sure didn't want to go into combat if at all possible. Of course, the military is not known for formulating its plans based on the wishes of its troops. And he would serve his country however they, and his God, saw fit.

A month later Dad called with the news that he would be boarding a flight in a few days, headed east. He wasn't allowed to say exactly where or when, but based on the few conversations they'd had leading to this moment, Blake Kershaw, and his mom, Katy, could only assume he was headed to the Middle East.

December 16, 1990 was the day Cecil Kershaw boarded the chartered American Airlines flight headed to Saudi Arabia.

. . .

SADDAM HUSSEIN INVADED Kuwait in early August of that year. The most obvious explanation for his actions was his lust for the oil. It came out later, Iraq had accrued a considerable debt to Kuwait, so the invasion served to cancel the debt and seize the resource all at once.

After much bluster by the UN, and sanctions leveled by the Security Council, Hussein was not intimidated. He simply annexed Kuwait and declared it a province of Iraq.

NATO, the UN, and King Fahd of Saudi Arabia knew that, if Hussein went unchecked, his next logical move was to attack the largest producer and exporter of oil in the world at that time. On November 29, 1990, the word was given and mobilization of forces from America and an international coalition set course for Saudi Arabia.

Saddam Hussein's recalcitrance set Operation Desert Storm in motion on January 16, 1991. Air power—mostly American—was brought to bear on Iraq, raining incredible destruction on their defenses and infrastructure. That done, the allied forces turned their bombing attention to the forward deployed Iraqi forces in Kuwait. This prepared for the launch of Operation Desert Sabre on February 24, which aimed to force the Iraqis out with ground troops. The effort proved overwhelming as the less well equipped and trained Iraqi conscripts were quickly pushed over the Kuwaiti border and pursued one hundred and fifty miles into southeastern Iraq.

The last stand for the elite Republican Guard was at Al-Baṣrah. They were summarily defeated, but not before launching numerous Scud missiles into Saudi Arabia. President George Bush declared a cease fire on February 28, 1991.

. . .

WHEN THE OFFICIAL-LOOKING sedan pulled up the drive, Blake dropped the bag of trash he was hauling to the burn pile and returned to the house. As he and his mom came through the door to the porch, two men in uniform exited the car. The sight of a cross on the collar of one of the men hit the woman and boy like being plunged into utter blackness.

One of the Scud missiles launched from Al-Baṣrah found its way to the main logistics center warehouse in Saudi Arabia, blowing their beloved husband and father out of their lives. Cecil Kershaw transcended to eternity in a flash on February 27, 1991.

3

THE OPPRESSION OF guilt returned to seize Blake's heart. Compounding the normal grief of losing a father, Blake could never shake the parasite attached to his conscience, as it replaced halcyon memories with the conviction he was to blame for his father's death. The stupidity of a kid playing with fire resulted in his father being consumed by it.

He was amazed at how his mom dealt with losing the only true love she'd ever known. Unlike others Blake saw over the years, her sadness ran deep, but it never consumed her. Blake's perspective may have been skewed by how his mom was more concerned about him than herself, but even in her taciturn moments, when he knew she was missing her husband, a cloak of peace was ever on her shoulders. Maybe that Scripture about believers not grieving like those with no hope was real. For Blake, guilt and hope could find no common ground.

There was another burden Blake carried; he'd failed to protect the most important woman in his life. One of the many life lessons his father wove into his character was chivalry, the ancient virtue—mostly mocked in post-modern society—dictating man's responsibility to protect anyone who could not protect themselves, especially their women and children. It was an ethos reinforced throughout his military training, but one he'd failed to uphold.

The weight of this failure and the secret igniting it could be hidden no longer when Blake was making preparations for his first military deployment. He sat down with his mom, and with his last will and testament, he also presented his guilt. He told her the story of his responsibility for burning down the barn and the loss of their husband and father. Blake did not show emotion readily and it was rarely an asset in his line of work, but reliving his crime before the one he loved most, and hurt the most, released unstoppable tears down his reddening face. His mom's response was to reach across the table and cover his clamped and trembling hands with her own. Though he knew his mom wouldn't fly into rage, she never had, Blake almost wished she wouldn't try to comfort him either. Maybe punishment could at least be a down payment on the debt he owed.

Nonetheless, Blake's burden lightened a bit that evening—confession has that effect. His mom was visibly surprised to hear his story, but she doubted his guilt, based on the fire marshal's investigation, and said even if it were so, she did not hold him responsible for his father's death.

He never had reason to think his mom had, or ever would, lie to him, but her assurance did not assuage his sense of failure.

They talked for another hour about how she would manage in his absence and generalities about where he was headed and what he'd be doing. They prayed together—rather, she prayed—and with a hug and kiss, they parted, still devoted mother and son, but not quite the same. Blake often wondered who'd changed in that confessional.

Just as the black memories of the next blow to his mom by his hand started scrolling across Blake's thoughts . . .

∙ ∙ ∙

BLAKE'S SENSES AND training stopped the replay when he caught movement at the far edge of his left peripheral vision. The big buck emerged from the tree line into the center clearing. He'd missed the does leading the way.

Good thing I'm not in combat . . .

This one sure looked like the image captured on the game camera. It strode into the clearing with an ease learned over years of no hunters on the land, but still alert.

BLAKE SLOWLY SWUNG THE Model 700 to his left to acquire the target. The buck was about a third of the way into the clearing, but facing Blake. Four more steps and it presented a perfect broadside target. At this distance, there would be very little ballistic declination, especially considering he'd hand-loaded his .30-06 rounds with as many grains of powder as the shells could handle. His bullets left the barrel at better than 3,000 feet per second.

A gentle breeze almost imperceptibly stirred the trees beyond the deer, so windage would also be negligible. Blake zeroed in on the front shoulder and drew in a slow breath. He started exhaling and drawing back on the trigger at the same time. He'd taken up nearly two of the two and a half pound trigger pull when the cell phone in his breast pocket buzzed.

Damn!

Under combat conditions, a mild distraction of this sort would not have stopped him from downing a target, but this wasn't combat and these circumstances called for different priorities. Among other things, he now had a wife and son who might need him and couldn't wait for him to field dress and extract a 200-pound animal.

Blake lowered the rifle, pulled his phone out, noticed the ID was blocked, and answered without using his name.

"Jacob Hunter?" a female voice asked.

"Who is this?"

"If this is Jacob Hunter, I'm calling for Colonel Johnson."

"Authenticate, blue horizon."

"Five of diamonds . . . Please hold a second for the colonel . . . "

"BLAKE! HOW ARE YOU son, "Bob Johnson here. It's been what, eight, nine years? I'd love to catch up, but that will have to wait. I thought of you after a CIA briefing yesterday. We need to talk."

"Colonel Johnson, I heard about your promotion and new posting. I'm sorry I couldn't send my congratulations. My cover still has me on a pretty tight leash."

"No need, Blake, and for now, Bob will do fine. I think I know the answer to this question, but are you by any chance on an encrypted phone?"

"No, sir, I'm out hunting. I have one back at work."

"That's too far."

"Uh, sir, how did you . . . oh never mind."

"Blake, I know you've been through a lot and you've done more than your fair share of service for your country, but I need to talk to you about a problem I'm confronting. How quickly could you make it to Fort Lee?"

"I could probably be there in under three hours, if I hustle."

"I'd appreciate it if you could. I don't have much slop in this timeline. I'll arrange for a private room in the headquarters building equipped with an SVTC. Just check at the security desk when you get there and say you have an appointment with the commanding general. It will be under Jacob Hunter."

"Sir, can you give me anything to go on before I get there?"

"Sorry, Blake, I know about your current situation, but you'll just have to wait until we can talk securely."

"Roger that, sir."

Blake broke the connection, let his imagination spool a bit, but gave up quickly and started collecting himself to dismount the tree stand and trek back to his truck.

On his way out, he pulled his cell phone again and said, "Call home."

After two rings his wife's voice came on. "Hey, honey, how's the hunting going? You get a big one already?"

"No, I'm afraid not. I was just about to drop the one I've been looking for when Bob Johnson called . . . "

After the expected pause for concern he knew Alia would have, Blake continued. "He wants me to run over to Fort Lee to talk about something."

"I thought he was promoted to Delta commander at Fort Bragg."

"He was. He needs us to talk over a secure line and the nearest one's at Lee. I can only assume he has reasons for not wanting me to come to Bragg."

"I'm not sure I like the sound of this, Blake."

"I know, Sweetheart, but Bob's been a trusted friend for a long time and maybe the best boss I've ever served under. He at least deserves to be heard."

"Sure, I understand. When do you need to be there?"

"Right away. It's still early enough; I should be able to get over there and back before I'm too late for supper. I'll call if I get delayed"

. . .

THE DRIVE GAVE BLAKE plenty of time to ruminate on why, after so long, his old boss would be in need of him. The possibilities were numerous, counter-terrorism was a 24/7 mechanism and it seemed it would be for many years to come. Even though he had been out of the intel loop since returning from Iran and taking the job at the CIA Farm, the news outlets delivered a steady flow of reports from every nook and cranny on the planet. The world was not doing well against the spreading Caliphate.

The lines of battle blurred almost every day as nation-states around the world came under the ever-widening impact of radical Islam. Political correctness and corruption continued to play into the hands of the many factions seeking a global Islamic state, even in America. While various "freedom fighters" pursued the violent overthrow of moderate governments, cultural Jihad was being pursued in virtually every western country. Some, like Denmark and the UK were already using sharia in their courts and their parliaments were being increasingly populated by Muslims. King Frederik of Denmark and King William of England were not long for their thrones.

America was not far behind Europe. If not for a remnant of those still holding tenaciously to the founding documents, the United States Council of Muslim Organizations, the political party founded by the Muslim Brotherhood in 2014, would probably be the dominant political force in Washington. They continued to push for disarming citizens and making any offense to Islam a crime, but resistance held them mostly at bay. The states succumbing to gun control legislation and integration of sharia were adding up, but so were their crime rates and acts of civil disobedience. As freedom-minded people fled those states, the declining tax base pushed the governments closer to bankruptcy. Fortunately for Blake and Alia, Virginia returned to its roots after the Obama regime's agenda unfolded and was holding to its sovereignty against constant attacks from within and without.

That was the main reason Blake was not pursuing active duty again. The flaccidity of the U.S. government's foreign and domestic policies— the work of career politicians chipping away at the Constitution in thinly veiled collusion with the Muslim Brotherhood—was fundamentally transforming George Washington's homeland. It was becoming impossible to know for whom he would actually be working. Blake was as passionate as ever about crushing America's enemies, but the military, under a series of dilettante presidents and legislators, was more social laboratory than fighting force.

Blake wondered how Bob Johnson was able to hold up under the present administration. Between budget cuts and policy shifts, a warrior like him must be finding it hard to function.

He knows I'm not in my twenties anymore and that I've been out of operations for a decade. At least my training post helps keep me off the fat farm.

At any rate, it was Bob and it was still the country to which Blake pledged his oath, and that oath came with no expiration date. *I'll go and I'll see what he has in mind.*

4

OMAR'S MATRICULATION IN the technical school of Islamic Jihad continued to amaze even his recruiter and mentor, Abu Hamza. He once told his faith progeny he considered changing his name to Abu Omar. Omar fulfilled for Abu Hamza the role only a prized first-born son could. He could not imagine being prouder, or loving more the natural product of his loins. During his early training, Abu Hamza gave Omar his new operational name, Abu al-Wafá. He was being renamed Father of Faithfulness.

As they sat at the small table outside *Qahwah Qasar*, their favorite café, Abu Hamza ruminated on how far his protégé had come since they first met. The cowering, battered boy of seven was now a brazen and clever warrior for Allah. By his multilayered training in Quran, *Hadith, Sira*, combat, and strategy, Abu Hamza helped Omar channel his resentment of a derelict father and the abuse of infidels into glorious Jihad.

Now they were here talking about Omar's latest mission and plans for the next. They choose this spot because the owner's allegiance was unquestioned and talking in low voices outdoors made eavesdropping almost impossible. Nonetheless, they kept the details buried under reference and code. Their years of working together made communication virtually telepathic at any rate.

The need for Abu Hamza to hear every detail of Omar's actions had long passed, so these meetings were usually more celebration than formal debrief. Since Abu Hamza ordered the attack and outlined most of the planning, his only concern was to know of any intrinsic flaws in the operation they could handle differently next time. He no longer had any doubts about Omar's abilities or obedience. Those evaporated after the first few operations on which his star pupil was sent.

Even at seven, on his first foray into Israel, Omar showed more composure and courage than some of the much older recruits. Posing as shepherds from Syria, they carried weapons for Palestinian freedom fighters. He executed his role as he might a trip to the market for fish. He carried an equal load and stuck exactly to the plan. The possibility of capture or death seemed to have little effect on Omar's eagerness or execution.

Upon his return, Omar's only concern was about how soon he would get to go again.

It wouldn't be long before Omar would be conducting detailed post-mission analysis with his own subordinates. In fact Abu Hamza knew it would be sooner rather than later. He'd stopped leading actions several years earlier and the onset of illness and advancing age would take him all together from the cell he founded long before his heart was willing.

He'd known almost from the day he recruited Omar into The Brotherhood that he was destined to lead. The only thing that might slow Omar's decision to take his place was his loyalty and the passion he had for being the one to pull the trigger or push the button. Surely, Omar knew the day was quickly approaching, but he never broached the subject and veered like a caroming soccer ball whenever the subject arose.

There were certainly others in the network capable, and even desirous, of Abu Hamza's post, but none came close to the expertise and trustworthiness of his beloved adopted son.

Looking up from his pita and hummus, Omar caught the familiar look in his mentor's eyes. The look he'd longed for from his father and never got. On the other hand, he never doubted his mother's love and care. And though his father's adherence to Islam and hatred for infidels was unquestioned, it was his mother's teaching and passion that formed the bedrock for Omar's path.

That night long ago as Omar awaited sleep, listening to the hard raindrops falling on the tin roof of his Beirut home, he could smell the sea water carried by the wind even with the doors and windows closed. That winter was particularly brutal. They did not have heat in their one-bedroom house and the outside cold crept in through the many gaps in the walls. Omar and his six other brothers slept huddled like chicks, drawing heat from one another. Mattresses were spread all over the tiled floor of the main living area, military style. The boys slept on one side, girls on the other.

As he was lying there, the day's teaching looped through his head. The story Mother told the boys in their home in Madrasah was of a great ancient martyr for Allah. Omar was captivated by the story and the reward the martyr received.

After dismissing the other boys for the day, she held Omar's face in her hands and said, "My, Omar, you are very special; the things you'll do for Allah and Islam will be great. My son, if you kill a Jew, your hand will light up in heaven before Allah's throne. That is what the *Hadith* by al-Bukhari of Islam says..."

He knew then his destiny was to kill as many Jews and other infidels as he could before giving his life for the cause and claiming his rightful place in Allah's eternal kingdom. There, he would be served by virgins with nothing more on their minds than to fulfill his every desire.

Maybe then Omar's father would finally realize his worth . . .

· · ·

HIS LATEST MISSION, THE one from which he'd just returned, was to plant a bomb in a popular night club in the Zehlendorf district of Berlin, Germany. The club was a regular weekend gathering spot of soldiers from nearby U.S. Army Berlin headquarters. It was renamed "Ford-Goins" after the soldiers killed in a similar bombing at a discotheque in 1986, before the reunification. The club was just upscale enough to attract officers as well as enlisted. The loss of life would be felt all the way to the Pentagon. One of the best weapons in the Jihadist's arsenal was the short memory and inevitably lowered guard of westerners.

The operation was set into motion after another cowardly drone strike on the leadership of *al-Jam's al-Islamiyyah al-Muqatilah*, otherwise known as Libyan Islamic Fighting Group in Benghazi, Libya, or LIFG. The Hellfire missile killed the aging founder and a couple of his aides, but missed the new head of operations.

The local and international press was as helpful as usual in spreading the story of the innocents killed in the attack, a wife and teenage son, though there were no bodies offered to back it up.

America would finally go after the head of the organization complicit in the deaths of their ambassador to Libya, Christopher Stevens, along with Sean Smith, Tyrone Woods, and Glen Doherty.

Ansar al-Sharia and Al Qaeda in the Islamic Maghreb were the groups of primary interest in the area to international intelligence agencies, which is why LIFG was brought up to spearhead the attack on the compound in Benghazi. They weren't particularly well-trained or equipped, but their hatred for America would suffice. Weapons could always be supplied. That maneuver proved unnecessary when the Obama administration took to the stage to perform a farce so ridiculous, the best Islamic propagandists could not have come up with a better narrative. Omar still marveled at the gullibility of Americans, or perhaps they just believed what they chose to believe. In any case, their stupidity was a priceless asset in global Jihad.

Over time, with constant pressure from a few zealots in the U.S. Congress, and a president hoping to keep his polls up, the trail finally lead to LIFG and Abdel-Hakim Belhadj. Against the advice from several on staff and the minority leader in the senate, Operation Stagehand was authorized by the White House.

Though he assumed the irony would be lost on the current military leaders in the area, this sequence of events was the exact reverse of 1986 when America bombed Tripoli and Benghazi after finding that Ghaddafi and his East German consulate were behind the deaths at the discotheque, Omar found it too poetic to ignore.

• • •

WORKING THROUGH THE Turkish embassy in Berlin, Omar flew in under diplomatic passport, one of many he held. He was given a car and he drove south about fifty minutes. There he met with the team arranged by Abu Hamza through the Sura Council and the head of Jihad operations in Germany. The Directorate-General for Strategy and Operations in the Federal Ministry of Defence converted to Islam and was radicalized during his two year posting at the German embassy in Yemen. A captain at the time, Heinrich Bota met the most beautiful woman he'd ever seen during a dinner held at the embassy.

She won his heart with her affection and his head with horror stories of growing up in Palestine under Jewish occupation. He started attending mosque about a year after arriving in Sana'a and swore allegiance to Allah's Holy War weeks before being transferred back to Berlin. His intelligence moved him up the ranks of the Bundeswehr, his passion procured favor with a local imam who was the leader of the German Sura Council. Having Bota in one of the most powerful positions in the German government was pivotal to the ultimate overthrow of the Federal Republic of Germany and the installation of an Islamic state under sharia.

Bota supplied Omar with essential plan elements including digital maps marked with ingress and egress variables around the target, components for the bomb, and a member of his personal contingent to serve as security and clearance.

When Omar arrived at the safe house in Brandenburg, he found the team already assembled. Code phrases were exchanged but no names, the less each knew of the other the better. Being tasked by their handlers was all the security they required.

The bomb-maker chaired the chemistry department at Stuttgart University and was in Berlin conducting a guest lecture series at Technische Universität Berlin on the advances and impact of chemistry on leading-edge technology. His personal passion was visiting ever greater devastation on Zionists by creating explosive devices that could be delivered for the widest possible applications. His latest composition was used to kill a busload of students from Tel Aviv University returning from a football game. The six kilo device all but vaporized the bus, leveled the two storefronts next to it, and shattered windows in a two-block radius.

The driver, once a professional on the European rally circuit, now owned a taxi and limousine service in Berlin. He would be driving an unregistered taxi to deliver the bomber to the venue.

For security, a major in the KSK Kommando Spezialkräfte from Bota's office would make sure the team members had safe conduct during the operation and, if necessary, take out any interference or possible witnesses. He was one of a growing number of the German military being recruited to the new world war.

Omar was pleased with the team, which seemed well selected from the local network and suited to their jobs. One more member would be added just before execution of the plan; a woman, Lamia, from the Fazle Omar Mosque in Hamburg, would walk the bomb into the nightclub.

. . .

LAMIA WAS CAUGHT talking to a man not of her family, and to raise the offense, he was from the West. When the dishonor was reported to her parents, they dragged her before their imam. What they didn't know was the imam was actively searching for a martyr for Omar's operation.

While Lamia and her parents were expecting something like a beating or house restriction, what the imam declared was a shock. Under sharia, imams have unquestioned power based on their interpretation of Islamic writings.

"I was also given a report of Lamia's offense," the imam said. "I discovered that the man she spoke with has ties to a Christian organization."

"But, I did . . . " The words were across her lips before she could stop them. Her compulsion to defend herself overwhelmed ingrained decorum. She stood before the imam, but kept her head lowered.

"Silence! Have you not shamed your parents enough already?" The imam banged his fist on the table that separated him from Lamia's family.

Addressing her father, the imam said, "Since we cannot know exactly what was said between them, we cannot know to what extent she fell under the persuasion of the infidel. The only way to insure Lamia's allegiance to Allah and purge this dishonor from your family is for her to sacrifice herself in his holy cause."

Lamia's mother could not restrain a barely audible gasp while her father's only reaction was a slight widening of his eyes.

Lamia lowered her head and sobbed. She knew it was risky, speaking to the man in public, but he was so handsome and charming. Her fear was traded for the feeling of worth he gave her. As most Muslim women, she'd been trained to believe she had roughly the value of a cow or goat in the eyes of Muslim men.

Living in Germany with its many western influences was slowly chipping away at this ideology and pulling at Lamia's deep-set need to feel wanted. Her dream was shattered, and her body soon would be also. Escape was not a remote option. Even if she could slip the grasp of the imam, the shame it would heap on her parents was not conscionable. She would be held at the mosque until she was taken to do as instructed by the Jihadists who would insure her follow- through. Her only remaining hope was that Allah would accept her sacrifice so her temporary bondage would be bartered for a place in jannah.

The imam came to Lamia after morning prayers two weeks into her sequestration and told her she would be picked up in a few hours and transported to the place where she would bring honor to her family and praise to Allah. She was given no specifics other than to obey without pause every direction she was given. The one operational detail made clear was that the explosive device would have a remote trigger as well as the one she would be expected to use. If she did not detonate as told, it would be done by another, and Allah would not receive her on the other side.

Two women came into Lamia's room after the imam departed. They had western clothes and makeup. An hour later, she could not have been distinguished from any well-heeled German woman. The clothes were uncomfortable and the makeup made her face feel soiled.

So this is what western women do to make themselves attractive. What would normally bring shame to a Muslim woman was here considered righteous deception.

A woman carrying documents bearing the name Mary Mueller exited a cab as it paused for only a moment in a gap between two street cameras a few doors away from the Blue Door nightclub. When the recordings were examined later, they would show a cab moving slowly down a busy street, the angles obscuring whether it contained a passenger. Even if they chose to track down the cab, the search would be a dead end.

The bomb used in 1986 was effective, but the chemist's work, combined with engineering innovations, meant a device nearly twice as powerful delivered in a smaller, lighter package. It was easily concealed in the outside lining of the purse carried into the club.

"Mary" entered the nightclub and moved through the pulsating crowd to the bar located at the mid-point of the establishment. She clutched the bag slung on her shoulder with her right hand on the embedded trigger in the strap, her lips moved in a silent prayer and then, as loud as her strained voice allowed, she proclaimed, *"Allah Akbar!"*

A few seconds later, the three-story building containing the Blue Door nightclub was rubble.

Two blocks away, atop a condominium, Omar and his security escort turned and left. This was the moment Omar always savored most. The planning and preparation was fulfilling and allowed him to apply his intellect and skill, but watching the curs of the Earth sent to Hell eclipsed sexual climax.

Omar arrived home after a circuitous return from Germany. The carefully planned and executed bombing had confirmed kills of eighty-seven and a hundred and twelve injured. He was always grateful for the intel supplied by the international media. The replay from the scene along with names and nationalities documented his exploits better than having his own film crew along.

What the media never knew was who was behind these daring plots. If the media had no clue, international law enforcement was no better. Absolute secrecy, planning compartmentalization, and strategic leaks worked together to allow Omar and his compatriots to execute Jihad with nearly assured impunity.

For this mission, the dogs were put on the trail of neo-Nazis trying to push Americans off German soil. It wasn't much of a stretch, and the Americans were always ready to run with any narrative that did not raise the ire of their Muslim population.

• • •

AT THE CONCLUSION of their operational agenda, Abu Hamza informed Omar of the council's approval of his ascension to take his place at the head of Al-Asifa, the unit he founded nearly fifty years earlier.

"Ya-Baba, I'm not ready to fill your shoes or head our group. Without your leadership, I know we will lose our focus."

"Nonsense my son, you've been ready for some time now. It has been my need to stay in the fight that has held you from this so far. You are ready."

"But what of the others, are you sure they will follow me? You know there has been at least one strong rival almost since you recruited me. I think he will not react well to taking orders from me."

"Omar, I'm not moving to Bali. I'll be here and available for counsel and support whenever you need. You will take full control of operational planning and coordination with our brothers on the council. You will have no trouble from anyone in our ranks, I will see to that as we make the transition."

"As you wish, I will do as you say and strive to honor you in this responsibility, by Allah's will."

"I know you will. Let us return to the mosque for prayer and then I want to speak to you about something I've just learned about one among us."

Omar motioned the owner/server over and handed him several times more than enough to cover the bill. Loyalty was always encouraged with generosity.

The two rose from their chairs. Omar turned in the direction of the mosque and glanced behind him to be sure his beloved adopted father needed no aid, then slowly started down the sidewalk.

Omar was one stride from being past the wall dividing the café from the neighboring rug shop when the gates of Hell opened behind him. The wall of partitioned glass at the front of the café disintegrated and flew from the building like a giant shotgun blast. In its wake came twisted tables, chairs, and fragments of the few customers who chose to eat inside. Then followed the flames from the ruptured gas line and whatever tinder remained.

Omar and Abu Hamza were lifted from their feet like marionettes and tossed on their faces into the street. Because Abu Hamza was a meter or so behind Omar when the bomb went off, he caught more of the concussion and shrapnel. He was dead before his body hit the pavement.

5

Moving toward consciousness, Omar's first thoughts were a confused, almost dream-like state as he clawed his way back to the present. Was he on a mission gone wrong, was he in Beirut, Berlin, Damascus . . . was he in danger?

Allah, help me!

Open your eyes . . .

Through slits, Omar saw a blurred mix of forms and smoke. As his eyelids parted further, his irises and lenses did their jobs, a face appeared. Abu Hamza's eyes, wide and unblinking didn't look back and yet pierced Omar to his soul.

Ya-Baba . . . my father . . .

He moved to get to his feet and immediately discovered that was not going to happen. As his senses came back on line, awareness and pain merged. His back and legs seemed to be on fire. Though he could see chaos and people running about, very little sound was making it through his ears. Barely able to push onto numb and wobbly arms, Omar managed to drag himself over to Abu Hamza, or what was left of him.

The blast of shattered glass and metal reduced most of Abu Hamza's body to an oozing pulp. In surreal contrast, his feet and face appeared untouched.

Omar draped himself over the only man from whom he'd ever felt love, wept, and committed him to Allah's mercy.

His convulsions slowed as sorrow moved to anger, exploding in his heart as an inferno of hatred. He would find who set this bomb and make him suffer for many days before finally being sent to Hell. *I swear by the name of the prophet, I will not rest until I have visited vengeance on the Shytan who has taken you from me . . .*

Having spent the last ounce of strength he had left on his oath, he felt the universe close to the distant tone of sirens.

A block and a half to the southeast of the burning café, atop a residential building, a man lowered binoculars from his face as a satisfied smile spread across his dark features.

. . .

THE NEXT TIME Omar opened his eyes he found himself in a small room lying on his stomach as he was the last time, but this time he was in a bed. A hospital bed. He could see through the vertical rectangular window in the door to a hall where a few people flashed by. He started to roll and was reminded of his injuries, so he decided to stay put. A tube ran from his left arm and back out of sight. A couple of wires came from the neck opening of his gown and went the way of the tube.

He could feel the effects of drugs, but past that, his head throbbed and his back and legs reminded him of a beating from his father. With the pain came the indelible image of Abu Hamza lying in the middle of Bakkar Street. Omar started to close his eyes as seething anger returned.

The door opened and before it passed forty-five degrees, Omar knew it was his wife. The sight of Suzan was better than he ever imagined seventy-two virgins could be and he was instantly back on the bus during the spring of 2006 . . .

. . .

Omar awoke the morning he first met Suzan and was delighted with what felt like an overnight arrival of spring, his favorite time of year. The winters in Beirut were often brutal, though he never liked cold weather, no matter the degree.

With his first cup of tea in hand, Omar headed to the backyard. The brightness and warmth of the spring sun was a celebrated victory over the terrorizing winter. The lemon and orange trees were covered in brilliant white, star-shaped blossoms. The air was saturated in a sweet fragrance he could almost taste. The citrus-flower infused air, occasionally spiced with the rising aroma of black tea, made Omar wish he could stop the sun in the sky indefinitely, but alas . . .

He had to get going to make the first bus to Bourj Hamoud, a suburb of Beirut. It was a short ride made long by the crowds. Omar was never anxious to make this trip, but it was important to Abu Hamza and the cause, so he would go and tolerate the overpopulated area. The mass of people in the bus stations and streets were not the worst part, it was the composition and the memories.

Since being taken in by The Muslim Brotherhood and Abu Hamza thirteen years earlier, Omar never again experienced the beatings he once received at the hands of the Armenian boys. He nonetheless hated this part of town, and the infestation of Christians that just kept growing.

They started coming here from what was now Turkey when the Ottoman Empire went from imposing civil and financial restrictions on them to murdering them outright. Omar would always remember the stories his grandfather told him of that time. The first modern genocide of the Armenians began in 1915 during the First World War. The Empire with its capitol in Constantinople was defeated as part of the Central Powers and from there declined through revolution until the Caliphate was abolished in 1924, a dark time in his grandfather's life.

Since many of the Armenians took the Allies' side during the war, going back to Turkey was not a happy option. A great many of them joined those who fled during the genocide to Lebanon. In bitter irony, Omar's mother's family was forced to flee Constantinople as well, when the glorious Muslim nation fell. So the purging of the infidel Christians from the Turkish Empire ended in the blending of the two peoples.

His grandfather's voice still echoed in Omar's memories. "Glory to Allah. Allah in his great wisdom gave Talaat Pasha the great victory to cleanse one and a half million infidel Christian Armenians from their home, and occupied their land by bringing real Muslims from the region to inhabit it.

"My children it is our duty by Allah and Muhammad to abolish our enemies the Jews and Christians; they are nothing to us. In Quran 5:60 Allah calls them apes and pigs. My children we took their prized Christian state of Constantinople. This is where five big Christian churches were converted into mosques. We are the followers of the prophet of Allah and will do exactly as we read of him in the *Sira* of Muhammad. We will rule the Earth. We will fight those who believe neither in Allah nor the Last Day, nor hold that forbidden which hath been forbidden by God and His Apostle, nor acknowledge the religion of Truth, they who were People of the Book, until they pay the *jizya* with willing submission, and feel themselves subdued."

Omar received directions for these trips from Abu Hamza's assistant, Abu Youssef, who he'd come to trust as the voice of his mentor. This was one of many techniques used by their organization to keep anyone trying to track them off their scent.

A skilled tailor, trained and commissioned by Al-Asifa opened a shop near the center of Bourj Hamoud and staffed it with locals recruited to Jihad for the purpose of intelligence gathering and operational planning when the need arose. Omar was the only conduit from the main group to this plant and his job was to collect regular reports and run closed meetings on site with other business and religious leaders. Electronic communications of any sort were not trusted with the most sensitive discussions.

One of the things Omar enjoyed about this job was his specific instruction to keep the intimidation of the tailor's staff on high. He'd recently discovered one of them was talking with the pastor of one of the orthodox churches, about what, they did not know for sure, but that didn't matter. A two-man team was dispatched on a motorcycle, one armed with an AK-47. The young man and two others of his family were gunned down in an open market and four bystanders were wounded.

Omar climbed aboard the old yellow bus he'd been riding from his neighborhood for as long as he could remember. He handed the bus attendant fifteen Qurush and sat on the narrow, cracked-leather seat just behind him. The old diesel-driven box laid down a smoke screen and accelerated toward downtown.

At the big central bus station, masses of people from every nation and tongue milled about going from point A to point Q.

I wonder if this will be the way on judgment day, Omar thought to himself.

Inshallah, there will be no lines for martyrs.

Omar was remembering the teaching of Abu Hamza. "The only way to please Allah, my son, is to die as a martyr. The Quran says, 'All Muslims will have to go to Hell first.' Think not of those who are slain in Allah's way as dead. Nay, they live, finding their sustenance in the presence of their lord. They rejoice in the bounty provided by Allah. 'They glory in the grace and bounty from Allah, and in the fact that Allah suffereth not the reward of the faithful to be lost.'"

Praise Allah who has mercy on his slave Omar. The bus bound for Bourj Hamoud finally arrived.

As Omar turned from paying this driver, his eyes were arrested by a girl standing near the back of the already-crowded bus. There, in a white and blue summer dress, was something he'd never seen or even dreamed of before. Though the dress was modest, it was certainly not the proper attire of a Muslim female. The pious thought flew through Omar's mind so quickly he might not have actually thought it. Observers might have mistaken Omar's reaction as being hypnotized.

Oh my Allah; can there be such beauty on Earth?

It was then he realized he wasn't breathing, as his lungs expanded in survival mode. His tongue was like a dried fish and the inside of the bus was wavering in his peripheral vision.

I think I'm having a heart attack. Am I? What do I do? I have no training for this. Why was this not covered in madrasah? Allah, help your slave Omar. I'm so sorry, Allah. I know this is beneath you.

Omar blushed for the first time in his life, but lost time was made up by intensity. He thought the flesh on his face was melting.

His efforts to collect himself were futile.

This must be how Adam felt when he met Eve for the first time.

I now understand why Adam would eat the forbidden fruit.

The smile on her face was an embarrassed summons. The line of people behind him were done being patient and started pushing Omar toward the girl, he was in the gravity of providence.

Destiny was finding expression as though his story was being read from jannah by Allah. The paths of their lives were to cross here and now. They were soon to be face-to-face, breath-to-breath. The ethereal and terrestrial merged on a bus rolling through downtown Beirut.

This is supernatural.

The hand of Allah pushed the crowd to the back forcing Omar arm to arm next to her, then their hands touched. Something like megawatts of electricity shot through Omar's body, but it was nothing like the jolts he got on his construction job occasionally, it was pure pleasure.

She smells better than a grove of lemon trees.

"My name is Suzan. What is yours?"

"Oh my name is . . . eh . . . yes—yes, it is Omar." The moment his name came out he realized it was loud enough for the entire bus to hear.

Oh my God, I am speaking to a Christian woman . . . I am dead . . . I am dead for sure.

As Suzan looked into Omar's eyes, his heart left him. He knew it because he could no longer feel the thrum in his neck or the thump in his chest. Perhaps he was dead . . . could he be dreaming?

"Here is my stop," said Suzan. "I must go now."

Omar was caught off what little guard he had in reserve, and before he could recover, she was halfway down the aisle.

Speak you camel head, speak.

By then Suzan was off the bus and Omar was left to the falling bricks of regret smacking him in the skull.

I didn't ask how I could see her again.

How do I find her?

Does she have a phone number?

So, this is how a jackass behaves.

Suzan stood on the sidewalk waving as the bus drove away. The expanding distance between Omar and the girl was like being jettisoned from an orbiting spacecraft and realizing you forgot the tether.

I should stop the bus or jump out the window.

For days after the encounter, Omar traveled to Bourj Hamoud taking the same bus, traveling in the same hour, but she was not to be found. She was gone and, in a way, so was Omar.

Spring worked through its cycle of exchanging blooms for leaves and fruit, but Omar was back in winter. His favorite sister noticed his dark and cool demeanor. Makkyiah tried without success to get him to tell her why.

She said, "Omar, you must have lost something very special."

Summer rolled in on the Mediterranean Sea breeze, and the smell of sage on the hills mixed with the brine of the water to create an intoxicating recipe. Omar loved the sea from his earliest memories. It came to symbolize the beauty he saw on that bus. At sunset Omar would watch the sun taking a bath in the Mediterranean and pray he'd find her again. He watched until the red sun and golden water surrendered to steely gray.

I'll see you and maybe her tomorrow.

A few days later Omar was once again downtown boarding the bus. He turned from the driver to find a seat when his eyes caught the purest kind of light, bouncing off strawberry blonde hair, glowing argent skin, carmine lips, and eyes that seemed to reflect eternity. Her face was carved on the retina of his eyes. He would have recognized her from across a stadium.

"Suzan? Suzan is it you?"

She sprang from her seat at the end of the bus and ran into Omar's arms. With tears sliding down her cheeks, she said, "Omar, where have you been? I've looked all over for you. I cried to God many times over."

Omar's eyes held an impossible well of tears until he opened his mouth. It was a destiny heaven made.

"Do not do this to me again. I can't live without you, my Suzan."

By the end of summer Omar and Suzan became one and Omar found his heart again in holy matrimony. She was a Christian Armenian and she would share with him her love for her God. He would share with her his devotion to his God. They both knew they did not speak of the same God.

From his earliest teaching at home, Omar was told women were put on Earth by Allah for two reasons only: to bear children—preferably males—and to care for Muslim men. His mother taught him it was best to marry a Muslim woman, but not only was there no shame in marrying an infidel; it was another kind of religious conquest. The infidel woman would be dominated by the man and she would bear followers of the prophet.

The teaching held no connection to his love for Suzan.

Something stronger, something greater, something was moving within the hardened Jihadist. It was like Heaven on Earth every moment Omar was with his bride. He was no less committed to his life of advancing the Caliphate, but he was starting to know another life. Suzan often spoke of the unconditional love of her God, but Omar could not comprehend such a God.

It was their secret, no doubt. Nobody would ever know the love of Omar's heart was the very Christian he was commanded to kill or dominate. There would be another secret held even tighter by Omar; he could never tell Suzan what he did in his travels. From the time they met, Omar told Suzan he worked for an export shipping company whose ships moved cargo mostly around the Mediterranean. He said he'd worked his way up from deckhand to sales manager. It worked well as cover for missions when he'd have to be gone in some cases for weeks, working out deals with foreign clients.

· · ·

"Omar, my love, I'm here, can you hear me?"

"Yes . . . uh yes. I'm sorry; I was lost in my memories of how we met."

"What happened to you, Omar? I'm told Abu Hamza was killed in the blast that put you here. What happened? Why did this happen?"

The pleasure of remembering the best part of his life was instantly replaced with pain and rage at the loss of the only man he'd ever loved.

He reached to his cheek and clasped her hand as he closed his eyes and compressed his emotions to protect his beloved. Moments passed before he could bring his emotions under control enough to be able to look at Suzan again and speak.

How can I tell her without putting her in danger? She and our sons are all that matter to me now.

Suzan had always known about Omar's close relationship with the man from his mosque and the hole he filled in Omar's life left by his blood father. She'd never really come to know Abu Hamza well, because she did not attend mosque with her husband. She did know Omar looked to him often for advice, counsel, and companionship. Even with that, the emotion and radiating anger from her husband was like she'd never seen and there was something so dark about it, she was frightened. She would lay that aside and care for his wounds, inside and out.

Perhaps the Spirit of God will use me in this horrible event to show Omar His unfailing love and eternal hope.

"I don't know why this happened or by whose hand, but I will find who it was and they will pay a dear price."

"My Omar, I understand your grief and anger, but we must focus on your healing. The doctors tell me your back was broken in two places, you have a very bad concussion, and it will take weeks for your burns to heal. Thanks be to God you were not closer to the explosion or more of your burns would be third degree. As it is, your lower back will have some scarring, but with graphs and a new burn therapy they told me about, the scars will not be pronounced.

"My dear, I know you loved Abu Hamza as no other and I cannot say how sad I am for his death and your loss. I liked him too; he was a good man. We will get through this together, but you must not allow hatred to fill your heart where your love was. You can cherish your memories of your friend and let the authorities find his killers."

"How long have I been here?"

"Three days. You were in such bad shape they induced a coma until repairs could be made. They said you'd most likely wake this morning. I've been here since I was notified of the bombing. Surgery fixed your spine, but you will need months of therapy to regain full mobility.

"I could have lost you . . . " Suzan could contain herself no longer; she lowered her head and wept into her hands. "You must tell me why this happened. I have had questions from our beginning about where you go and what you do. I must know the truth."

"I have wanted to tell you for some time about who I really am, but I feared losing you. I see now this choice has been made for me. I chose to be who I am and do what I do long before I found you. I should have given you the choice as well."

For the next hour, Omar told his wife of his childhood and the pivotal point of his life at age seven, leading to the present. Suzan only stopped him twice to ask questions. Almost from the moment he began, Suzan's tears ceased and her being was overwhelmed by the realization of what she'd previously only vaguely feared. Her husband was her mortal enemy and the enemy of her family, and her family of faith. At the same time, he was still the man she loved completely. The emotions, thoughts, and foreboding threatened to rip her to fragments. Then came the statement she feared most.

"I do not want to lose you Suzan, but I give you the choice now that you know the truth. Of course our sons will remain with me. Not only because that is our law, but to insure our safety."

She took a breath and opened her mouth to respond . . .

6

A KNOCK ON the door coincided with its opening. In walked one of Omar's fellow Jihadists, Cairo. They'd known each other from the beginning, when Omar first joined the Muslim Brotherhood. Cairo was about a year older and much larger in build. He was recruited from an influential family in Beirut, from the bloodline of Abu Hamza. Though Omar and Cairo came to the organization at about the same time and had their initial training together, they never formed a friendship. From the time Cairo joined Abu Hamza's cell, his arrogance was like a splinter under a fingernail to Omar. He was strong and took well to training, but it always seemed to Omar he didn't consider himself part of the team. It was as though he was passing through on his way somewhere and on his way, he took every opportunity to put others under his boot.

The reason Cairo started focusing his efforts against Omar was the favor he received from Abu Hamza and Abu Jihad, their trainer.

The rivalry between Cairo and Omar started their first day at the secret camp near the coast, the most exciting place the seven-year-old had ever seen. Located behind a high wall, the main facilities were surrounded by obstacle courses, firing ranges, and urban assault structures.

Omar was picked from the group within minutes of arriving to start small arms training. Abu Jihad swung an AK-47 off his shoulder and handed it to Omar. He'd never held anything so powerful or inspiring and his enthusiasm was obvious as his finger went immediately to the trigger. Abu Jihad quickly intervened and proceeded to instruct Omar in how to safely handle the rifle. He proceeded to show him how to hold, aim, fire, and reload. Every explosion sending lead downrange seemed to energize Omar. The sound and concussion was to his spirit what food was to his body. Though he was exhilarated by the violence of the full auto setting, there was something more satisfying about the precision of sending one round at a time into the head of the human silhouette fifty feet away.

After the lesson, on their way to lunch, Cairo sidled up to Omar.

"That was fun, wasn't it?"

"I liked it."

"It seems you are liked as well."

"What do you mean?"

"The instructor picked you to go first and he took more time with you than the rest of us. I guess he could see right away you would need extra help."

Omar stopped and glared at Cairo, who kept walking to the dining hall.

Omar was not the type to gleam in the light of attention. He never really took it as a compliment when someone shrouded him in glory, nor did he take it as a slight when he was not recognized. His life trained him to withhold trust and that made him believe most adulation was disingenuous. Cairo on the other hand, had a thirst for praise, the type that quenched his undying need to be accepted, even exalted.

One night the boys rolled out their pallets on the ground and prepared for bed as usual. Before most of the others finished, Omar was stretched out with his back turned to the clamor. As he started to close his eyes, he overheard Cairo boasting to a group of boys.

"My grandfather, the Great Imam of Bakker Mosque, invited the Grand Mufti, Abu Hamza, and *three* viziers from the Lebanese government for dinner at our home last summer."

His audience emitted a wave of audible amazement.

"THAT'S RIGHT! AND GUESS who got to eat with them?" He said pointing to himself.

"You wouldn't believe the food. Legs of lamb bigger than your head! Couscous with pearl onions and tomatoes. Baba ghanoush and huge bowls of hummus and fresh olive oil. And last but not least, homemade *kanafa* for dessert. The best of the best."

"Well what did you talk about?" One of the boys asked.

"Nothing worthy of your ears, *ya missqeen*." Cairo laughed and spit at his feet.

The rest roared with laughter.

"But I will tell you, since you are all surely desperate to know, they had a lot to say about me! My grandfather says one day I will be the next Abu Hamza. So kiss up now, because sooner or later you'll be answering to me."

Omar huffed in amused scorn to himself, thinking of Cairo as little more than a drum full of air.

From that moment, Omar noticed a change in some of the boys. It was as if they believed themselves to be less than before; they took the position of subordinates to a superior, and followed Cairo around like his personal staff. Of course, not all the boys fell in line; many felt the same as Omar and were disgusted by the stink of Cairo's arrogance.

In contrast, Omar commanded a sense of respect. His inner confidence and fair nature made him rise as a leader as well. The boys who fell under him were rich and poor, strong and weak, encompassing a full range of different talents and lifestyles.

Sameer, one of Omar's closest friends during their initial training, was of a similar wealthy bloodline to Cairo. Because of this, Cairo often sought Sameer's presence, assuming they were equals and aligned. But Sameer was more kindred to the spirit of Omar, uninterested in big-headed conquests and lavish lifestyles. Their strength, acumen, and confidence made the pair an unstoppable force. As such, their relationship sickened Cairo more than anything, and the rivalry between him and Omar continued to build pressure.

The main difference that emerged between Omar and Cairo was their sense of mortality. Cairo clung to his; Omar was ever ready to exchange his for Allah's favor, bypassing the grave, and assurance of jannah.

One day Abu Hamza came to all of the boys with a request.

"Syria has given us a green light to go through the Goulan Heights and take weapon caches to the Fedayeen, 'the Martyr Brothers.' I would like to know which of you will go."

The room stood silent for a while, as the boys looked down and away from one another. From the crowd the newly dubbed Abu al-Wafá stood and said, "We will go, Sameer and I. The mission is ours."

"Good. I would proudly see you both go."

A smile stretched across Abu Hamza's face as he turned and walked away.

As he exited the room, Abu Jihad shouted, "Our god is greater and higher than any god! Now, what is our creed?"

The boys yelled back in unison, "Allah is our objective, the prophet is our leader, the Quran is our law, Jihad is our way, dying in the way of Allah is our highest aspiration, Allah Akbar, Allah Akbar, Allah Akbar."

As the sound faded, they returned to their training.

One hot summer day, the boys shuffled through training, stripping to the barest articles of clothing they could to stave off the heat. The main obstacle of the day was to crawl through a series of land mines under a barbed-wire fence and come out the other side unscathed. Two went at the same time and raced to the end of the obstacle. The purpose of the exercise was to instill bravery and competition.

Omar went through for the first time and returned to the back of the line victorious. Sameer was obviously nervous as be scanned the obstacle and saw what it did to some of the boys.

"Don't worry," Omar said. "It's pretty easy. Just make sure you keep yourself on a straight path and crawl as fast as you can"

Omar was in his element and even took pleasure in wiping away the sweat and mud on his face. His enthusiasm was more encouraging to Sameer than his words.

"Alright, I can do that. Hopefully 'you know who' won't cheat and throw an elbow like he did yesterday"

The two laughed and talked until it was Sameer's turn to race Cairo. Once at the front, the two boys got on their hands and knees and waited for the go ahead. It was a vicious competition between the two; they were neck and neck the entire way. As they got near the end of the obstacle, Sameer was gaining on Cairo when one of the mines exploded, ripping Omar's friend to pieces.

Cairo was pulled from the course, bloodied and blubbering. They pulled shrapnel from his arms and hands, as he had apparently used them to protect his head from the explosion.

Days later everyone wanted to know what happened, what he saw. Cairo's reaction was to turn red, don a pitiful expression, and cry sullenly without shedding a tear. While others patted him on the back and expressed their regrets that he had to endure such a thing, Omar knew he was insincere, he knew Cairo was not capable of feeling sorry or sad. Most of all, he knew Cairo was somehow responsible.

As Cairo entered Omar's hospital room, he held a similar miserable expression and Omar's stomach dropped. Suzan stifled the words she was ready to deliver and quickly put a tissue to her face as she rose to greet Omar's "workmate." She'd only seen him a few times. He was never in their home and Omar rarely spoke of him. There was something repellant about him, but she would never say anything of the sort to Omar. Many things were becoming clearer.

"I will leave you to talk," she said. "I'll check on our boys."

Cairo brightened slightly, "It is good to see you, Suzan, though I wish it were under better circumstances."

"Thank you, Cairo."

"Omar, I'll be back in a few minutes and I'll bring your sons. They are very anxious to see you."

As soon as the door met the jamb, Omar spoke. "What do you want, Cairo?"

Cairo took the seat vacated by Suzan. "Abu Youssef asked me to come. Your wife told him you'd likely awaken today, and we need to hear from you about what happened."

"Why send you? Why did he not come himself?"

"He has taken over for Abu Hamza at least temporarily. The High Council wants him out of the public as much as possible until we can get to the bottom of this. He resisted, but I volunteered to come on his behalf, and he accepted. However, you should know our leaders are also concerned about how this may draw unwanted attention after your most recent mission and their political successes in New York. I'm here to get your report."

Omar pondered the implications of Cairo being in a meeting with al-Zawahiri. "I have little to report. A demon planted a bomb in the café where Abu Hamza and I were having lunch. I can only assume we were the targets, but Allah has spared me for his reasons. I pray he allows me the honor of finding and crushing my enemy. The strange thing to me is the timing of the bomb; had it been detonated even a few seconds sooner, I would be with Abu Hamza now. What do you know of this?"

"No more than you. We are interviewing our eyes and ears around town, but nothing of substance has been gained yet. There is some speculation about this being the work of the Israelis, which is to be expected, but it would be unusual for them to place a bomb in a public place. The cowards would rather lob them over their borders. The other thing opposing that scenario is we discovered the explosive used was not unlike what you've used in recent operations. Perhaps the one responsible used your supplier."

"You should know that won't lead us anywhere. I use that material because its chemical composition cannot be traced to a single source. So much has been made and in so many locations, it's impossible to trace the origin of a single device. This information does help me somewhat though."

"Yes, how so?"

"That is for me to ponder for now. When I'm back on my feet I'll keep Abu Youssef informed. I will find who did this and . . . they . . . will . . . pay."

The glare from Omar's eyes into Cairo's caused him to blink as though his retinas were being burned. He averted his eyes and shifted in his seat.

"I spoke with your sons before I came to your room. They are growing into fine men. You must be proud."

Jarred by the abrupt subject change, Omar's countenance softened, and he said, "Eh, yes, Mohammad and Youssef are gifts from Allah. All praise to him. I assume you spoke of nothing regarding the attack."

"Of course not, that is not for me to do. I only told them how sorry we are at work and we are praying for your quick recovery and return."

"How old is Mohammad now? Nine? Ten? Is it not time to bring him into the Brotherhood?"

It was probably a good thing for Cairo his colleague was in no condition to move, much less react as his emotions motivated. He managed to roll slightly to his right side and raise his head. His eyes narrowed to slits. It was hard to tell if his trembling was from weakness or rage.

In a measured, low voice that dropped the temperature in the room to about twenty degrees below zero, he said, "You must listen to what I'm about to say as though your life depends on it. My family is none of your concern, especially my sons. You will not speak to them again unless I am present and you will never speak of them to me. I am their father and you have no part in their lives and never will. My sons will walk the paths Allah and I have for them, and Allah will not protect you from me if you violate this vow."

Seconds or perhaps hours passed before Cairo rose and turned to leave. He pulled the door open a few inches, turned, and said, "You might want to take care how you speak to the man who may soon lead Al-Asifa." He was through the doorway before Omar could react.

Cairo brushed past Alia, Mohammad, and Youssef in the hall as though they weren't there.

Alia quickly put her arms around her boys and ushered them in to see their father. Foreboding enclosed her heart. She left a trail of prayer down the busy hospital corridor.

7

Blake turned into the main entrance to Fort Lee and pulled up to the guard shack. A young PFC asked for his ID and placed it face down on his tablet.

"Mr. Hunter, welcome to Fort Lee," he said. "You're expected at the headquarters building, do you know where that is?"

"Thanks, I think so soldier, but is there one place better than another to park?"

"You'll see the main door as soon as you approach the building; there should be open visitor slots right up front."

"Thanks again."

As he drove away from the gate, Blake was a little disturbed at what seemed to be rather lax security around the base. The soldier at the gate only had a sidearm and the others he saw moving around carried no weapons at all.

You'd think they'd have learned by now after the attacks at Fort Hood and the other military installations around the country. I hope Bob isn't going to ask me to work on a base. At least at the Farm, no one's supposed to know we exist.

Several blocks from the gate, Blake followed the signs and pulled into a space facing the headquarters building a few yards from the door.

He approached the security desk and told the female PFC behind the desk he was there to see the commanding general. She scanned Blake's ID and printed a visitor label for his shirt. She touched her screen again and said Jacob Hunter was there to see the general. The voice on the other end said to send him up.

A couple of brief directions sent him two floors up and to the general's outer office where his civilian secretary rose from her chair and said, "Mr. Hunter, we've been expecting you, the Secure Video Teleconference is right through here." She showed him to an adjoining conference room.

Inside the windowless room, there was a fifteen foot oval table surrounded by leather office chairs. At one end of the rectangular space, a video panel that looked to be about eight feet wide was mounted on the wall.

The secretary asked if he needed anything to drink and, when he declined, she exited and pulled the door shut behind her. When the door met the jamb, Blake heard the ping signaling the room being electronically sealed.

At the same time an easeled tablet on the credenza under the video panel lit with the words "Welcome Blake" and a voice said, "Please press your right index finger to the screen and have a seat." A second after Blake touched the tablet, the "Welcome" disappeared and the video panel displayed the Army Special Forces logo.

Blake sat in the chair at the end of the table closest to the monitor.

Bob Johnson appeared on the screen. "Blake Kershaw, it's great to see your face," Bob said. "I must say though, the plastic surgery has certainly made you unrecognizable to folks like me who knew you before you went to the dark side. Don't worry; the only folks here who know you are still alive, other than me, are two of the guys on the team who pulled you out of Iran a decade ago. We told them because you'd served together. In fact, two of the other guys from that team are now retired and the other two are doing different jobs so you need to keep that in mind as we get into the substance of this discussion. I doubt you'll ever run into them, but they do know your face."

"Being dead has its perks, but the downside is worse," Blake replied. "You may not know, even my mother thinks I am dead."

"I don't need to tell you my reaction when I was told," Bob said. "Of course then I didn't know you'd gone to work for the Agency. You'd really be dead and I'd never have known the truth had my team not been tasked to pull you out of Iran. I've never found anyone to replace you. Look, I hope we can catch up on things soon, but I need to get on with business."

"Go. I'm ready to hear what's so urgent."

"As you probably know, Blake, the foreign policy coming out of Washington the last couple of decades has not made our work very easy. We're supposed to keep America safe, but we're not given the tools or permission to get it done. In fact, it seems the only time we're cut loose to go after bad guys, is when the politicians need a boost with their constituents."

"Yes, sir, I've been paying attention. How have you managed under those conditions? I know you to be a badass warrior."

"Let's talk about that another time. For now, let me give you a context for why I called you.

"We've been spending a lot of time and assets following the strands of hundreds of terrorist organizations and cells operating on every continent looking to take out the leaders. A pattern is forming that's doing real damage to our long held belief that these groups answer to no central leadership. That theory took a huge hit after we got Bin Laden. Taking him out had no discernible effect on Al Qaeda's operations. It certainly didn't lower the attack rate. Between the numerous factions who at times even fight each other and the theological chasm separating Sunnis and Shiites, we've assumed we were fighting a disjointed and somewhat anarchistic enemy." Johnson paused a beat and then continued.

"That day is gone.

"You probably know the UN has granted special status to the second largest alliance of nations next to them; The Organization of Islamic Cooperation, or OIC. It was one of the last blows to international security Obama managed to land before leaving office. Of course his successor is not much better, but the rancor during the election cycle and the ongoing grassroots uprising since then has given us a little space to pursue things strictly forbidden under Obama. As if the UN wasn't enough of a threat to our national sovereignty, with the OIC on the Security Council, we think all Hell is about to break loose.

"They make no secret of the nations you would expect to be aligned with Islam, including those we know to be fomenters of Jihad. They are based in Saudi Arabia and have official agreements with seventy-two other nation-states including the likes of Iran, Turkey, and Malaysia. It's the ones they don't advertise we should be most concerned about. We believe the United States Council of Muslim Organizations is their connection here. Are you aware of them?"

"Yes, sir, but only from what I see on the Net. I confess, my cynicism about all accessible sources of information keeps rising. I know they had a much larger presence during the 2016 elections than most thought they would, but they still seem to be pretty small compared to the other parties."

"Now's not the time to go into the American political side of this discussion, Blake, but hold those thoughts for later.

"OIC's public purpose is to be the voice of Muslims worldwide and to protect the interests of their over two-billion members. They also use words like: education, good governance, democracy, and human rights. While the gullible continue to buy into this line, we can't afford to be that lazy. We have good reason to believe this is in fact the governing body for the Caliphate they've pursued since Mohammad. They are closer to fulfilling their dreams than anyone wants to think.

"I need you to come to Bragg as soon as possible. We've collected a pile of intel you will find interesting and which will explain why I need you back at Delta. I wish I could explain more now, but as secure as this line may be, I have to go SCI on this one."

"Roger that, sir. Do you have a specific timeline for this?"

"As I mentioned before, I have no time stretch, so I'm gonna have to ask you to be here within forty-eight hours or I'll have to go another way. I really don't want to do that, so I hope you can get your ass over here. Your background is exactly what we need applied here. If you decide not to come back for this, no harm, no foul, but I think you're going to at least want to know what's going on."

"Sir, I'll need to talk this over with my wife. Would it be okay if she made the trip with me?"

"You bet. She's cleared for this level of intel, though it's probably not a good idea for her to be in on your briefing. Let me know as fast as you can and I'll make arrangements for you to stay overnight."

"Thank you, sir. I'll be back home in a few hours and I should be able to get word back to you by late tonight. How do you want me to contact you?"

"I'll ping you when we're done here and you can use that to reply. Thanks for coming, Blake. I've always been able to count on you."

"You've more than earned my trust over the years, sir. I'm honored you still want to work with me. I hope I can be of service."

"I know you can, Blake, now it's just a matter of whether you will. I'll look for your message later. God bless you and give my regards to Alia."

"I will, sir."

With that, the screen returned to black and the ping sounded again, letting Blake know he was free to leave the room.

Since Blake's last mission and medical recovery, his relationship with Alia was not what they'd once had and he wasn't sure what to do about it. This was not going to help. Though she'd been involved in military and clandestine work for most of her life, the possibility of losing her husband, and now the father of her son to it, was a strain.

After years of combat and high value missions, Blake was finding it hard to be at home. He loved his wife and son more than his own life, but not having a focused purpose outside of them was not working well with his metabolism.

He took the position at CIA's secret base in eastern Virginia doing training for paramilitary operations because it meant being home every night, and it was at least close to the kind of work he loved. Even though he was never read into the missions, it was always a pull when one of the teams he trained would be called to action. After all, he found his wife on his first clandestine operation. He was caught between the competing sentiments of wanting to be home with his son and the woman he owed his very life to, and his powerful instinct to be in the action. It was just part of his DNA and there was little he could do to change it.

When Blake and Alia met, he was blind. The first job he took with The Agency changed everything about his life. His job was to take on the identity of a prison convert to Islam which would gain him access to an isolated terrorist training camp in Garj Valley, Pakistan. There, intel compiled over many months pointed to nuclear weapons being prepared on site to be transported to multiple targets, most likely among them; America.

An essential part of assuming the identity of Grant Reinbolt was facial reconstruction. When Blake awoke from surgery, a woman was there he at first assumed was a nurse. That notion was dispelled when she introduced herself as Alia, special assistant to Colson Atwater, CIA's deputy director of operations. She was there to give him an intense emersion into all things Muslim.

He was both anxious and in dread of having the bandages removed. Being without his sight was one of the worst experiences of his life. However, he had become so enamored with Alia, he was afraid of what his eyes would first take in. He would be devastated if her appearance didn't match her voice and touch. He had nothing to fear.

Blake and Alia were married by his mentor, General Sam, on the general's farm as soon as he could stand on his own after his last mission. Thanks to Alia, he'd been pulled out of Iran after guiding a bunker buster onto the heads of that country's top leadership. He was closer to the blast than sanity dictated. His best man was ready to catch him just in case.

· · ·

BLAKE MADE IT home in time for dinner, much to the delight of his eight-year-old son. He was particularly excited this evening because he'd been selected to play on the football team of his choice in their homeschooling co-op league. His mom was not terribly happy about her son being pounded on the gridiron, but she'd given up trying to buffer the recreational activities of her men.

After getting their Sam into bed with prayer, Blake and Alia retired to the front porch for a glass of wine and to talk about the day. Alia was ambivalent about hearing what Blake found out at Fort Lee. She needed to know, but she felt a foreboding in her chest.

Blake filled her in on most all of what Colonel Johnson told him, which of course wasn't much and was known by Alia anyway. She was no longer active with the Agency, but she held her clearance and was called on occasion to consult as a freelancer. It was usually something comms intel gathered that needed to be filtered through someone fluent in Arabic and Muslim culture.

She was well aware of OIC, and even of them being a front for activities not listed on their Web site. However, she knew little more than that and no specifics. That was no barrier to speculation though, as it was easy for her to connect the dots between what OIC may be up to and Blake's experience and expertise. She already didn't like where this was headed.

Alia came out of Islam and for good reason. She knew of its inherent malevolence and the cancerous danger it was to the world. She joined the CIA to fight it and there had been no diminution in her acrimony for Jihad and the demons behind it. She'd also seen the only man she ever loved almost killed twice in that fight.

Blake on the other hand was finding it difficult to completely quash his invigoration over being wanted back on the teams as he told Alia why Colonel Johnson wanted them to come to Bragg. His rather feeble attempt at playing it down reminded her of her son trying to convince her how safe football was.

Even greater than her willingness to oppose Islam, was Alia's immutable commitment to her marriage and family. She knew Blake struggled with feeling useless as he tried to show her his devotion by taking a non-combat posting. She also knew it was building a cloud of resentment between them. That was not tenable.

She would go to Fort Bragg with Blake, not just for him, but this way at least she'd know what he was doing and perhaps she could even find a way to help. She would arrange for their favorite sitter to stay with Sam and keep him up on his lessons while they were gone.

Before turning in, Blake found Bob's message on his phone, hit reply, and typed in: *We will arrive tomorrow evening.* Since he'd already taken the time off for his hunting trip, there was no need to notify his boss at The Farm. If he returned to Delta, the brass would have to work out his transfer.

8

T HE DRIVE FROM Aylett, Virginia, to Fayetteville, North Carolina, took six hours including a relaxed lunch at one of their favorite mom-and-pop barbeque places south of Richmond. The meeting with Colonel Johnson was scheduled for the next morning. Johnson had replied to Blake's confirmation message with the request he arrive early enough in the day to allow for a few hours of reading to prepare.

They pulled through the Longstreet gate at Fort Bragg and headed to The Landmark Inn. All the arrangements were in order to receive Mr. and Mrs. Jacob Hunter. After getting their key-cards for the room, the desk clerk retrieved a sealed envelope with a receipt attached, which he asked Blake to sign before transferring it into his possession. From its heft, Blake and Alia wouldn't be getting much time together that evening. A sense of excitement flooded Blake's emotions and he silently contemplated, *I'm back in the game. Feels good. Don't let Alia see I am eager to do something operational. Who am I kidding? She knows me too well.*

After settling into their room, Alia decided she'd head to the Exchange to pick up a few things and get something special for little Sam. Since Blake was going to dive directly into his homework, she would also get some take-out for them both. As she was retrieving the keys, Blake stepped behind her and wrapped his arms around her waist. His tender kiss on her neck brought a feeling of security as well as passion. But she knew it was just his way of saying thanks for supporting him in his efforts to save the world.

"I really love you, Alia; you know that don't you?"

"Of course, Blake, I do know that and I love you too, with all my heart."

Blake released his grip on his wife and gently turned her around to face him. His look was serious and somewhat puzzling to Alia.

"What are you thinking, Blake? You have an odd look on your face"

"Well, Alia, I think it's time for us to stop using my real name. While you have never slipped and called me Blake in front of anyone, I am concerned about our Sam. It could be very confusing for him if either of us ever slips up and uses my real name. We have to accept that Blake Kershaw is dead. Everyone knows me as Jacob Hunter anyhow. I just think it's safer all around to use Jacob, even when it is just the two of us."

Alia was relieved. "Jacob, is that it? I thought that you were about to confess to loving another woman." She smiled and turned to leave.

Blake broke the seal on the envelope and pulled out a sheaf of about a hundred pages of documents, maps, and photos. The cover letter from Colonel Johnson explained how reading through the enclosed material on the OIC would save them considerable time in the meeting and allow Blake to prepare questions they would no doubt invoke.

The first few pages recapped with a bit more detail about OIC's origins and current status, from their first official meeting in 1970 with a handful of attendees, to their recognition by the UN and a seat at the Security Council table even Germany couldn't attain. Blake was almost amused by a line from their Web site; "The Organization is the collective voice of the Muslim world and ensuring to safeguard and protect the interests of the Muslim world in the spirit of promoting international peace and harmony among various people of the world."

That statement didn't sound much like the instructions given the Muslim people in the Quran. The passage from Surah 4:89 always came to Blake's mind when he heard things like this from the Caliphate. "Those who reject Islam must be killed. If they turn back from Islam, take hold of them and kill them wherever you find them . . . " Blake briefly reflected on the time he'd spent living in the Afghan mountains while on his first mission for the CIA. Under deep cover, Blake became one of them and was more familiar than most about their theology as well as their methodology. This whole OIC thing was just a big propaganda program but few Americans had figured that out, in spite of the progress the hardcore Islamists had made in their quest to dominate the world for Allah.

Further into the reading material, the connections between the OIC and America took shape.

Concerns about the infiltration of Islamofacism into every level of society, which had been on the intelligence radar for decades, finally hit the national conscientiousness after September 11, 2001. So-called fringe groups warned of the dangers presented by Islam long before, but they were pushed off audible frequencies with chiding mainstream chants of "conspiracy theorists," "Islamophobes," and "hate speech." Even "Christians" and "churches" piled on in defense of Muslims.

Under the Obama administration, any pretense of supporting and defending the U.S. Constitution against all enemies foreign and domestic was dropped. They enlisted cabinet members, department heads, and staff from organizations known to be part of international terrorism. In one interview on French television, Obama told the reporter, "If you took the number of Muslims in America, we would be one of the largest Muslim countries in the world." In perhaps the most telling act of all, when calling on the King of Saudi Arabia, he bowed at the waist to put his head lower than the king's. This was an unprecedented act by a U.S. president and shed light on how the OIC was able to gain so much ground in America in so little time. A Saudi prince, four years prior to Obama, declared a Muslim would be the next U.S. president.

A section of the material was dedicated to immigration's impact on the metastasizing of radical Islam within U.S. borders. Not only was enforcement not tightened after 9/11, laws on the books were blatantly ignored and others concocted from thin air by the White House. All to the function of keeping those who hate America on station and making the inward flow unhindered.

This is where the intelligence package funneled into actionable discoveries. It began with the accidental partial exposure of how the terror network in America functions. A young man, recently hired to do odd jobs at a used car lot went looking for car washing supplies one day and found a room stacked with weapons of all sorts. He was smart enough to keep it to himself until he got off work and could call the police.

By the time the red tape was processed and officers dispatched, the owner was gone and the office and storeroom cleaned out. Forensics found residuals from weapons and ammunition, and interviews and record tracing lead to a Pakistani native in the country illegally. His cover was good enough to allow him to fade into the shadows.

The one thing they could not completely control were the car registrations required to move them from state to state. That was the key to how they moved weapons, money, and people around.

The network was sophisticated enough in compartmentalization as to minimize the damage in losing one operation. However, the opening in their veil was the view counter-terrorism needed to get a foothold. From the scraps they learned in running down every lead from the Atlanta, Georgia car lot, every branch of U.S. law enforcement had agents tracking and infiltrating small businesses all over the country. One crumb left on the trail was the extra document needed to move cars to and from Mexico.

Progress was bogged down by restrictions put on the agencies by the Justice Department and budget cuts primarily reducing field agents. The worst of all, though, were the shadow cells within every law enforcement branch. There was no other way to explain how the key players in the terror network were always gone by the time an arrest warrant was issued. Of course it also didn't help that most of the illegals swept up in the raids were released by circuit court judges.

This was all very interesting to Blake, but he wasn't sure how this would necessitate his return to Delta. Their operations were never on U.S. soil, so this must somehow lead to dealing with the up line of OIC overseas.

· · ·

Alia returned from shopping and had take-out food from the Greek Odyssey restaurant. It wouldn't be as good as Alia's, but her acumen in the kitchen developed a regular craving in Blake for lamb, spanakopita, and baklava. They sat at the desk, ate, and talked about what Blake read while she was gone. Because Alia previously worked for the CIA, she still had a TOP SECRET clearance. In fact, she only left her job there to be at home with their son, Sam, who was named for Blake's old mentor, Lieutenant General Samuel V. Wilson. Blake felt comfortable sharing the contents of the file with Alia and secretly hoped she would be persuaded that he should accept this mission, whatever it was. He needed to get back to what inspired and motivated him most, *action*!

Colonel Johnson asked Blake to meet him at the Special Warfare Center at oh-six-hundred so he and Alia retired early. Blake wanted to get up early enough to get in a five-mile run and they were both a bit tired from the day's activities.

.   .   .

After arriving and going through a biometric screening, Blake was escorted to the operations room in sub-basement two where Bob Johnson and an Army Intelligence officer were waiting. After brief cordialities, the three moved to a group of chairs facing a wall bearing six large video panels. On the top center screen was the picture of a *keffiyeh*-clad man with the name Iyad Ameen Madani printed at the bottom.

Blake recognized him as the secretary general of OIC who took the post in January of 2014. Born in Mecca and educated in America, he held positions in the Saudi monarchy and worked in print and media before being nominated to lead the OIC.

Then a picture of another face familiar to Blake appeared below Mandani's.

"You probably recognize this guy," said Johnson. "His full name is Ayman Mohammed Rabie al-Zawahiri. He's been front and center in the so-called war on terror since he and Bin Laden hit the international scene in 1998 and the U.S. embassy bombings in Africa. He's kept a low profile for the past several years. We now know why.

"The OIC has become the overseer for terrorist operations worldwide. There are still a few groups maintaining their autonomy, but most of the best financed, equipped, and staffed organizations have thrown in.

"Madani is the store front. He's the pitch man and diplomat. His job is to sell the over-the-counter brand of Islam and he and his agents are doing a hell of a job. There are probably no more than a handful of college campuses around the world that don't have a controlling Islamic influence embedded by Prince Talal of Saudi Arabia. They have also managed to get every major textbook publisher in the world on board as the one religion taught under the guise of cultural studies.

"Our work over the last several months has shed some light on the operations side of OIC. That's where al-Zawahiri and his brother Muhammad come in. The elder heads the directorate that vets and coordinates the missions initiated by, or tasked to, the various organizations. His brother does the onsite meetings and leads an enforcement team, a rather nasty bunch."

"Do we know where they work from, can we get to them?"

"Don't get ahead of me, Jacob. I've always appreciated your 'strap it on and get it done' MO, which is why you're here, but we need to take this one step at a time. The empty suits in Washington swing between not wanting to do anything and knee-jerking when they think it'll get 'em on the talking-head circuit where they can pound their chests and raise their polling. Those of us who have been at this while elections come and go have to work around the dilettantes.

"While we're on the subject of Washington, now's as good a time as any to cover the political realities we face. Our government is schizophrenic at best. Since the uprising of the Tea Party in 2009, the establishment has been scrambling to hold on to their seats while the insurgent Constitutional conservatives have flipped the switch on the klieg lights making it tough for the globalists to work. People are paying more attention than they have since Kennedy. Unfortunately, for those of us who simply want to do the job of defending America, the corrupt system built over decades of political avarice and electoral apathy has deep roots.

"That's why I'm asking you to come back to Delta. The combination of your "nonexistent" status and extraordinary skills in counterterrorism will make it possible for us to conduct the operations our intel has indicated as crucial, while keeping a low profile on the Hill. We can compartmentalize you and your team to insure security and freedom of movement."

"Roger that, sir. How do we proceed?"

Colonel Johnson motioned to the Intel officer and a map appeared on the upper left screen. It covered an area from Portugal to India and from the UK to Niger. Red starbursts were posted on numerous points.

"The bursts on this map show where attacks and other terrorist operations have been carried out over the last ten years." Johnson waved his hand again and all but eight of the starbursts disappeared. "Based on Humint, comms collection, and forensics, we think we've found someone these events have in common, the most recent was the nightclub bombing in Berlin—more on that in a minute. We know he most often goes by Abu al-Wafá and we are ninety percent sure he operates out of Beirut. Of course the bad news is that's probably not the name he puts on rental agreements and utility bills. The good news is we have a contact in Beirut who will be able to help."

"Let me guess, this guy is somehow a link to al-Zawahiri and the OIC."

"Sharp as always, soldier. We want to use Abu al-Wafá to get to the leadership and at least slow them down, if not make them fold. The Germany bombing is primarily why we have been able to plow through most of the political BS we're normally mired in and why we've been able to move so quickly to calling you back. The brass at the Pentagon have finally found a pair to put in their jocks. They lost two excellent officers in that blast and one of them was spearheading our OIC investigation through NATO. The other was the son of the army chief of staff. I don't think the Jihadis knew who was in the building or they might have reconsidered. Even a bear knows better than to stir up a hornet's nest. It's also possible their hubris was bigger than their brains.

"I'm prepared to offer you a direct promotion to lieutenant colonel and the freedom to select a team. You'll have full tactical and intelligence support, but everything will be run through me. You will be on a special roster few people have access to in order to cover the fact you are back in the army"

"I like the sound of that, sir, but I wonder if I might be able to ask two things first."

"What's on your mind?"

"Before my requests, just confirm for me that the mission is to capture Abu al-Wafá, hoping he will lead us to Zawahiri. Do I have that much right?"

"Yes, Jacob, we need Abu al-Wafá. Given some of our newer interrogation methods, including a new category of drugs, Abu al-Wafá will tell us what he knows regardless how much of a tough guy he thinks he is. He will lead us to the leadership of ninety percent of the terrorist operations in the world today. Blake, this is as big as the missions you have run at the agency. I realize you stopped a nuke attack on Washington a few years ago. And the mission in Iran was incredible. But I'm serious when I tell you—this is just as big."

"I'd like to be able to have Alia read into the basics of our ops and I'd like to be able to run this by General Sam."

"I don't see a problem with either of those requests; in fact, Alia and the general can only be assets to what we have planned. However, as I've told you since disturbing your deer hunting, this is extremely time sensitive. This organization and its top operatives are as slippery as they come. We must move on this ASAP to have any hope of success. I'll need your answer in twenty-four hours and if affirmative, you'll need to have a team selected and assembled here within a week."

"Yes, sir, I think that's doable. Alia and I have already been able to talk some about the threat the OIC poses and she's no less at war with Islam than ever. I'll call General Sam when we leave here and see if we can connect on our way home."

The rest of the meeting was spent going over the broad aspects of how they would go after Abu al-Wafá and what to do with him. They broke in time for lunch.

. . .

Blake RETURNED TO the hotel, collected Alia and they left Fort Bragg. Talking in the car was secure and would give them plenty of time to cover all the bases. General Sam was more than happy to receive them and give them a room for the night at his lake house. Blake could read General Sam better than most. The sly smile that appeared on his face when Blake and Alia came through the front door was just a little unusual. And the way the General sounded on the phone when Blake called to see if they could meet almost made Blake think the old war dog was expecting his call. Then it dawned on him. Sure he knew. Johnson called General Sam before he contacted Blake in the first place. Johnson knew Blake would not take on a mission like this without consulting with his mentor.

Over dinner, the three discussed Colonel Johnson's request and plan for Blake's return to active duty. As usual, General Sam knew more about OIC and the operational arm than Blake was given in his briefing. He filled in a few blanks about their command and control and other suspected key players. Though it was not essential to the immediate task, Blake always liked having as much information as possible about the opposition.

The old warrior well knew what it was to be inactive after years of being on the front lines of the fight. He said nothing to discourage Blake and in fact added some points of his own as to why Blake was the man for the job. Of course taking a small assault force into Beirut on a snatch and grab was rife with inherent jeopardy and there was never assurance of a plan going by the numbers.

Blake went over the stratagem using maps projected from his new phone on loan from CIA's Counter Terrorism Center. Ingress and egress were pretty straightforward, with variables for each. It was the onsite op about which Blake had concerns. They only knew with any certainty that Abu al-Wafá worked out of Beirut, but they had no hard intel on where exactly or when he'd be there. That was all to be tracked when they got there using an Israeli contact posing as an expatriate Palestinian bike shop owner. They might be there a month or more waiting for the tumblers to fall into place.

General Sam found the plan to be sound and had only one suggestion of a piece of equipment they should have. Alia suggested Blake have a different exit option than the current backup.

General Sam assured Blake he'd be available to Alia and Sam while he was away.

Finally, Blake's most trusted friend and confidant outside Alia gave Blake a failsafe in case things really got out of hand. If he could not make contact with operations and needed immediate help, he was given a phone number and a passphrase to be used when it was answered by Global Reparations. Blake's curiosity was overruled by trust.

9

Blake and Alia had an early breakfast with General Sam at his favorite café before they headed home. He walked them to their car, gave them each a hug, and told them he'd be praying for them. He asked Alia to give Sam a big hug for him.

They rode in silence for about thirty minutes, listening to news on the radio.

"We talked about Colonel Johnson's proposal last night as though the decision was already made. Is it?" Alia was not one to fall prey to assumptions.

"I think it's something I need to do, but I also need you on board. If you have concerns or reasons to be against this, I want to hear them."

"Blake, I know we're losing the war against the spread of radical Islam and I know there are few as well suited to take the fight to them as you." Alia reached over and placed her hand on Blake's thigh. Without turning his head, he could see the tears glazing her eyes. In a tremulous, halting voice, she continued. "I'm conflicted. If by you responding to this call, we can hurt them, I'm all for it. On the other side, we have a son and a much different life from the one we started. I want you home with us, and I don't want a chaplain coming to me with bad news."

"I know, Love, but . . . "

"Please let me finish while I have my thoughts in order. I know it's been hard for you to be training when you'd rather be doing. We've talked around the edges of this for a while now, but I can see the Lord working through this situation to force the issue. I've been afraid of making it worse by going straight at it before now. Since you took the job at the Farm, you've slowly moved away from Sam and me. I urged you to take that job even though my heart told me yours wasn't in it. I both hoped you'd grow to love it as much as running missions and knew you wouldn't. You've neglected nothing and our son knows you love him, but our intimacy is dying . . . "

Blake could feel Alia's words crowding his heart, making it hard to think. He wanted to tell her he had no idea what she was talking about, but valor won and he remained silent.

"I love you more now than the day we stood at General Sam's farm and made our covenant before God, and I know you love me. I know you've not purposefully pulled back, but I also know I can't keep feeding you slack. I loathe the thought of losing you, no matter the cause. When I put my emotions aside and try to think rationally about this, I know there is no better man for this job than you. I married you in part because you are the kind of man who loves this country and is motivated by that love. But, Blake, I am your wife now and I can't stop feeling deep concern for your safety. You just have to expect that from me as I am no different from any other woman who loves her husband. I know you want, and probably need, to make this move and I give you my full support, but I ask one thing."

Blake pondered what he just heard for a moment, letting it sink in. Had she just agreed to support him taking this mission? Was she saying she was *all in* on this? He was not sure what to say next. Finally he responded, "Alia, I will do whatever you ask, and you should know that."

Although he was watching the traffic ahead, he could feel her gaze to his core as she said in a determined tone, "I choose you and your calling, so go get this guy, and when you get back, you and I need to go somewhere for some remedial marriage building, a cruise maybe."

Blake felt a strange emotion, the result of colliding feelings. He loved the woman next to him heart and bone and knew she was chosen for him by The Almighty. She was a woman of incredible courage and skill, both of which she brought to bear to save his life on his last mission. She was also a wife and a mother. He spoke softly. "I've been telling myself I've held it together pretty well, I'm sorry. I do love you, so when I'd feel what could only be resentment, I refused to deal with it because I didn't want to lay it on you. You've nailed me, and rescued me, again.

"I will get this murderer and then we'll head to the high seas. Besides, I may be getting too old for this commando stuff." He turned to see a smile on Alia's face.

"Hurry and get us home, Blake. I want to start our post-mission cruise activities a little early . . . so speed it up, my commando."

Now Blake was smiling as his right foot moved closer to the floor-board of the truck.

"I'll call Colonel Johnson when we get home and give him our decision and condition."

. . .

BLAKE WAS PACKED and headed back to Bragg within twenty-four hours. On his way there he started thinking through the selection process for his team. He would need specialists in comms, intelligence, medical, and of course, a sniper.

Harry Chee would be his first call. Not only was he the best comms guy in the business, he was the man Blake most wanted by his side when things went sideways, and in his experience, they always did, one way or another. They'd saved each other's lives more than once and there wasn't an operator anywhere he trusted more. Having Harry would fill several needs at once; along with communications, he would be his second. He was strong in surveillance and he spoke several Arabic dialects. Having him meant they could go in with five instead of the more common six which would make them lighter, faster, and less visible.

He could choose anyone he desired but he had to consider more than the capabilities of the team members. After all, Blake was officially dead and had been for a decade. Only the men who rescued him in Iran a few years ago knew he was still alive. He thought back to that moment when he expected to die, not realizing Alia had contacted Colonel Johnson in Iraq and pleaded with him to throw caution aside, break the rules, and send a team into Iran to save Blake. He had to hand it to Johnson; he put it all on the line that day when he launched the extraction team. Blake finally decided to stick with the guys who knew his story; the guys who literally pulled his ass out of the flames.

Having thought through it pretty carefully, Blake knew his next selection would be Aaron Page, the sniper who won the "Nationals" two years earlier at Camp Perry, Ohio. He was good, really good, and Blake needed him for more reasons than his marksmanship. His knowledge of weapons from around the world was unmatched. Aaron, like Blake, was a man of strong faith, which gave Blake a buttress. He was also an EMT with excellent medical skills. He'd also cross-trained in Special Forces communications so he would be a great back up for Harry.

The fourth man on the team had to be up to date on the latest intelligence methods, technologies, and techniques as well as the latest software programs. They would be relying on current intel coming from the CIA and the rest of the IC on tablets and their new PDAs which were now miniaturized and imbedded in watches. Each man would have one of these, but someone had to be able to teach the team how to use them. That meant the next choice would be a retired Sergeant Major, James Randall, known by most of his friends as "ReeRee." No one was sure how he got the moniker, but he was the best in the business with technology and intel analysis. His current job in the CIA "Ground Branch" made him readily accessible so he was an easy choice.

Blake decided on one other who'd come through his CIA training course at the Farm. Daniel Steele, from Tennessee, showed exceptional acumen for tradecraft, and he loved to hunt, which gave him and Blake something to talk about other than the mission at hand. After leaving Special Forces, where he was a trained medic, he returned to Vanderbilt and majored in pre-med. But like Blake, he was a man of action, and he knew he simply did not have the patience to spend another eight years in training. He chose instead to join the agency and became a case officer and para-military operative. He was up-to-date on the latest interrogation drugs and techniques.

Blake always thought highly of him as did ReeRee, who had been on several missions with Daniel during their time in Ground Branch. The team was complete and Blake felt good. He could not think of a better crew for this job. Things were shaping up well. Blake never considered this to be anything but voluntary and that any of the men could decline the opportunity to be part of the mission. He knew these men and he knew every one of them would accept the assignment with the same enthusiasm he had. All systems were go, now he needed to get them all together; and ASAP.

• • •

THE TEAM WAS assembled at Fort Bragg forty-eight hours later. The Special Operations leadership had shown a great deal of foresight thirty years earlier when they built a "Black Site" on the western edge of the post. Situated in a remote area, the facility had everything the team needed to train and prepare for the mission, including seclusion. All the intel pipes came into the site so they could tap live intelligence from drones as well as analyzed reports from human sources. NSA provided a "cleared" analyst to help the team sort through the SIGINT reports, which consisted mostly of emails between the key terrorist players in Beirut.

Blake's first order of business was to brief the team on the mission and then pore through the intel with them. The intel briefing generated many questions from the team members, as Blake anticipated would happen. These were real pros and they knew what questions to ask to insure the highest probability of success. Blake could see the excitement growing among his team members as they calculated the impact this could have on the terrorist network.

No man on the team was under any illusions about the difficulty of the task, nor about the risks involved, but they were not deterred by either. The team's *esprit de corps* solidified, and with it, Blake's confidence. Colonel Johnson was there for an hour or so each day, mainly to see if they needed anything. Otherwise, Blake was running the show.

The next two weeks were spent training for the mission at hand. Each day began with physical training and then off to the range for weapons practice. The men trained with suppressed weapons of varying calibers. Aaron briefed the team on the most common weapons used in the area of the op. Harry schooled them on important phrases in the local dialects and reviewed digital topography maps of the region.

Even with the latest technology, it was still impossible to find a truly silent weapon. The team was leaning toward a new sub-machine gun fresh off the H&K bench. While none of the team members really liked a 9mm caliber weapon, these new "Silent Sabres" were indeed as close to a silent weapon as could be found.

Weapons training was followed by lunch and then an intel update in the operations center. The afternoons were used for planning as they awaited nightfall. Their operation was sure to be executed in their preferred environment of night. Night vision equipment gave them a huge advantage. Many of the bad guys had NVGs as well, but they were always on the downside of the technology curve. The difference between the old cumbersome "green blob," monocular devices they had and the flush mount HD goggles Blake's team were using was like comparing a Sopwith Camel to an F-36.

The Black Site was perfect for night mission training in an urban environment as the facility had an array of movable facades, allowing them to build their own scenarios in minimal time. The staff at the site was not read into the mission, but they all had clearances and they simply asked no questions of the team regarding the mission or destination. They arranged the buildings into the requested configurations and moved out before the exercise began.

Every night, the team trained for hours, practicing the "snatch-and-grab" mission. Using live rounds and conducting "Close Quarters Battle," the team was quickly becoming an alloy of precision. Potent execution depended on each man being able to anticipate the actions of the others.

Planning included every detail down to only one of them surviving the mission going to Hell. They all knew each other, with the exception of Steele, and he caught on quick, which helped abbreviate the time it took to be ready to deploy.

Having trained and planned for two hard weeks, the team was ready for action. The final task was to pack for the trip to Beirut. They needed to travel light and maintain an inconspicuous posture. Uniforms would be the street clothes of the city. There was serious discussion among the team members about body armor. Should they risk taking it and potentially being compromised because of the extra bulk and weight? This mission had high enough risk without adding more. But there was an equal risk of not having it when the lead started flying. The consensus was to leave it and Blake agreed.

The rest of the equipment was fairly straightforward. Foldable tablets with the latest software were essential. To a casual observer, they looked like every other personal digital device. The embedded encryption was virtually undetectable.

Weapons and ammo would be the heaviest things they would carry. After much testing and discussion, the team decided to go with the new H&K sub-machine gun even though the team was unanimous in their dislike of 9mils. The composite hollow points they carried assuaged some of their disdain. The sniper rifle Aaron packed was handmade and collapsible.

The other items included mini GPS systems, hand held communications devices and a single mini-satellite radio that could be easily concealed. Equipment packed, the team was ready to rock.

They left Bragg before sunup on a chopper to Charleston where they boarded the military version of the Gulfstream G800ER. Unlike the version celebrities and senators flew, this one had the interior configuration of a commercial airliner. But that's where the similarity to a commercial flight ended. There would be no visible record of the aircraft leaving the U.S. or its flight plan. It would return under a previously filed round trip. The downside to the plane's range was the time they'd be on it getting to Egypt.

From Egypt, they took an older twin turbo-prop owned by a U.S. import/export company to get into Lebanon by way of a small airfield near the gulf of Jounieh.

From there a disguised panel van moved them the twenty-five kilometers to the Cornish Al Manara district on the coast, where the team unloaded quickly and moved their equipment into what on the outside was an old beach house, but on the inside was a CIA safe house where the agency often kept and protected important recruited agents. Blake knew this game well and only hoped this one had not been compromised by local intelligence services or, worse, by the terrorists.

Blake looked at the driver in the dim light emanating from a porch light of the house. The man looked familiar. Then it came to Blake; he had seen him around CIA headquarters. Clearly Lebanese, he was obviously with the CIA station in Beirut. He could be a great asset for the team. He looked the part.

They were equipped to present a civilian comportment until they were ready to grab Abu al-Wafá. Acting as trade agents looking for commodities to market in America gave them freedom of movement and a favorable reception from the local constabulary. That, combined with a cover as representatives for several electronic machine manufacturers meant their luggage and sample cases were not closely scrutinized.

The import/export imbalance that plagued Lebanon's economy for decades was made worse by the influx of Syrian refugees in the early 2000s. Many of these chose to stay, despite the new Muslim regime, rather than return to the continuing conflict in their home nation. Any chance to increase the flow of foreign money to the government coffers was encouraged.

The pretense of U.S. moral objection to Muslim theocratic rule was nothing more than a mask on a stick most politicians could throw up when the climate called for it and the camera light was on.

It was past oh-one-hundred the next day by the time the team settled into the well-stocked beach house in Beirut, between the south end of Rafic Hariri Stadium and a small inlet to the Mediterranean. They quickly went over the plan for the day before getting some sleep.

• • •

EARLIER IN THE day than any of them would normally prefer, the team was up and moving. Blake and Daniel headed out by cab for the bike shop on Al Habib in the Mazraá district just beyond Mar Elias, near the Russian embassy. Harry installed surveillance and comms equipment in the van with the help of the driver who identified himself as Asam, which Blake knew was an alias. Aaron did a function check on all the weapons while Harry sent out his second SITREP, the first was upon arrival, just to let the folks back at Bragg know the team arrived safely.

Blake and Daniel entered the small bike shop. Approaching the shop owner, Blake spoke first, "I am searching for Canadian made bike shoes. Do you carry those?"

The shop owner looked at Blake as if he was sizing him up before answering. "No, my friend, but I have a variety of French-made shoes?" The bonafides were properly exchanged, completing the connection between the two operatives. Bashaar swung the sign around on the front door and locked it. He turned to Blake and Daniel and flashed them the international sign for "silence." The three men moved to the back workshop and descended a flight of stairs to a depot for parts that doubled as a secure area to communicate.

The Sayeret Maktal deep cover agent had been in Beirut for the better part of ten years and was integrated fully into the local cultural fabric. He was particularly popular with the young boys in the neighborhood because he always dealt fairly with them, often let them use his phones, and had regular free Coke days. Keeping them peddling and happy provided Bashaar with a constant flow of information. Over the years he'd even managed to recruit a few for even more precise intel collection.

He'd been tasked to concentrate on the tentacles of the OIC for some time, so he was prepared to help the American team quickly narrow the search for their target. Due to the infiltration of The Muslim Brotherhood and other Islamist organizations in the American government, this kind of specific real-time intelligence was no longer transferred in any way easily traced back to the source, which was why they had to wait to get to Beirut to interface directly with the Israeli agent. The loss of a number of embedded foreign agents, mostly Israeli, during the Obama administration all but severed the close ties once enjoyed by both sides. Fortunately, there were still individuals who trusted each other.

When word came from Tel Aviv about the American operation, Bashaar started collating what he already knew with recent events and rumors. One of the best leads he had came from a bomb attack on a café about four kilometers from his shop. Seven people were killed and another dozen injured in the blast. One of the dead was known to him as Abu Hamza, the leader of a terrorist group which had been operating out of the Dar al Fatwa Mosque by Al Azhar Al Shariff since before he'd arrived. One of the injured was with him when the bomb went off.

"The injured man was taken to American University Hospital with a broken back and burns," Bashaar said. "He was released some time later. I've had my radar up on him for a while, though he must keep a low and tight profile because I haven't been able to make a direct connection between him and any specific event . . . until now. He goes by Abu al-Wafá which means, the roots of faithfulness, loyalty, and truth to the call.

"I was told he'd just returned from somewhere in Europe before the bombing, but I don't know where he lives. He's not seen around much and he's not the social type. We have managed to get voice prints on Abu Hamza and some of his men. The connection to Abu Hamza is enough for me to assume he's in the upper ranks of their cell, and rumor has it he may be Abu Hamza's successor. Going to the hospital would probably yield more crumbs from his trail."

Blake looked at Daniel who needed no more instruction. He turned and left the shop with nothing more than a quick nod to their host.

Blake stayed long enough to be sure he had the timeline and locations down, thanked Bashaar, and headed back to the beach house. He had the cab driver take a tourist route to get a general lay of the land between the Mazraá district as far north as the governmental palace and back to the coast. Blake prayed they'd find this guy not too far from their egress point. This was a busy town full of people moving around at all hours.

The team regrouped when Daniel returned from the hospital, where he'd posed as an American hospital administrator attending a lecture series at the Lebanese American University. His interest was in record-keeping procedures used at the various hospitals in town. Quick work by the embassy gained him access by the time the cab pulled up to the visitor entrance after departing the bike shop.

"I think the guy we're looking for goes by Omar al Qobbani, or that might even be his real name. He came in with the injuries Bashaar told us about. I got an address, which may or may not be good, but I also found what will probably be a complication for us."

"What's that?" Blake asked.

"It seems our target has a wife and two sons."

The table went quiet for a few moments. None of them wanted civilians to get caught up in this and certainly not women and children.

"We'll deal with that when we have to," Blake said. "Okay, first thing tomorrow, we spread out and start scoping out the area around this address. Aaron, take a taxi and find an overlook for yourself and make a diagram of the area, especially breaching points for an assault. Stay in the taxi and do the best you can and be careful of the driver. If he figures out you are on a recon, he might report it to the wrong people. ReeRee, take a second taxi and get some photos but be careful not to get compromised. This may be a hot bed of activity among the bad guys so don't even stop if it looks questionable.

"Harry, you'll need to see if there's any way to use the van for a static surveillance platform or if we're going to have to find something in the area to rent. That will be risky, too, but let's explore all options.

"I will start looking for several exfil routes with time variables; we may not get to choose our favorite time of day to pull this off. We're gonna need to get some shots of this guy to confirm with Bashaar and to transmit to the boss along with what we have so far. Let's get this done tomorrow so we can set up and get a bead on this guy as soon as possible."

Instructions issued, Blake was now curious and a bit stunned by the information Daniel gathered. He had to ask the obvious. "Dan, how in the heck did you find this all out in such a short time?"

Daniel donned a sly smile and responded, "Glad you asked. Turns out the hospital administrator is an American from Knoxville. We speak the same language, if you know what I mean. I can spot an east Tennessee drawl in a crowd, Bro. Anyhow, he was delighted to meet a fellow hillbilly and he was a talker; it was like downloading a server. I asked him about the bombing and he gave me chapter and verse. All I had to do was throw out a few simple questions and he did the rest. I didn't put him on the poly, but I am betting he has some pretty good intel."

Blake was satisfied, but he had one more question. "He wasn't a Vanderbilt fan was he?"

Daniel grinned. "Naw, he's an LSU grad. We discussed football too."

10

A FAMILIAR ROBERT Burns phrase always cycled through Blake's thoughts when planning an op, "The best laid schemes of mice and men, go often askew."

The address lead the team to a small apartment complex on Ouzai, nestled between Beirut-Rafic Hariri International Airport and the coast. The area was old, but well kept. It made sense this would be where they'd find a terrorist. Asam told them the district's recent history as an ignition point for Lebanon's civil war when the PLO and The Muslim Brotherhood in the area massacred thousands of Christians.

Multi-family dwellings were never an ideal venue for a surreptitious operation, but the good news was the street was wide and busy, so the "plumber's" van fit the décor. They found a spot, across the street and down a few doors, with a good line of sight where they could park the van without looking out of place.

A drive-through confirmed another of Asam's points about the neighborhood; it would be unwise for any of the team to be seen on foot. It would be the proverbial scene from an old western when the stranger walks through the swinging doors of the saloon, alerting the community to the presence of outlanders, and it would not help the plan.

Harry set up the van to be operated by remote satellite control from the safe house. He could monitor the comings and goings using the roof-mounted 3D camera disguised as a dome radio antenna. This way they could also get precise measurements for diagramming the layout.

After three days of surveillance, the camera recorded nothing to indicate their target, his wife, and two boys lived at that address. The only interesting appearance was an old woman who frequently sat in front of the building using her phone.

The address must have some significance to their target to use it at the hospital, so Blake asked Colonel Johnson to arrange with NSA to erect an electronic fence around the building for a four block radius. With that, they could gather all landline and microwave traffic, including video, voice, text, and email.

Two days later, Harry burst from the room containing the data collection equipment.

"I think we've got something. I just listened to the old woman talking on the phone to who I think may be our guy. It happened at oh-eight-hundred, so it's only minutes old. I've already requested a geo-location on the other phone and should have it shortly."

Blake was up and waving the team to the room before Harry finished his report, "Let's hear it."

Harry cued it, hit the play icon, and then hit pause to translate each part of the exchange for the team members who did not understand Arabic.

Hello, Ya-babibi, my beloved first son. Finally, you call your mama.

Yes, Mama, it is me and I suppose you know this by the number I am calling from. Please remember that you are to give this number to no one.

Yes, yes, I know. You tell me the same thing each time. How are your injuries? I have been worried. Praise Allah that you were not killed by the blast. Allah the merciful has spared you for a reason.

Yes, Mama, I know. How are you? Are you eating well?

You would not have to ask if you visited me more often. Why do you never come and see me? Why do I never see my grandchildren? You do not visit because of the infidel you are married to? I am a mother and I know these things. You prefer to spend your time with the infidel rather than with your own mother.

Please, Mama, do not start this again. I called to check on you. You must stop complaining about my wife. It only leads to arguments between us. Now tell me how you are doing.

I am a lonely old lady who misses her son and grandchildren. Bring them to see me. These children need to see their grandmother.

Mama, I have told you before that I cannot come into your neighborhood. There are too many eyes watching and many of them are looking for me. I am doing the work of Allah and that makes me a target. You know this, yet you still insist on something that cannot be done safely, so please do not ask for this. I will have a driver pick you up and bring you to my home so that you can see the children. It should be obvious to you that I am a wanted man since they tried to kill me. Please, Mama, try to understand.

Okay, my son. When? I will be ready when the driver comes. When? Will he be here today? This evening?

No, Mama, but tomorrow, Allah willing. He will come tomorrow. And you can stay for a few days with us here in our home. I will call you before he comes.

Will the infidel be there?

Mama, stop this now. Yes, my wife will be here and she welcomes you. I will see you tomorrow, and please be careful what you say around her.

Harry hit the stop icon on the screen and turned to Blake. "How do you want to proceed?"

"First, get this off to the boss and see if they have any voice prints to match, then transfer a copy to my phone. I'll take it and see if Bashaar can help us verify if this is Abu al-Wafá."

"We're going to need to move at light speed on this. If there's any chance he called from nearby, or better yet, his home, we have high probability he'll be there tonight and we'll need to strike."

"Harry, when you transmit the file to Colonel Johnson, give him the SITREP and our projection so he can have his analysts step on it. Oh, and get Asam over here.

"Daniel, you're with me to the bike shop.

"Aaron, you and ReeRee prep the equipment for a 'bank robber' op.

We're going to have to hustle if this checks out, and I want to be as far ahead of the game as possible.

"We'll regroup here at thirteen-hundred, sift the intel, and go from there."

.   .   .

Harry was the first to speak after they'd settled around the dining table and he'd placed two sheets in the middle. "NSA located the emanation point for the phone call, a house surrounded by a high wall on Rafic El-Hariri. It's only three kliks south along the coast from here. I took the liberty of asking them for satellite shots for a quarter mile radius and electro-magnetic imaging of the house, and I've loaded them to these flex-slates. Unfortunately, they built something into the roof that makes wave penetration dicey. They can't get clear pictures inside the house for anything but a rough layout. It's not as good as we could do on the ground there, but it will certainly expedite planning." At that Harry turned and looked at Blake to take over.

"What security can you see?" Blake asked.

"The muscle looks like a couple of guards packin' AKs and RPGs. Looks like maybe they have a position on the roof and one patrolling the grounds. I would bet they only man it at night. What I can't tell is whether there are cameras or a security system. That's not unusual, considering home security technology these days. Even here, the ones with a little money can get state-of-the-art wireless systems. When we get the van close and take a reading to be sure of what we're dealing with, we can get NSA to black out the UHF before we go in. They will probably fly an EW Predator out of Larnaca for the job. I'll run our ground comms on ELF and, Blake, the mini sat-radio you have will not be affected," Harry explained.

"Can we take the guards out, ReeRee? What think ye?" Blake asked.

"No problem, Boss. I can take one from the ground and Aaron can get the one on the roof with the sniper rifle. There will be enough ambient noise in the area that we should not attract attention, with the suppressors on these weapons."

Blake turned back to Harry. "Have you found a spot where we can put the van?" The wheels in Blake's head were spinning.

"There's a parking lot for an office building about two hundred meters northeast of the house. We could park it on the south side closest to the service entrance. Asam can stay with it until we call him forward. To deploy, I suggest Asam ease down the road and we just roll out of the van a couple of hundred meters away and make a stealth approach through the shaded areas next to the road."

Harry made an air circle with his finger around a spot on one of the displays. "Aaron can probably get in an overwatch from the high ground in this open area about three-hundred meters away. That gives him a good view of anything approaching the house from the front. He can guide us into position by radio. If there is any reaction to the assault from outside, he can take out anyone approaching the house. That is provided he thinks he could hit anything from that far . . . "

Aaron used his right middle finger to pull down on his lower right eyelid while staring at Harry. "If I can see it, I can hit it."

Blake paused a moment to allow the guys the levity and to look at one of the slates. Not only did Blake appreciate the exchange along with the others, but humor always helped to keep operators loose.

"Okay, moving along, how about voice-print confirmation?" Blake asked.

"Colonel Johnson says they have a match for Abu al-Wafá, he's ready to green-light the mission as soon as you have a plan to run by him," Harry explained.

"Good!" Blake nodded. "We also have confirmation from Bashaar. Aaron, are we ready to gear up?"

"Yes, sir. The rifles and sidearms are oiled and loaded and we have suppressors for all. We have NGVs for everyone and two gas-powered pistols, one for the outside team and one for the inside team. The syringe darts have a special cocktail mixed up by Daniel. I kind of wish we'd brought vests now that we're going in on snap count."

There were nods all round.

"Daniel, what can we expect from your darts?" Blake asked.

"It's comparatively mild. I modified it a bit when we found out kids could be involved. It's still strong enough to put a two hundred pound man out for about thirty minutes. We'd be wise to hog-tie the target, just in case."

"We can make modulations after we get there and watch a bit, but for now we'll plan to execute at oh-two-hundred. That gives us a little margin to exit the van, move through the shadows, and watch for a short while before we go in." Looking back down at a flex-slate, Blake zoomed in on the wall and house, and then continued. "Harry and ReeRee will scale the back wall after Daniel and Aaron take out the guards. You guys need to coordinate the shots on the guards so they're simultaneous. Daniel, I am guessing you will need to shoot your guy through the grates in the front gate. It appears he is fairly fixed in that general area and only makes rounds a couple times an hour. Aaron, you have the guy on the roof. Once they are down, Daniel and I will go through the gate or over the wall in the front.

"Harry, you and ReeRee move to the windows on the back side and see what is visible. Call if you see anything we need to know. Then stay there and make sure no one escapes out the back. I am hoping they'll be in the back of the house and not upstairs, so Daniel and I can do a surreptitious entry on the front door and not have to deal with stairs. Once inside, we'll move slowly to find the bedroom, where I expect him to be that time of the morning. We'll grab him, drug him, and haul his ass out the front door.

"Asam, when you hear the exit signal, get the van out in front of the house ASAP. When we've cleared the wall, we'll signal you, Aaron, and you get down and out and we'll pick you up as we head north to the extraction point."

"If all goes well, *by your grace, Lord*, we'll board the CIA boat out of Larnaca for the trip back by oh-two-thirty. From there a military jet should have us back to CONUS by lunch.

"Any questions on the plan? It's almost exactly what we rehearsed. Are we clairvoyant or what?"

Harry spoke first. "Yeah, Boss, I have one. That is, do we go on the assumption that whoever we grab is Abu al-Wafá, or do we need con-firmation from a biometric scan? That's going to take a few minutes to transmit and get an answer."

"No, Harry, this is his home and he's in there. We grab the adult male in the house and scat."

Then Aaron chimed in with more of a point to make than a question. "Since I am operating as a loner, could I get my choice of seats on the exfil boat? I get seasick."

No answer was provided.

The van cruised down the street at oh-one-thirty, stopping first to allow Aaron to step out while the van was still moving. He moved rapidly up a steep knoll that was fairly open with only scattered olive trees dotting the area. Aaron quickly found a perfect overlook position giving him good visibility into the walled home. His first task was to assemble his weapon followed by a quick check with his range finder to get the exact distance to the roof. Three-hundred twelve yards was the reading. *Piece of cake, even at night.*

The van continued down the road slowly as four more men ejected from the rear. Harry and ReeRee crossed the street to approach the house from the beach. Blake and Daniel lopped south one hundred fifty meters, then crossed the street to approach the house from the south where there was more cover. Once in the shadows, the team found concealed positions and went prone to listen and watch. Traffic on the street was non-existent. The only ambient sound came from the surf. All else was quiet. Harry could smell Turkish tobacco and figured one of the guards was having a smoke.

After five minutes in a static position, Harry and ReeRee made their way to the back wall where Harry whispered the ready code, "Blue." The encrypted in-ear two-way made Harry's voice sound as though he was standing right next to each of the team members. They kept low and quiet, waiting for the report from Aaron and Daniel that would mean the guards were down.

Colonel Johnson was able to retask a satellite so he could watch the mission in real-time and supply the team with additional observation behind the walls. No news was good news. Unfortunately, he was having the same trouble getting images from inside the house.

Blake knew he had to make a final call, but he was already determined to execute the operation if the call did not go through quickly. He keyed the microphone to his mini-sat radio. "Jagged Edge, this is

Blue Moon. Arapaho. I say again, Arapaho." This was the code word that would tell Colonel Johnson his team was ready, and to cue the NSA blackout, the bird had already been orbiting the site for an hour. He would wait no more than ten seconds for a reply and then he was going to execute the mission. The reply from Johnson came in five, "This is Jagged Edge. Concord. I say again, Concord." Blake smiled, *game on, let's roll.*

After ten minutes of waiting and listening, Daniel moved out, first easing to the gate and watching for a glimpse of the guard inside. Blake followed several paces behind, being careful where he stepped to insure he did not compromise the whole operation with a false move.

Suddenly, Daniel stopped in his tracks. Blake knew instinctively Daniel had the guard in sight. Daniel gave Blake a quick hand signal letting him know he was ready to engage the guard. He then clicked his teeth together three times to "Break Squelch" as a signal to Aaron he was ready for the shot. Aaron returned the signal with two clicks to say he had his target on the roof in sight and was also ready.

Blake's command was a whisper, but clearly heard, "Execute."

The time separation between shots was humanly indiscernible. As if a life switch was flipped, the sentries on the roof and in the front yard simultaneously folded like dropped blankets. Center-mass head shots reduced the sound reaction to dull thuds not heard outside a fifteen foot radius.

Aaron, then Daniel whispered, "Message delivered."

Harry cupped his hands for ReeRee to place his foot in. With his rifle slung, ReeRee stepped into his teammate's hands and was atop the wall in an instant. Then Harry slung his weapon and reached up to grab ReeRee's open hand for a little aid in getting to the top before they both dropped to the other side.

Harry and ReeRee leapt from the rear wall and each took a window at either end of the back of the house. They saw no movement through their night vision goggles, so Harry moved to another window, looking into a living space while ReeRee checked for a hard-wired alarm system. He found no overt signs, but he cut the landline to the house as a precaution.

"Clear," whispered Harry.

Blake and Daniel were at the front door ready to breach the deadbolt after silently forcing the knob bolt back. At Harry's signal, Daniel slid a thin piece of metal into the deadbolt's key slot and pressed a button on the fob-sized handle. A dim green light glowed from the end of the handle and, with a counter-clockwise quarter turn, the door jarred.

Daniel stepped back, stowed the burglar tool, and retrieved his dart pistol, as Blake moved past him through the door.

● ● ●

Since Omar's confession to Suzan in the hospital months earlier, neither had returned to the subject. The time was spent getting Omar back on his feet. There was a marked difference in their relationship, but Suzan did her best to maintain stability for her sons, and to keep Omar's secret from them. The addition of guards and a security system was explained to the boys as the result of threats against the company for which their father worked.

She knew the situation was untenable. She could not continue to support a man who stood against everything she valued. It was one thing to be from different religions, it was quite another that he killed for his. Neither could she abandon her sons to follow their father's path. Since they were born, she'd read the Bible to them and taught them the tenets of her faith without disrespecting her husband. She knew it was between them and God what they chose, but she wanted to insure they had all they needed to make an informed choice.

Most nights since that day in the hospital found Suzan awake and in prayer into the middle hours. Only the sovereign grace of the Savior could lead her from this conundrum. The more she prayed, the more she felt the minutes compressing to some sort of answer, an event, a release. It was not comforting, but her trust was unshakable. Peace was her bedrock, tension covered her world.

"Omar," she said. "Did you hear that . . . Omar?"

"Uh . . . what . . . what is it?"

The two of them were in their bedroom where Omar was sleeping. His wife sat beside him on the large bed.

"Did you hear that thump on the roof?"

"No. It was probably Abdullah or Rafiq."

"Maybe, but then I thought I heard something at the front door."

"I'm sure everything is fine or the alarm would have sounded, but check on the boys if you want. One of them might be up for something to eat. I'm going back to sleep."

Suzan swung her feet to the floor, opened her nightstand drawer, and removed a .380 pistol which she slid into the pocket of her robe. "I'm sure you're right," she said. "I'll be back shortly."

Mohammad and Youssef still shared a bedroom, even though their new home had enough rooms to go around. She slowly opened the door and found both in bed making the sounds of deep sleep.

Something's wrong.

. . .

Blake and Daniel finished sweeping the first floor and converged in the center of the house before moving to the staircase. Blake led the way and signaled Daniel to stay wide and watch their six.

Suzan reached into her robe pocket, gripped the pistol stock, and crept to the top of the stairs. Two silhouettes, one a couple of steps ahead of the other, were about to reach the bottom step. She pulled the pistol and, without aiming, fired two rounds.

As the second bullet exited the .380, Blake's H&K was sending two 9mm composite hollow points in return. The first made the second unnecessary as it expanded on impact and disintegrated Suzan's heart. She fell back, just out of Blake's sight. Her pistol dropped to the floor and clattered down two steps from the landing.

He paused to be sure there was no movement and that no one else was approaching.

Harry's voice came over the radio, "Blue Moon one, this is two, SITREP . . . "

"Contact, one down I don't think is our target. Muzzle flash, hard to be sure, I think it was a woman. Stand by."

"Copy that."

. . .

AT THE SOUND of the .380 going off, Omar bolted from the bed and into the hall. Mohammad was coming through his doorway and saw his father coming through his.

"Baba!"

Omar motioned him back into his room. "Lock your door and look after your brother."

The boy instantly obeyed.

Omar turned to move down the hall and saw the motionless form lying at the top of the stairs. The darkness was no barrier to Omar's horrified realization. *Suzan . . .*

Rage momentarily clouded Omar's judgment as he dropped to crawl to his wife instead of retreating to his bedroom for a weapon. He was almost to her when he heard movement on the stairs. He moved to return to his bedroom for a weapon and realized just as quickly there was no time. An ethereal voice that sounded very much like his wife came more to his soul than his ears, *Jesus, I commit my family to your care.*

In that pause came Mohammad's voice from the hall. "Father!"

· · ·

BLAKE WAS WITHIN five degrees of being able to see the landing when he heard a boy's voice and saw movement. A man was rising from a crouch to run down the hall.

"Daniel, hit him with the dart," he said. "There he goes. Hit him quick."

Before Blake could reach the landing, Omar was at a door at the end of the hall. Blake leveled the H&K and shouted again, "Come on, Daniel, I have him cornered. Dart him."

Daniel was not to be seen. Where was he? What to do now? Shoot to kill? Shoot to wound? *Where the hell is Daniel? No time left, act now.*

The door opened. Omar had his right hand on the knob, his left at head height on the jamb. Blake fired, trying to hit him in the arm. Splinters flew from the door jamb, but Omar was through the doorway and, by the time Blake made it to the door, it was locked. He took one step back and rammed the sole of his boot into the door next to the knob.

As the door swung open, Blake rolled right to avoid return fire from within the room. Nothing.

That's when he realized Daniel was in trouble. *I can't stop now.*

He crouched and rolled left to peek around the door jamb with his H&K out front. Nothing.

A quick check revealed no one in the room, closet, or attached bath. *He's gone, but how?*

"Blue Moon Two and Three, this is One, any movement your way?"

"This is Three, nothing here."

"Negative, One. You got him?"

"Negative. I thought I had him cornered, but he vanished."

"Say again, One."

"Never mind, check the perimeter."

"Copy that."

"Blue Moon Five, SITREP."

"Five, come in . . . "

"Two, I think Five is down near the first floor stairs. Get in here."

"Roger that. On my way."

"Blue Moon Three, keep watch on the rear. Blue Moon Four, cover the front."

ReeRee and Aaron confirmed in order.

Leaving the room, Blake noticed something on the floor; a severed finger. *I guess I hit something after all.*

He picked it up and stuffed it in his left thigh pocket then proceeded to be sure the rest of the second floor was clear.

Colonel Johnson's voice cut through everything flying through Blake's hyper-active mind. "Blue Moon, this is Jagged Edge. Signals just caught an EHF burst coming from your location. No ID, but you best exvac. Out."

"Everyone, listen up," Blake said. "We're leaving, *now.* Blue Moon Six, we'll rally out front in five, be there. Four, keep eyes on until we're mounted, then close up shop."

After three responses came in, Harry's lower than normal voice said, "Man down, One. It's bad."

"Roger that, Two. Get him out. We've run short of time and options."

"On my way."

Blake paused at the body lying in the hall. *Damn! It is a woman, probably his wife. Dear Jesus . . .*

By the time Blake made it to the van, the others were aboard. Daniel was laid out in the back with Harry and ReeRee hovering over him.

"How is he?"

Harry looked up and spoke. "Not good, Boss. Chest wound. He's breathing, but just barely. I've got the bleeding stopped, but he's still out. He must have hit his head pretty good on that tile when he went down."

"Let's get Aaron fast. Asam, screw the low profile, we need to move."

Before Blake could finish speaking, Asam had the throttle to the floor.

Asam whipped the van around to head north. He'd reached nearly sixty miles per hour when two modified trucks flew past them headed south. The most visible modifications left no questions about who they were, or where they were headed. Each had a rear-mounted .50 caliber machine gun.

Aaron's assessment was not as dire. Daniel had a collapsed lung, but no arteries were hit. Getting him to a hospital ASAP was advised nonetheless. His pupils indicated a concussion, but he was coming around.

Blake radioed the SITREP to Colonel Johnson, who agreed with the plan to bypass the local hospital and get Daniel out by boat. With Omar on the loose and his wife dead, they had to exfil Beirut immediately, if not sooner. They would have to stick to the boat plan, but the colonel would arrange a Cypriot SAR chopper evac for Daniel as soon as they were a safe distance from Lebanon.

When Blake and the rest of the team arrived at Larnaca, a CIA case officer met them and took them to a safehouse for debrief. In four hours, all pertinent intel was recorded, along with a chronological script of events. The case officer uploaded the files to Washington and transmitted a redacted Sensitive Compartmented Information brief containing the after-action report to the U.S. Consulate in Beirut.

11

F AILURE WAS NEVER in Blake's mind when a mission was launched, and he'd been blessed to get the job done many times, though he often had to purchase success with his blood and bones. Not only had they not been able to capture Abu al-Wafá, but the operation put Daniel Steele in the hospital. Fortunately, thanks be to God, his life was not threatened, and there'd be no permanent damage.

The worst of it, however, was the death of an innocent woman. As many times as Blake told himself he was not to blame, blame himself he did. He was one of those warriors who exemplify sinew and heart. From his earliest recollection, his father taught him by talk and walk to be lethal and compassionate. Even killing a deer was done with precision to avoid suffering. He would bear the burden of this kill for the rest of his life.

Col. Johnson's debrief was perfunctory. They didn't get the target, but the intel gathered by the team and received from the Israeli, would be useful. Johnson knew what the guys did was an incredible feat in itself: finding their target and getting into his home with little time and even less firepower. Unfortunately, Abu al-Wafá was off the grid and would likely stay there for some time. The team was released to their previous jobs until another operation could be formulated with caution for heightened vigilance for a while.

All except Lieutenant Colonel Hunter.

The other major operational concern about Abu al-Wafa's escape was the killing of his wife in the failed op. Based on Colonel Johnson's real-time oversight of the mission and the debrief of the team, he did his best to reassure Blake that he did what had to be done and he was not to blame. Of course, Johnson's personal knowledge of Blake was all the evidence he needed. Johnson had seen Blake in action before and knew he would never harm anyone who was not a threat. And that was the point Blake was not dealing with well. The woman fired on him and his team, and the only thing to do was shoot to kill. He wished Blake could just put it behind him, yet Johnson understood why Blake was struggling. It was simply who he was, and that was one of the reasons Johnson trusted him so much. However, that would most definitely not be how the terrorist would see it.

Here again, Blake's alias of Jacob Hunter came in handy. Even if the terrorist network had the resources to track him, they would follow the trail to a dead end. That said, both Bob Johnson and Blake Kershaw were old enough models with enough miles on their odometers to know you didn't get cocky and take your eyes off the road. NSA would be sending them daily reports compiling signals intelligence from the entire Middle East. They would also stay in close contact with Bashaar, both for intel and his safety. Likewise, they would stay in close contact with the U.S. Embassy in Beirut in case they got intel on emerging threats against Blake or the team.

The big concern they had was for Daniel who undoubtedly had left DNA behind. These days just about anyone could extract the identity of a person from a single drop of blood, saliva, or a hair. Chances were Daniel left all three on the floor of the terrorist's home. Ever expanding U.S. government control mandated the gathering and digitizing of all health records, including biometrics after the implementation of universal healthcare in 2014. Push back from the Pentagon and a few congressmen and senators didn't even slow the inclusion of military records in the massive database. "Secure" was the word they used to assuage public concern, but like so many in the twenty-first century, that word held no meaning.

. . .

DANIEL WAS STABILIZED on Cyprus, transferred to Landstuhl, Germany, for surgery, and then shipped to Walter Reed in Maryland. The records there would show him being discharged a week later, when in fact, he was moved to a civilian hospital in Tennessee under an assumed name. Even his family would not know until a reasonable threat window closed.

. . .

AS PROMISED, BLAKE was given two weeks to fulfill his commitment to Alia.

While Blake was in Lebanon, Alia checked out several cruise lines with routes leaving within ninety days of his departure, assuming he would return within that ninety-day period. She found one leaving Venice and ending in Haifa eight days later. As soon as she knew he was headed back, she called up her agent and had her reserve the flights and a starboard side cabin with a balcony. From Blake's cryptic message about the mission on his way back, Alia knew there'd be more than their marriage needing fortification on this trip.

. . .

BLAKE RETURNED HOME from Fort Bragg thirty-one days after leaving. Sam all but tackled him before he could make it through the front door. Past the joy of holding his son, Alia could see something morose in his eyes. When Sam finally stopped gushing about his recent accomplishments and asking a thousand questions, Blake took Alia into an embrace like nothing she'd felt for years.

After dinner, the three of them took a walk to the neighborhood park so their son could bleed off some excitement and energy before bedtime. Sam saw some of his neighborhood friends and bolted to the playscape as his folks took a bench nearby.

The retelling of the gunfight in Beirut and the death of the target's wife strained Blake to the point of breaking, but he held on. This was not the first time Alia had been confronted with the grisly reality of violence, especially in the world of Islamic terror. This was the first time her husband had to deal with causing collateral damage. The phrase went through her mind as rote, but it seemed non sequitur in this context. While she wanted to say the obvious to Blake, she refrained. Her instinct was to say, *Just get over it because she fired first and she was part of the terror network. She is one less terrorist or sympathizer we have to worry about.*

Alia had no sympathy for anyone who supported or tolerated Islamic terrorism because it was these fanatics who duped her Down Syndrome brother into strapping on a body bomb and committing suicide for some foolish notion of heaven with virgins. The poor lad didn't even know what it all meant, but he was tricked into being a suicide bomber. So as far as Alia was concerned, they all needed to die. Her Christian faith was often in conflict with her emotions.

Alia could see and hear the change in her husband, a change it would take time to understand. There was palpable regret and sorrow, which could very well be guilt. If it was the latter, she would need to help him find the only place for healing, God's grace. She knew she needed the same grace to overcome her hatred for Muslims.

"My Love," she said. "I cannot know what you must be feeling and I know words will have little effect, but I love you and I see no blame for you in what happened. I grieve for this woman's sons who have lost their mother, but I now have greater contempt for the man who put them in that danger."

"We took a huge chance trying to grab him from his home in the middle of the night, but we saw no better option," Blake replied. "I must have missed something we could have done differently to avoid harming his family. It would have been less risk to his family had we gone after him while he was moving in a vehicle or on foot. We went to his home because we thought it was safer for the team. We have good reason to believe his wife, Suzan, was a Christian."

"Then perhaps we can have hope she is now with the Father, Blake. You must stop this line of thought. You have a family too. Yes, it was safer to go into his home at night, and that is all the more reason it was the right thing to do. I know I don't have to tell you that you have a responsibility for your men as well as your mission. Blake, there was no other option and you need to accept that. "

"Maybe . . . "

"We have even more need to get away together for a while. I'll call the agent and book our tickets. It's all arranged." Alia pulled her phone from the pocket in her skirt and, in five minutes, hit END. "We'll need to leave Thursday to get at least a day in Venice before the boat departs. I'd love to spend more time there, but our time together has to be the primary focus of this trip.

"Sam was pretty upset when I told him we would be leaving again, but he mostly recovered when I told him Maria would be staying with him, and she plans to take him to a Nationals game. I had to sweeten the deal with a promise you'd take him hunting when we get back, as well."

"I think he's ready for that. He's gotten pretty good with his .223 and he can probably manage to be quiet in a stand for a while. Now I'm anxious to get this cruise over with and get back for deer season."

Alia delivered a solid right cross to Blake's shoulder which almost caused him to slip off the bench.

"But, not as much as I am to be with you on a boat!"

Appeased, she took his hand and they watched Sam play tag with his friends for a while before heading home.

The emotionally charged reunion and conversation funneled into fervent, almost manic passion in the couple's marriage bed that night.

• • •

NEITHER BLAKE NOR Alia had ever been in Venice, so within a few hours there they were already planning to return. The Royal Mediterranean cruise ship was almost as big as Venice, but much newer. The cabin was, as promised, on the starboard side, with a balcony, and hot and cool running attendants. It, and his beautiful wife, came close to taking Blake's mind completely off Beirut, Lebanon.

. . .

Wᴴᴬᵀ Bʟᴀᴋᴇ ᴍɪssᴇᴅ in the room from which Omar and his sons vanished was the sliding panel inside the closet. Behind it, a chute with a sloped end dropped to a tunnel under the house where it merged with another from the master bedroom. From there, the tunnel exited near the base of a slope leading to the water, disguised as a storm drain.

He was also unaware of the EHF burst transmission beacon Omar set off before exiting the boys' closet. Had Omar not been distracted by his wife being gone when the gunshot awakened him, Blake and his team might not have made it out of Beirut.

In the tunnel, Omar grabbed a backpack from a hook on the wall and removed the first aid kit. He extracted a roll of gauze and quickly and tightly bound what was left of his left ring finger and secured it around his palm. Reaching again into the pack, he pulled a cell phone and hit the power. Five seconds later the phone bore the message, NO SIGNAL. He threw it back into the backpack. He would contact Abu Youssef after he was clear of the area.

Omar, Mohammad, and Youssef scrambled to head north on the beach. Along the way, Omar had to put his sons off as they wanted to know about their mother.

"Where is Mama," Youssef, the younger, asked when they landed in the tunnel.

"Not now, my son. We must hurry, danger pursues us. We will talk about this later. Keep quiet and move quickly."

"But, Baba—"

"*No!* Do as I say!"

He threw the backpack strap over his shoulder, grabbed Youssef by the hand, and led him as they stooped to trot down the tunnel. He glanced back a few times to see Mohammad on their heels.

They emerged from the tunnel and immediately turned right to run up the beach along the base of the slope.

When the house was no longer in view, Mohammad called after his father. "Baba, where is Mama? What happened back there? Where are we going? Did I hear someone speaking English?"

Omar retraced a few steps and took his eldest by the shoulders. "My son, I swear I will tell you what you ask, but we cannot stop now. We must get out of this area. You are good sons and I love you. We must keep moving to survive."

Youssef started crying. He was old enough to assume the worst when his father refused again to talk about their mother.

Omar released Mohammad, whose expression was morphing from confusion to shock. He quickly wheeled, seized the younger boy's arm, and all but dragged him forward. What neither son could see in the darkness was the amalgam of pain, rage, and grief contorting their father's face.

When they were nearly a kilometer north of their home, the roar of a vehicle gained volume as it came up behind them. Omar pushed his sons behind him and drew a sub-machine pistol from the backpack. After pulling the magazine from the stock to make sure it was full, he slammed it back, and racked the charging handle.

He brought the pistol up just in time to hear a familiar voice call his name from the approaching vehicle. The emergency plan was working.

"Abu al-Wafá, we are here to help,"

"Abu Youssef, you are here?"

"Would I not respond to a distress call from my favorite warrior?

"May I put my sons in the truck before we say more?"   "Go sit in the truck," he said, waving his sons toward the vehicle. "I'll only be a minute, then we can leave."

Youssef stopped, grabbed his father around the waist and in a fear-pitched voice said, "Baba, who is Abu-Wafá? What is happening?"

"My son, get in the truck. We will talk about everything later."

The look on his father's face repelled Youssef's impulse to push. He dropped his arms and followed Mohammad to the truck.

Abu Youssef ushered the two boys into the back seat of the king-cab Toyota Tundra. Mohammad paused to stare at the machine gun mounted on a tripod in the bed of the truck. Abu Youssef shut the door and turned to approach Omar.

"What has happened?" he asked. "Two teams are at your home now and their initial report said nothing of anyone being there. They found your wife . . . she is dead. I'm sorry."

"I couldn't save her!" Omar cried bitterly. "At least two intruders attacked our home and killed my wife. To save my sons, I hit the beacon and left with them before they could reach us. I'm almost grateful our teams did not find them. I will want to extract my own vengeance. Have there been any reports from other stations? They must try to hide or leave from somewhere."

"So far, there have been no other reports, but I have our entire group on alert for anything out of the ordinary. If they are foolish enough to still be in Beirut, they will not live long."

"Abu Youssef, I must beg your indulgence. I have tried to protect my sons from my life of Jihad until they were older, but as with many things lately, my choices do not matter. Now we have lost their mother to an infidel dog and all will change for us. We must go somewhere safe to make ready for these changes."

"Of course."

. . .

THE FATHER AND sons spent the next two days sequestered in a small apartment a block from the Dar al Fatwa Mosque. They wanted to be sure the infidel murderers were no longer a threat. Abu Youssef ordered his men to set up a perimeter around Omar's home and to care for Suzan's body.

Abu Youssef also wanted his subordinate to stay in hiding a while longer, but Omar would have none of it. He had to call and cancel the pickup for his mother. She was angry when he called and she responded in a way that nearly drove him over the edge.

"It is the infidel woman; she does not want me in her home. You care only for this evil woman who separates you from your mama."

Shut up, woman, you don't know what you are saying!

Omar checked himself as the sadness of his loss was deepened by his mother's criticism of his now dead wife. His blood inflamed by revenge demanded action against those who had taken his children's mother. This was personal for him now, and he would seek revenge.

"Mama, Suzan is dead. I cannot speak with you on this now. I will call another time."

"My son . . . " Her words fell into the abyss of a severed connection.

He told his sons a band of assassins broke into their home to kill him and instead shot their mother. They wept together and he swore an oath to them before Allah that he would track these devils to Hell itself, if necessary, to bring back their heads

When they asked why this happened, he told them he'd long been a warrior of Islam, but he told them no stories of his exploits or details of that life.

"Islam has many enemies who want us all dead."

Youssef was confused. "Mama was a Christian, Baba, why would they kill her? Mama taught us to be Christians, will they kill us also?"

"No, my son. You will move under the protection and will of Allah from this day. You will become a mighty warrior for our cause and wreak vengeance on all infidels for what they have done to our family. The day of vengeance is *now*, Allah willing!"

Youssef seemed even more confused, but he said no more.

Mohammad remained silent during this exchange. When he looked up to meet his father's gaze, had it not been for his red eyes and wet cheeks, Omar could have been looking at a face carved from stone. This was not a parallax; something had shifted in his son. He was not seeing him differently, he was different.

The boys were carefully instructed to say nothing to anyone about the death of their mother other than that bad man broke into their home and she was killed. The narrative Omar gave Suzan's family was that criminals trying to rob them were surprised when Suzan got out of bed for water. The funeral was left in her family's hands; Omar only insisted it be brief.

The first thing Omar did after taking Mohammad and Youssef to stay with his sister was to make contact with his informant in the U.S. embassy. The man from the CIA station was trusted by the Americans so he had very good access to the most classified information available. Twenty-four hours after initial contact, Omar carried 50,000 U.S. dollars to a meeting to exchange for information. Inflation in Lebanon meant the payment could fund a middle class lifestyle in Beirut for years or the high life for months.

The man placed a file on the table in the rear of the café and the terrorist slid a thick envelope next to it. When the man reached for the package, Omar slammed his hand atop it, a couple of heads turned and then quickly whipped away.

"Did you bring the specifics for which I asked?"

"I have the names for you, but we have no access to details about them. I can't probe without attracting attention to me, and then to you. You asked for information on the team that attacked your home and I've brought you all I can. According to the after-action report, one of them was critically injured, and the leader of the team killed a woman."

"Show me."

The man flipped open the file and on top was one sheet bearing a photo with the name Jacob Hunter. The rest of the form was redacted of other information specific to the subject. The four sheets beneath had the same for the other team members. The after-action report was at the bottom of the stack.

"We don't know anything about these men other than they are American and probably current or ex-military, though this was a CIA operation. Whoever they are, they went to a lot of trouble to keep their whereabouts cloaked."

"That will do, though I'm not sure it's worth the payment."

Sweat broke out on the man's forehead and his eyes widened a bit.

"But we may need more later . . . " The stolid terrorist slid the envelope to the man, grasped the folder, and rose to leave.

Jacob Hunter, you will soon feel the wrath of Allah and his slave. Your appointment is with the abyss, Allah willing.

12

OMAR STOOD JUST inside the balcony door of his eighth-floor hotel room. The opening looked out on the harbor in Haifa Israel. He hated this place. Not only because the Jews occupied this land, but this place in particular because of the childhood memories it evoked of a failed mission in this very harbor. His team had come in Zodiac boats only to be destroyed by the Israelis. Had it not been for a Lebanese fisherman, what was left after the fish were done with him would be on the floor of the Mediterranean today.

And kill them wherever you find them, and turn them out from where they have turned you out.

This time, by Allah's mercy, he would succeed in killing the American pig and redeeming his past.

The one-hundred eighty degree view from the room was what tourists paid millions of dollars every year to experience. The current occupant of this particular room was only interested in the view 175 yards straight out.

Had anyone been in the room with him, they would have been irradiated by the waves of hatred emanating from the man watching through a pair of binoculars as a cruise ship eased into port. The huge ship was the perfect symbol for his enemy and all those like him. Millions of dollars wasted to build an altar to self-indulgent pleasure. The focus of his vengeance would most likely be in a stupor from alcohol when he sent him from his decadence to the torment of Hell.

Just under a month earlier, Omar met with Abu Youssef to seek his help in tracking down the man who killed his wife. He was told the high council shared his interest in finding and killing the American. This violation by the infidels caused them to alter plans that had been under development for months. They would like the opportunity to capture this man to get information, but killing him would have a helpful outcome as well.

Omar was given full access to the OIC network, under Abu Youssef's supervision. Messages were routed to every cell in Europe, North Africa, and the Middle East with instructions to contact Beirut if the name Jacob Hunter appeared on any immigration documents entering that part of the world. The process was tedious and slow, but no operation of this size was worth compromising valuable assets.

This was his only hope to catch his wife's murderer since all attempts to learn more about the target and where he lived came back void. Even having agents in the leadership of the Pentagon and the ironically named Homeland Security did not help. What *did* help was having a U.S. president who sympathized with the Muslim cause. He was perhaps the most useful idiot The Muslim Brotherhood ever had. It was astounding that, with the years spent getting their people into every level of American society and government; they could not locate this one man. Omar was left to wait and pray to Allah for his quarry to come to him soon.

The rest of the band of murderers and accomplices were not so difficult to find. The one his wife shot disappeared after getting treatment at the military hospital near their capitol, but it would just be a matter of time until he surfaced. They would all be killed along with their families by the justice of Allah. However, Omar could not risk sending his prime target underground, so he must be first.

A message came back eight days earlier informing him that Jacob and Alia Hunter of the United States would be landing in Venice, Italy, but would be there only one night. The office from which this information came could not supply further details.

Working through the Al-Rahma Mosque in Venice to check car rental agencies, airfields, and harbors, Omar learned that the Hunters would be arriving in Haifa on a Royal Mediterranean cruise ship six days later. In what could only be the mercy of Allah, he was also given the name and phone number for one of their men who was an officer on the ship. Cruise ships were one of the best platforms for transporting arms and other material from all over the world to the Middle East.

He now watched as the mechanical island cast its mooring lines to the dock hands. Omar pulled his phone from his pocket and hit send on the present number.

"Hello, who is calling?"

"This is Rassule," Omar said.

"Yes, this is Hakim. I was told to expect your call. What do you require?"

"I need access to a couple on your boat. I must know where they sleep and how to get to them."

"I can get that information for you, but you will only have tonight. All passengers leave us tomorrow. The people you seek may still be in Israel after, but I will have no way of knowing where or for how long."

"Tonight will work well. How soon can you get me what I need?"

"If you can hold one minute, I can access that information right here. What are their names?"

One minute after Omar gave him the names, the voice came back to the line. "They are in stateroom C401, that's on deck ten, starboard side. I can get you in that room. Tell me what time you want access; you can meet me on the dock and I'll take you up. You can pose as a harbor official."

"While they are eating the evening meal," Omar said. "They should be out of the room. I'll also have the cover of darkness for my departure. Is there a way to know when this will happen?"

"Allah is smiling upon you and providing your way. They have a reservation at the captain's table for the cruise finale at eight o'clock, which should keep them out of their room for at least two hours."

"I will be near the stern of the ship at seven-thirty. I want to verify they depart the room."

"As you say."

That left him eight hours to facilitate the rest of his plan.

Omar next sent a coded message by text for which a reply came in under a minute. The answer was an address and time.

· · ·

WHEN HE ROUNDED the corner to the sidewalk café, he saw someone he'd known since childhood. The first mission on which Omar was sent by Al-Asifa was moving weapons and ammunition to the PLO through Syria posing as sheepherders.

When he reached the other side of the tunnel crossing from Syria to Israel, the team receiving the delivery also posed as sheep tenders. One of them waved Omar over. He was a couple years older than Omar and seemed experienced. Omar carried a heavy backpack containing a couple of handguns, several AK magazines, and twenty pounds of explosives. As the boys transferred the backpack from Omar to the sheep they exchanged names.

The two would see each other on several more missions and got to know each other well. Rami and Omar became friends and trusted allies. Once again, Rami was at the ready when Omar needed him for this operation. Rami had risen to prominence in the PLO and had many people and resources at his disposal.

· · ·

"SALAM ALAKE, RAMI," Omar said. "I didn't expect a man of your position to come to a meeting like this."

"My friend, you should know I would not pass an opportunity to help you in any mission, but especially this one," Rami replied. "I share in your grief in the loss of your wife, and I consider it an honor to play a part in seeing her murder avenged."

"Thank you."

JERRY BOYKIN AND KAMAL SALEEM

"So, what do you need from me?"

"I will need transport from the cruise ship *Sea Mist* in the harbor tonight. At approximately eight p.m. I will drop a rappelling line from the starboard side of the ship. Could you have someone in a Zodiac stationed beneath it by nine p.m. and he may be there for an hour or more?"

"Of course, will one man be enough?"

"Yes, I don't want to endanger others of your people. I will also need several weapons, a .40 caliber suppressed handgun I will carry, an assault rifle, and RPG for me in the boat. I would recommend your man come similarly equipped."

"I will have the pistol hand-delivered to your hotel; the boat will be waiting for you. How far will you need to go?"

"I will need to be taken directly to sea from the ship about eight to ten kilometers, to be met by a small freighter that will take me home. It would be helpful if your man could assure that the Zodiac has two outboard engines to guarantee we can outrun anyone who pursues us. As I leave the ship there is a small chance that might happen."

"It will all be arranged as you request. May Allah's mercy grant you victory over your enemies."

. . .

OMAR SAT ON the floor between the king-sized bed and the open sliding door to the balcony. His prey had been out of the room for over an hour. He held the suppressed CZ-75 at the ready, not knowing for sure when the door would open. The darkness of the room was daylight compared to the darkness in the man. Waiting found Omar replaying the scene of his wife lying lifeless on the floor, his finger being blown off his hand, and the narrow escape with his sons.

. . .

BLAKE AND ALIA were thoroughly enjoying their final night on the cruise that reset their marriage and moved Blake a distance from his emotional morass from the failed mission. The captain had many entertaining stories between courses of the kind of food you only get on cruises. Way too much, way too rich, and way too easy.

They were also looking forward to getting home to their son. Between them and him was one last romantic night on the boat and a day and evening seeing some of Alia's family who came from Cairo to Haifa. They planned to stroll the long way round back to their stateroom to take in as much of the boat's entertainment and the lights of the harbor as possible.

For dessert, Alia chose chocolate cheesecake and rolled her eyes when Blake chose simple vanilla ice cream. Neither could finish and both were ready to be out of their chairs and alone. They rose to excuse themselves and to express their gratitude to the captain for the cruise and the dinner.

B LAKE AND ALIA exited the grand dining room on the port side of the boat and took a right toward the bow. The evening was clear and a little cool so Blake held his beloved close as they walked along the rail. The sounds of late-night swimmers met them just before they passed the corner blocking their view of the huge outdoor pool. They wordlessly exchanged the question, but immediately dispensed with the idea.

They paused at the bow to appreciate the lights in the dome from sea level to Pleiades. The sights, fragrances, and their embrace proved Einstein's salient theory. They may have been there for seconds or eons. Finally, they were both drawn by the allure of their stateroom and their final night at sea.

When Blake and Alia stepped into the elevator, they found it empty for a change and when the door closed, an old tradition was revived as they shared a deep and committed kiss. All too soon, the familiar ping alerted them the doors were about to open.

"Could I have the room card?" Alia asked. "I'd like first shot at getting ready for bed."

"Of course, my Love, but try not to take too long. You know it only takes us guys fifteen seconds."

"Yes, I know, but I think you may not be unhappy with the wait."

Alia slipped the card in and out of the slot and pushed down on the handle, but to no avail.

Almost under her breath, she said, "Dang, I hate these things; they never seem to work the first time."

She took a deep breath and tried it again. Success. She turned to smile at her husband as the door swung open.

Just as Alia's head turned back from the hall, the unmistakable spit of a suppressed weapon came from within the room; two shots in rapid succession. Blake knew the sound and reacted immediately by reaching for his own pistol from the small of his back just as Alia recoiled into his arms. Blake's instincts were taking over and he had to fight the urge to leave Alia and charge the intruder to get a quick kill. Had Alia been one of the team, he would have done just that, but this was the love of his life. She had to be the first priority.

He had the sub-compact 9mm out and leveled to fire as Alia slumped into him. The impact moved the pistol enough for the shot to go wide of its target. Omar fired again and the bullet zipped by Blake's right ear as he was going down with Alia. The intruder bolted for the balcony shouting "Allah Akbar." Blake watched the shadowy form dash to the balcony and realized he had to make his next shots count.

Holding the inert body of his wife in the crook of his left arm, he fired. Another wide shot. He started squeezing the trigger again just as the shooter made it onto the balcony. Blake led him slightly, but that sent the shot into the glass of the other half of the slider and the door behind it. The hollow point rounds Blake always kept in his carry pistol shattered both panels of glass, but had no energy left to reach the assailant.

As Blake lowered his wife to the floor, he sighted down the slide of his LC9 to see the man vault the balcony rail, making another shot pointless and dangerous to anyone beyond the ship. The last thing he saw were two hands grasping the top rail before grabbing the rope looped around it.

Alia was grasping at Blake and moaning. She'd been hit in the chest, but the rapidly widening pattern of blood made it difficult to tell exactly where. He went from the floor to the bathroom in one motion to grab a towel to put pressure on the wound, and on the way back he snatched up the phone and tapped the zero.

"Medical emergency in C401, get help here now!"

When he got back to Alia she wasn't moving. Blake cross-trained as a medic when he was in Special Forces. Now he would need those skills more than he ever had in his life. Could he save her? He ripped open the top of her dress and found the entry wound just above her right breast. Blake knew from the amount of blood pouring from the hole, an artery was hit. He pushed the towel down as hard he could without crushing her and started cursing the time it was taking for help to arrive. He suddenly realized she had stopped breathing and started CPR. He used his sleeve to wipe the blood from her mouth before placing his lips around the outer rim of hers to begin alternating between breaths to force air into her lungs and chest compressions.

Twenty minutes after Alia was shot, the ship's surgeon and a nurse were working on her. She wasn't breathing when they got her to the infirmary, so as the nurse tried to get an IV started, the surgeon continued CPR. An ambulance was waiting on the dock to take her to Friends of Rambam Medical Center just a kilometer from the ship as soon as they got her stabilized. Two Israeli EMTs stood just outside the infirmary ready to take over as soon as the ship's surgeon gave them the signal.

The doctor was unable to revive Alia after several cycles of CPR and called for the defibrillator. Three attempts at shocking her heart back to life failed and he turned to Blake, who'd been standing in the corner watching and praying as he'd never done before. The doctor slowly moved his head from side to side then reached down to pull a sheet over Alia's body.

Blake stepped forward next to the doctor and kept him from moving the sheet higher than his wife's chest. The doctor and nurse silently slipped from the small room. Blake stood over the vacant shell left by the woman he loved more than his own life and took her hand in his. And yet, he didn't weep. His chest felt like a sinkhole and his blood seemed stagnant, but his dolor was not producing tears.

What's wrong with me?

Maybe I'm dead too . . . I hope so.

His spirit told him she was on the other side of the veil, his heart was in denial, and his mind was a blender of thoughts, memories, and emotions.

The concept and reality of death was known to Blake from as early as he could remember. The story of the death and resurrection of Christ was introduced to him long before he could read or start school. He lost his first dog to a rattlesnake when he was six and he killed his first deer when he was ten. But, the fullness of loss by death didn't come to him until that day the men from the army came to tell him his father was killed in the first Gulf War by a missile strike.

None of it in any way prepared him for losing Alia. He loved, almost worshipped, his father but even that was an order of magnitude short of the bond he had with his wife, the woman he thought the Creator made just for him.

How can she be gone? Our time was so short. Lord why have you taken her from me? From our son?

Then, like being hit in the forehead with a major league fastball, his tradecraft was triggered to replay a mental image recorded under duress; *The hands on the balcony rail . . . the left hand was missing a finger, the left hand was missing—the ring finger.*

He didn't take her. I gave her up. This is my fault, my doing!

I burned down the family barn causing my father to go off to war just to support the family, and it killed him. I killed that woman in Beirut, and now my wife is dead.

Lord God, forgive me.

Blake's emotions found focus and he wept as he never had in his life. He draped himself over the now cold and lifeless body of the woman he had planned to grow old with; the mother of his son.

Lord, take me, too, please. I can't live without her. I don't want to go on. Take me now . . . please.

As Blake sobbed almost uncontrollably, thoughts of Sam began to consume him and he slowly started returning to a world of reality.

How can I explain this to him? he thought. *Do I tell him the whole truth, that I am responsible for his mother's death?* Blake placed his hands on the ashen cheeks of his dead wife and leaned forward to gently kiss her one last time. His tears fell softly on her face and lips as he said his final goodbye.

. . .

THE MISHTERET YISRAEL officers were directed to the captain's quarters where they found Jacob Hunter slumped in an armchair facing a window, staring out into the blackness. He'd just disconnected after calling and telling Alia's uncle of her death. He promised to get with him later to tell him more when he was able to leave the ship.

The initial report from ship security all but removed the possibility of robbery as the motive for the shooting, so the Haifa superintendent sent a counter-terrorism officer along with the two uniformed policemen. The oldest of the three, bearing an onset paunch straining at his uniform blouse and a splayed beard waited for the subject to acknowledge their presence. He didn't.

"Mister Hunter . . . "

"Mister Hunter, we are policemen, here to interview you about what happened tonight. You have our condolences on the death of your wife."

"Alia . . . her name was . . . is Alia" The voice was firm, but had just enough propulsion to get it to their ears.

"Yes. Can you tell us what happened?"

"I'd rather not right now. Can we do this later?"

"Mister Hunter, we know you are CIA and that's why you had a weapon, otherwise you'd be in jail for this interview. That does not, however, exempt you from cooperating with our investigation. This crime was committed in our jurisdiction and we intend to catch Mrs. Hunter's killer."

America and its allies maintained a special agreement regarding the travel of counter-terrorism and law enforcement agents. Nations recognized the threats to the men and women on the front lines of the terror war were never off, so they agreed to allow agents from cooperating countries to be armed while traveling inside those countries. However, to honor the agreement, a level of transparency was required. Jacob Hunter filed travel plans with the CIA station chiefs in Italy and Israel twenty-four hours before he and Alia boarded their flight out of Dulles. The Israeli investigators were obviously aware Blake was one of those covered by this special relationship among friends.

To avoid any unwarranted attention by customs officials, clandestine operators always traveled with a custom suitcase fitted with an x-ray absorbing compartment large enough to accommodate a variety of weapons and ammunition, but compact enough to be unnoticeable during a cursory inspection. The monitors watched by the minimally trained transit officers could only see the contents of the main compartments.

As Blake attended to his wounded wife, he'd asked the head of ship security to contact the embassy in Tel Aviv and inform them of the situation. The name at the embassy Blake gave the ship's security officer was for a former Green Beret who he met during his last mission in Iran. He was now the CIA station chief. Because Blake was not on a sanctioned U.S. mission, the embassy was not required to give more detailed information than to verify his name and security status.

Approximately twenty minutes after the call to the embassy, Blake's friend, the Station Chief, boarded the *Sea Mist*. The grief on his face was noticeable. Blake was a legend in the CIA since his last mission in Iran where he never would have survived except for the initiative taken by Alia.

She went around all protocols and the chain of command for the operation and called for an emergency rescue of the man she loved. Otherwise, Blake would have died. The Station Chief knew the special love between Blake and Alia because he was on the team that came to Blake's rescue. Now Alia was dead and he wanted to know why, but the time for him to ask was not now. Right now, he just needed to help his friend.

"Mr. Hunter," the Israeli policeman said, "you could greatly shorten this process by telling us if you know why this happened."

As Blake sat pensively before the investigators, he began to consider the possibility the Israelis might catch the man who murdered his wife. He did not want that to happen. This was now personal and he would deal with it as such; an eye for an eye. Finally he spoke, "You won't find him here."

"We've had the ship searched and witnesses questioned, we know the attacker left by Zodiac."

"I mean, he won't be anywhere in Israel."

"How do you know that?"

Blake's discipline managed to break the surface of his grief.

"Call it a strong hunch."

"I don't know what that means"

"It means if he left by boat, I suspect he was not headed to land nearby."

"That may be, but we must conduct our procedures. Your countryman from Tel Aviv has arrived and is waiting for us in the conference room."

Over the next two hours Blake submitted himself to the probing of the policemen. The one not in a street uniform asked only one question.

"Mister Hunter, have you ever been in Iran? I mean, have you ever run any operations in Iran? I think I know a bit about you."

The two veterans made eye contact just long enough to make the policemen curious.

Blake ignored the question. This guy obviously was fishing, but Blake was pretty confident the man asking the question was well aware of how Blake infiltrated Iran a few years earlier and stopped a nuclear attack on Tel Aviv. Try as they may, CIA could hardly keep operations like that secret from Mossad. The Israelis knew an American saved their nation and this man was probably having a hard time believing he was actually meeting the man of such legend. Blake was coy, "I have explained to these gentlemen several times. Alia and I were here on vacation. Iran has been closed to Americans for decades." The Mossad operative got the meaning of the response as only a seasoned spy could. The meaning: *You already know the answer so don't push this issue in front of these other guys.*

The Yasam officer nodded to Blake, then to the station chief and turned to leave. He opened the door, and then turned to address his colleagues.

"I must make a phone call. I will contact you later to go over what you've gathered. *L'hitrao.*"

The policemen stayed only long enough after their colleague's departure to instruct Blake to stay on the ship for at least the next twenty-four hours at which time he was free to leave the ship, but not Haifa. The ship was held in port until forensics could do a thorough job.

"I have no intention to leave Israel without my wife. Assuming I have no say in whether you perform an autopsy, when will you release her body for transport?"

This time the younger officer spoke up when his superior waved at him and continued to make notes.

"We cannot know that yet. We will let you know as soon as we hear from the coroner. We will do what we can to expedite the process, but the time will also depend on what the coroner finds. I'm sorry we cannot be more specific and may I also say I am sorry for your loss."

"Thank you, officer. If there's a way I can leave the ship sooner than twenty-four hours, my wife's family is here and I need to get to them as soon as possible."

The older policemen lowered his flex-slate and looked up at Blake. Intuition developed over twenty years in the units told him this was a good man before him.

"I will file this report as we leave and I will request your immediate release from my superintendant. I will let the ship's security chief know as soon as I get an answer. However, I must insist you stay in Haifa until we have completed all our work."

Blake nodded and reached to shake their hands.

The Tel Aviv station chief, who had been silent throughout the interview, stepped from the corner of the room and approached Blake after the policemen departed and wrapped him in a bear hug.

"Colonel Johnson called me after the message about Jacob Hunter hit the system. I'm so grateful to know Blake Kershaw is still alive. I can't tell you how sorry I am about Alia. I didn't know her well, but I know she was extraordinary."

"Thanks, Stu, I appreciate you coming. Can you stay a little longer? I may need another favor if they don't let me off this boat soon."

"Of course, no problem, I was here on some business at the consulate when they routed the call from the locals to me, so sticking around is easy. You know I will do anything you need me to do."

"I know and I'm most grateful."

Though he would see Alia's family, which he was not looking forward to, he was more anxious to get to the consulate. He needed to get his wife's body released and the two of them back to the states, and that would only happen after he made contact with Colonel Johnson.

The only thing worse than the prospect of facing Alia's aunt, uncle, and several cousins was thinking of what he was going to tell Sam.

Blake returned to the armchair and the darkness.

14

B LAKE WAS RELEASED from the *Sea Mist* cruise ship just under twelve hours after the attack in which Alia was killed. He was given the news by the head of security on the ship, who also told him Mishteret Yisrael would call him when the autopsy was completed and his wife's body released. The expectation at that time was he should hear from them within forty-eight hours. Blake picked up their luggage and was off the ship in fewer than fifteen minutes.

The local police went through their stateroom from floor to ceiling and wall to wall. In the process they enlisted a member of the housekeeping staff to pack the couple's belongings after they'd gone through them. The killer was a professional. There were no prints or DNA left behind and the ballistics from the bullets taken from Alia and the walls matched nothing in the vast databases available to Israeli police and counter-terrorism units. This had all the markings of an assassination.

Blake headed straight to the American consulate to send a secure message to Fort Bragg requesting a video conference with Colonel Johnson. The reply came back in less than a minute with time and connection instructions for the resident comms tech.

Precisely on time, Colonel Johnson appeared on the wall of the small conference room next to the attaché's office.

"Blake, I don't have the words . . . Alia was one of the finest women I've ever known and I know how much you loved each other. How are you doing?"

"Not well, sir, but I appreciate your words and your quick response to my request."

"Of course, I got the ping from the DOD on the Israeli inquiry about Jacob Hunter and followed it up myself. I knew I'd be hearing from you soon so I was on standby."

"Sir, can you get us out of here right away? I must go to Alia's family. They came from Cairo for what was supposed to be a reunion. I also have to wait for the coroner to release Alia's body, but if there's a way to expedite things with the government here, I'd like to be home in a couple days at most."

"I'll have to go through our State Department which is never pleasant, but we are fortunate to have an ex-team member on the Israel desk who should be able to move things along pretty quickly."

"Thank you, sir. I'm also anxious to get back because I know who did this and I want to get back to work to finish the job I started. This is all my fault and I . . . "

"Slow down a bit, Blake. How do you know?"

"I only gave the locals enough facts to be credible in the interview. I withheld anything that would connect me and the operation in Lebanon. It was Abu al-Wafá, I saw his left hand. It was missing the ring finger. It couldn't have been anyone else."

"I don't doubt you, Blake, but I think we need to deal with the immediate and handle the rest later."

"Yes, sir, but I was hoping you could start gathering intel from last night and his probable escape route by sea back to Beirut. I guess there's some chance he's still here, but I'd bet against it."

"I'll send an intel alert asking the community to watch for this guy. You concentrate on taking care of yourself and what you need to do there and leave this to me."

"Yes, sir, but . . . "

"Blake, that's an order."

"Copy that, sir."

"I'll send arrangements for you through the office there as soon as they can be made. In the meantime, you'll be given a car and a safe place to stay. It would be best if you spent as little time as possible out in public. We can't be sure the assassin is out of the area."

"Thank you, sir."

. . .

ALIA'S FAMILY ONLY knew Jacob Hunter as they'd never met Blake Kershaw. The difficulty of going to them under the circumstances was exacerbated by the subterfuge he would have to employ to protect them and his identity. They only knew he worked for the U.S. military and they had no idea about Alia's past with the CIA.

Blake had to excise himself from them after a couple of hours, though they cajoled him to stay for his remaining time in Israel. He showed them the picture he had of Sam and they loved hearing about him. With that, they finally conceded to his need to see to the arrangements to get him and Alia back to the states. Blake really respected Alia's family as they were very courageous people. Their conversion from Islam to Christianity made them apostates under sharia, which was punishable by death. Undaunted, they held to their new faith and one even trained for ministry. These were good people, but Blake had other priorities he had to get to.

Knowing they would not be able to get to the U.S. in time for the funeral, Alia's uncle, who was a deacon in his church, conducted a brief but powerful memorial for his niece. His closing prayer was so emotionally and spiritually charged Blake could only manage to give them each a hug before collapsing into his borrowed car. It was several minutes later before he was composed enough to drive back to the safe house provided by the Chief of the Station.

On the way he marveled at the deep faith and compassion of these people. They'd just lost a beloved family member to the darkest kind of tragedy just hours before being reunited, yet their love and care for him was effusive. They mourned, but it was permeated with solace. It was the granite confidence they had in Alia's place in the presence of the Redeemer.

Blake wondered how their sympathy toward him might change if they knew why she died. He wanted to tell them and he didn't want them to know. Was his oath of secrecy about his work a convenient escape? Was his compulsion to tell them a selfish need to assuage his conscience?

Of one thing he was sure, outside a handful of people, he never saw such passionate faith in America as that in which he'd just been immersed. Maybe there was something to the idea that intimacy with God was refined in times of trial, much like gold being refined in fire. In the last decade, Christians in Egypt had been all but eliminated by execution or expulsion. These were warriors of Christianity. The kind of warrior he'd only otherwise known in combat. It made him hate all the more not telling them the whole truth. But these were bright people and astute as well. They lived in this world of violence and betrayal and experienced the daily struggle for survival. Most likely they knew this was not a robbery or a random act. Still, Blake could not tell them the truth about Alia's death; at least not now.

My Lord, please allow me to make this right with You and this family.

When he returned to the safe house, he found a packet bearing his name containing an airline ticket for him and transport arrangements for Alia to be on the same flight. Included was a message from Colonel Johnson telling him his friend Stu pulled strings with the police commissioner in Haifa to expedite the release of Alia's body. He even had it prepared for burial. He was free to leave in thirty-six hours.

If all went as he hoped, he would be returning to this part of the world shortly, but there was much to do before then.

Blake called Maria.

"Maria, it's Jacob. Please don't let Sam know it's me calling."

"Okay, is everything all right?"

"If Sam is nearby, please have him go to his room. Tell him to read while you're on the phone. That should give us enough time and privacy."

Maria left to do as he asked. A few moments later, she returned to the phone.

"He's upstairs. Jacob, what's wrong?"

"There's no easy way to say this . . . Alia is dead . . . "

Blake could almost feel the vacuum of Maria's drawn breath through the phone. There was a long silence and Blake could hear Maria's soft sobs as she processed what she had just been told. "Oh no . . . Jacob, what happened?"

"I can't tell you now, Maria, but I'll be home in a couple of days. I'll message you with the itinerary. Don't tell Sam anything. I hate to put you in this position, but I will need you to stay a while after I get back and I didn't want to spring it on you. Sam and I are going to need your help. I wanted you to have time to think about it and make arrangements, if you can."

"Of course, Jacob, I'll stay as long as you need. It's going to be very hard, Sam doesn't miss much, but with the Lord's help, I think I can manage until you get here." Blake could hear the emotion rising in Maria's voice, but he could also hear her strain to suppress the sobs she couldn't afford to let loose.

"God bless you, Maria, I'll see you soon. Please pray for us."

Not one to put such things off, Maria prayed with Blake before they disconnected.

. . .

FALLS IN VIRGINIA produce colors the makers of crayons could never hope to recreate but, for Blake, the world was reduced to grayscale. He held Sam close and they stared through pools of saline down into the perfectly rectangular hole in the Earth and its charge; Alia's carnal body encased in pine. Sam Wilson stood at the head of the grave and the other three sides were lined with friends and church family. Blake's teammates and their wives were there, along with a few of Alia's former CIA colleagues. Maria stood on the other side of young Sam.

General Sam delivered a eulogy C.S. Lewis would have coveted. He spoke of Alia's depth of passion for life and her family, he told anecdotes that produced tears and soft laughter, salting each with phrases from Scripture. There were a few around the grave discomposed by levity at a funeral, but they were also captured by the old soldier's probity and lyricism. He held no Bible or notes.

"We are rightly angry, and in soul-grinding sorrow as we must say goodbye to Alia from this life. Our time left here is diminished by her absence. However, we need not grieve as though we have no hope, nothing to seek beyond the grave. Alia is a child of the One True King who purchased her with His blood. She is experiencing even now what our finite minds are incapable of even dreaming. She is likely feeling sympathy for us."

His closing prayer ushered the assembled believers into God's throne room and even those who did not believe knew they were experiencing the Supernatural.

Blake only knew what was going on around him at the periphery of his senses. From the moment General Sam referred to Alia as a mother, his thoughts turned to his mother. Because of the sacrifice he made for his country, he'd been dead to her for more than a decade. She was not there when he married Alia, she didn't get to witness the birth of her only grandson, and she was not here now, as he released Sam's mother to eternity.

The weight of sorrow he'd invited into the lives of those he was supposed to protect was making it hard to breathe as his faith crashed on the rocks of failure.

Am I cursed?

Those I love most are suffering for my sin.

How can all this possibly be leading to anything good?

God in Heaven, I know You are sovereign and I know You say You love us, but I can't feel it. I can't see how any of this expresses that love. I have loved You, but I don't feel that toward You now. Could You not have prevented Alia's death? Could You not have put that bullet in me instead? Sam deserves better than me, he deserves his mother.

I thought I knew You—who You are—but now I doubt whether I ever knew anything about You. Please help me, for Sam's sake.

I don't think I can live with my mom being on the outside anymore. I can't imagine how I'm going to tell her everything that's happened. If things were reversed, I'm not sure I'd be able to forgive her. I'm not sure I should be forgiven. She should be given the chance to decide for herself. She deserves to know her grandson, to know about his mother.

I have no idea how or when, but I must tell her.

Blake felt a hand on his shoulder and he looked up to see General Sam next to Sam. People were beginning to drift from the grave, there was to be no reception. Blake had no idea how much time passed since the general concluded the service. Harry and Aaron came around to give Blake and Sam silent hugs before leaving. A few others stopped briefly to express their sorrow and love.

Maria took Sam by the hand. "Come on Sam, let's go to the car and give your dad a few minutes to himself." He was reluctant, so Blake squeezed his shoulder and gently nudged him in Maria's direction.

"It's okay Sam, I won't be long. I want to thank the general."

As though his mentor and best friend knew what he'd just been thinking, General Sam said, "Blake, there's no way to make sense of all this right now, but you will come to see Providence further down the path. Excoriating yourself is only natural, which is your first clue that it is not originating from on high. I confess, I have no idea why this happened, but I do know it does not change the character of God. Come on, let's go. We can talk about this and anything else you want later. For now, Sam needs you and you need him."

15

THE OIC ADVERTISED its administrative center being in Jeddah, Saudi Arabia, but that was part of the show. The political window dressing was indeed on Madinah Road, where it intersects with King Abdullah Road, in an opulent building designed to entertain international dignitaries and otherwise present a globally-minded body. But, the functional arm, the operational segment, had no fixed location; the leadership was rarely together or in one place. For that there were numerous reasons.

The sardonic brilliance of their structure enabled them to carry out Jihad all over the planet, pushing ever closer to a prophesized world-wide Caliphate. They planned to achieve this through their network of more than seventy member nation-states and their infiltration of many others while their respectable front kept aggression against them at bay. The operational division strategized everything of the sword, from assassinations to military campaigns, while the diplomatic façade lobbied for tolerance and cooperation.

There was a quintessential example of this back in July of 2014. Operations granted permission and gave logistical assistance for Boko

Haram to send a suicide bomber to a popular market in Maiduguri, Nigeria. The blast killed fifty people (among them opponents of sharia rule). Then, the general secretary of OIC publicly condemned the bombing. He went on to express his condolences to the victims and their families and his disappointment in the continuing violence. Lincoln might not have been able to consider how a perverse house purposefully divided against itself might stand and expand.

If genius is a word that can be used for evil, it would work here. Of course, this expanse of deception is heavily dependent on the ignorance, disinterest, and complicity of a narcissistic world. As they say, timing is everything.

What the OIC could not control was the resolute hatred between Sunnis and Shiites. An allegiance was struck under the flag of a worldwide Caliphate, but both sides saw their collective as a chimera. At some point, the disparate parts were destined to turn on each other. Each sect maintained its own Sura governing council. There would be no mixing of assets or leadership like the UN or NATO. Only the councils would communicate and agree, or disagree, on initiatives handed down from the OIC.

What bound them and divided them were the Quranic six steps of Jihad, mandated as the duty of all Muslims. Jihad in the way of Allah, Jihad of the womb to repopulate a culture, political Jihad through propaganda and character sabotage, Jihad by the sword, Jihad by sharia law, and Jihad by peace when weak—to be followed by numbers. Interpretation and implementation dug the chasm separating the two sects.

From the signing of the joint agreements, the minority Shiites were plotting for the time when the fight would shift from outward expansion to their disparting. Al-Taqiah, the doctrine of guile and lying ordained by the Quran, proved to be a sword cutting both ways within the OIC. Much of the overt inter-sectarian violence plaguing Islam since the death of Mohammad sublimated after Sunni dominance was asserted when ISIS aggregated forces, arms, and money from Tunisia to Iraq. This move occurred during the so-called Arab Spring, starting in 2010.

What started as ISIS (Islamic State of Iraq and Syria) became simply the Islamic State as it moved into Iraq to reconstruct what was once the Ottoman Empire. In 1916, in the fallout after World War I, the Sykes–Picot Agreement divided the Middle East between the UK, France, and Russia. Since then, Muslims looked to, and worked for, the day when the arbitrary carving lines negotiated by three infidels would be erased and the Caliphate rebuilt. This would be another leap forward toward Islamic world domination. The establishing of the new Caliphate capital in Damascus, which was then renamed "Great Syria," was the crowning achievement of decades of strife. The site was secured as preparation for the return of the Mahdi or Twelfth Imam, whose job it is to constitute the Caliphate and raise an Islamic army for global Jihad. In the process, he will also open the way for the Islamic Messiah to judge the Christians and Jews and destroy them. The prophesies were unfolding and the end of the world for the infidels was at hand.

The American government, with the help of social media, succeeded in convincing the American public there was no war on terror, only against Al-Qaida and radical Muslims. They made the Muslim Brotherhood out to be moderates engaged with the U.S. government in the war against that enemy. This effectively covered the truth, that the Brotherhood was a Trojan horse, rolled inside America to destroy its civilization. While the president promoted the "democratic" uprisings publically, he provided money, weapons, and even air support to those he knew to be elements of Al Qaeda and its many affiliates, all while he withdrew U.S. forces from Afghanistan and Iraq.

He got his hand caught in the cookie jar when he left four Americans to die in Benghazi in an attempt to cover the trail of the transfer of arms from the Libyans to ISIS in Syria.

Accepting the odds at that point, the Shiite organizations and their followers employed the same strategy within the OIC, as Muslims had for decades among the infidels: civilization Jihad. They joined the Sunni-led movement, keeping their identity and their governing structure while feigning comprisal. As with ideological strife among any large group, a few pockets of recalcitrance continued to complicate the OIC's master plan. To those paying attention, one such example played out in Syria, where the successes—like those won in Tunisia and Libya—were delayed when Hezbollah bolstered the Assad regime.

Conversions between Sunni and Shiite (along with being rare) were most often from Shiite to Sunni, but conversion was not required for collusion. As with any segment of humanity, Islam is not corruption resistant. Bridges over lines of Muslim doctrinal loyalty were as easy to erect with money and the promise of power as they were in Washington, DC

In addition to the empire lust each faction shared, there was a deep theological competition over which sect would usher the prophesied Messiah or Mahdi to the high throne of the Caliphate. In this the Shiites were much more driven by the interpretations of the Quran and Hadith and the resultant dogmas of their imams. It mattered not if they were fewer in number when the Mahdi rose from their people and completed the establishment of Allah's kingdom on Earth.

. . .

CAIRO WAS NEVER as interested in theology as he was in himself. He was dedicated to Islam and to the Caliphate; he just wanted to come out on top, regardless of which sect got him there. Being raised Sunni in a wealthy family in Beirut meant religion was important, but not paramount. He joined The Muslim Brotherhood against his parents' will because his father's shadow kept the light from shining on him. It was also a chance to mingle with lessers where it would require little work to rise to prominence.

His plan hit a wall when Omar landed in the same training camp. The little insect had the favor of the cell leader, Abu Hamza, which he could only assume transferred to being favored by the head of training, Abu Jihad. Before any of the other boys, Omar was given a Jihadist name, Abu al-Wafá. This sealed Cairo's hatred for him and set him on a course to bring Omar down no matter what it took.

The ground was well plowed and fertilized when the first seed of sedition was planted in Cairo's ego by the leader of a Shiite cell. The two made initial contact when Cairo was sent to Syria to foment the uprising against Bashar al-Assad among both al-Assad's sworn adversary, the indigenous Sunni population, and the non-Alawite Shiites.

They saw the Syrian leader as apostate because his was not a sharia-based government.

Sayyed Hasan Nasrallah leading Hezbollah, backed by Iran and Russia, sided with the Assad family in the Islamic power struggle. Cairo was sent by Al-Asifa to represent the OIC, to augment foreign funding and weapons, and supply recruitment and training assets to bring Syria fully in line with the OIC. Cairo coordinated these efforts through Abdel Jabbar al-Okaidi, one of the leaders in the Free Syrian Army, with who he first met in Aleppo in 2012.

While there, he was instructed to meet with a representative of Hezbollah forces in Syria. He was told to open negotiations for their withdrawal. When Cairo made contact, he was asked to meet at a bar in the Christian section of Damascus on Straight Street.

"Why would we meet there among infidels and in a hole of sin?" he asked.

"Because Allah cannot see us there, we will be able to conduct our business in secret."

It took much less coercion and bribery than even the shrewd Hezbollah leader thought would be needed. His offer of alcohol was accepted, his offer of women was not. What he couldn't know was how he fit Cairo's long distance aspirations. By establishing an alliance with Hezbollah, Cairo was given a lane and a promise in the other side of the race to the top of the Islamic world order. In return, he gave Hezbollah a key to the inner sanctum of OIC operations. It was a win-win situation for Cairo; he would be on the victorious side no matter the outcome.

The first order of business for the new axis was to address hindrances to Cairo's ascent within OIC. Those were easy to identify; Abu Hamza and Abu al-Wafá. The bomb that took the life of Abu Hamza and almost that of Omar was planted by a member of a Shiite mosque not far from the Dar al Fatwa Mosque where Omar and Abu Hamza first met in 1997.

A few days after a pack of Shiite boys chased Omar into that Sunni mosque so many years earlier they were visited by Abu Hamza and a few clerics. The leader of the gang of boys and a couple of his acolytes were weeks recovering from their wounds. The gang leader had no means of recourse at the time, and then life took over to distract his childish need for revenge, but he never forgot.

When he was approached by his imam about the chance to serve the Shi'a cause, his instinctive obedience was augmented by the fact that Sunnis would be targeted, but when he heard the name "Abu Hamza," he only wanted to know how soon. He had no way of knowing at the time his childhood prey would also be on the menu.

Posing as a delivery man with the help of his cousin, who owned a produce wholesaler, he brought a box of cabbage concealing a device powerful enough to level the café. The timing of the delivery was only slightly off.

Watching Abu Hamza blown to fragments was thrilling and satisfying to Cairo, but when Omar escaped the same fate, much to Cairo's amazement and frustration, he set immediately to his next plan. Trying the same kind of operation twice would increase the risk of discovery, so instead of using his countrymen again, he decided to use their common enemy.

Even greater care would need to be taken to keep his machinations from backfiring. Leaking tidbits of information to just the right people in the right neighborhoods, and having his Syrian ally feed electronic eavesdroppers a hint here and a lead there, brought a team from America to Beirut. For Cairo, a capture would have been almost as good as a kill. It would have taken his adversary out of the picture, at least long enough to give Cairo the opening for promotion he deserved.

When Omar survived and escaped again, Cairo had a momentary flash of doubt. He worried he was perhaps up against one of Allah's chosen. Working in Cairo's favor was his belief that Allah favored his people and the victors from among them; he gave no points for surviving, so Cairo just had to come up with another plan. At least Omar's ape of a wife was dead. Cairo's vacuous soul was nourished on the pain he knew Omar was bearing.

Maybe there is a way to bring his sons into this as well . . .

. . .

IT WASN'T UNTIL Omar disembarked the coastal merchant vessel in Beirut and got in his car that his suspicions were confirmed; his mission was not completed. The international news service his radio broadcasted relayed a story of a woman being killed on a cruise ship harbored in Haifa, Israel. No mention of the man. *Abin al haram!*

Quran 5:45, *And We ordained therein for them: Life for life, eye for eye, nose for nose, ear for ear, tooth for tooth, and wounds equal for equal.*

He would have to go to the Sura, explain what happened, and begin plans to reacquire his target. Omar was unaccustomed to making post-mission reports to his leadership that told of anything short of success. How had it been possible for this infidel to slip through his hands of death? The first time, his own sons made a way of escape for the infidel, but he had no third party to blame for the second. It had probably been foolish to even consider he'd not be armed.

America's steady reduction of armed citizens was one of the great blessings for the expansion of the Caliphate. The ever-tightening restrictions on travel with firearms made many Al-Asifa operations as easy as stomping an ant hill. He should have planned for this one to be armed. He would not repeat that mistake.

· · ·

W<small>HEN</small> O<small>MAR</small> <small>MET</small> with Abu Youssef the next day to make arrangements to go before the Sura, his friend and superior had much to tell him. They met in a windowless building and remained standing during their discussion.

"Abu Youssef, I regret to tell you I was unable to eliminate the son of a pig."

"Yes, I know, but you were smart to leave the ship when you did. We all knew the risk when you were given permission to conduct the assassination in Israel. Since you weren't going after an Israeli, and you were not inland, we thought it worth the risk. However, with other operations under development, it would have been a large problem for you to have been killed or captured there.

"This brings me to the next item. We have been summoned to Pakistan to go before Ayman al-Zawahiri. He wants to hear what happen in Haifa, since the final word had to come from him to allow it. I'm told he also has something to ask of us."

"What would that be?"

"Across this distance, you know I would not have any details. I can only assume it is a mission."

"I don't want to break off from my pursuit of the man who killed my Suzan . . . "

"I know that, but we do as we are told."

"Of course. When do we leave?"

"An aircraft is being sent for us. We must leave right away. You will have time to pack a few things and visit briefly with your sons."

"Yes. I will go to them now and then prepare to leave."

"We have other things to discuss. Flying for hours will give us the privacy and time we need. While you have been going after your wife's murderer, we have continued to investigate the bombing that killed Abu Hamza as well as the attack on your home."

"What have you found?"

"For now, just know we have strong reasons to believe the two events are connected, and Shiites may be involved."

16

IT MIGHT HAVE been better for Blake had he not been given a month leave by Colonel Johnson after Alia's death. Left to himself, the pain of loss and the abyss of guilt made breathing a cognitive function and he wasn't sure why he gave it any attention at all. He wanted to go after the animal who took his wife and he was bogged in the mire of self-pity, sucking him into depression.

He was raised by parents who faithfully read the Bible, both privately and aloud. They were active in the little country church not far from the family farm in southern Virginia. Blake was dutiful about listening when the Bible was read after suppertime. And while he got up for church without complaint most Sundays, the whole Jesus thing didn't make much sense until his teenage years. Of course that coincided with hormonal high tide and widening social and philosophical vistas at school.

When Blake lost his dad, the combination of his mom's veracious walk through that valley, and his confrontation with personal sin, pointed him back to the Savior of the Bible. There was no lightening flash, no feeling of being bathed in warmth, no shaking of the ground under his feet. He recognized the change within by the dissipation of guilt, clarity about living in the world, and his future in it. Unfortunately, guilt is a renewable weapon in the hands of a determined enemy.

Since that day, Blake faced many clashes between what he believed and what he experienced. Losing Alia as recourse for his actions was a singular challenge to his faith.

There was an unusual midday chill in the air for late fall in Virginia, but for Blake, sitting on his back deck, the temperature didn't register. He reached over to place his hand on his venerable 1911. He'd loved the feel of this gun from the moment he first held it in the gun shop. There was something comforting about the texture of the checkered walnut stock under his palm.

This could all be over in a millisecond.

What is the point of doing anything down here, when even your best intentions turn on you like your dog gone rabid?

How can suicide be wrong? If I'm a Christian, what's the worst that can happen?

At least I'd be out of here, and the trouble I cause with me.

The phone in Blake's pocket buzzed and then buzzed again. He contemplated not answering. His hand went from the gun to the phone.

I always thought the brain had to tell the body what to do.

"Hello."

"Blake, it's Sam Wilson."

"Hello, General, it is so good to hear from you. In fact, I really needed to hear from you right now."

"You sound like a man in need of a lifeline. You okay, Son?"

"I might try lying if anyone else was on the line. No, sir, the truth is I'm not doing at all well. I miss Alia. This must be what it's like to be eaten alive by cancer. Only mine is self-inflicted."

"Blake, I've known and endured my fair share of death and loss, but even with that, I can't know exactly how you feel. I do know you can bear this, you *will* bear this, but only if you look outside yourself."

"You know, sir, my heart says one thing and my mind says another.

I know all the Scripture about how He knows and helps, but in the middle of this, I don't see much connection."

"It's only in the middle of our darkest times, Blake, when we're on our backs, that what we believe is really put to the test. You say you know all the Scripture? Maybe you do, but you'll soon find out what you believe about them and about the Author."

"Roger that, sir. I'm grateful you called, it was going downhill fast around here, but it makes me wonder if you've figured out a way to spy on my thoughts."

"I do have an asset there Who supplies me intel. His cover name is Spirit of God."

"I can live with that kind of surveillance."

"Well said, my boy. Now let's talk about Sam."

Blake and General Sam were as close as two men could be, outside a father and son by blood. Through the years and miles, the general regularly amazed Blake with his profound, penetrating wisdom. He was the closest he'd ever seen to a mystic—someone who seems to live in the spirit world as well as the physical. Yet, there was nothing mysterious or eerie about General Sam V. Wilson; he simply left no doubt about Who he served and why.

Without ever broaching the subject directly, General Sam made the inviolable case for why Blake needed to get out of his self-indulgent anger and back in the fray, human and spiritual. He reminded Blake there is but one Final Authority over life and death, and no mere man or woman could put that on their résumé. Of course, young Sam needed his dad more than ever, but there was also so much left to do in the war against metastasizing evil in the world.

Abu al-Wafá.

• • •

MARIA RETURNED WITH young Sam after a day at the zoo on a home school co-op field trip. Sam told his dad he enjoyed the zoo and being with the other kids, but Blake could see the change in his son. His normal exuberance was muffled, as though the loss of his mom had the same effect on him as a dialed-down rheostat on a light. He also knew his son was reflecting what he'd been getting from his dad. It was time to set a new course.

Blake gave Maria the next three days off, which was all that remained of his bereavement leave. Blake and Sam spent all their time—except bed and the bathroom—together. They'd missed deer season, but Aaron Page from Blake's team had acres down in Suffolk County and it was bear season. With the right bullet, Sam's .223 would be plenty to bring down the average black bear roaming the woods of southeast Virginia. They planned to spend a day preparing, a day hunting, and a day just goofing off before Sam would have to double down on his school work.

They didn't bag a bear, but listening to the hounds chasing them was almost as much fun. Their relationship made a quantum leap as they moved together and spoke in the rawest terms about everything. Sam's view of life and death through a biblical lens would have astounded Blake had he not known Sam's mother so well. Just as a sub-atomic particle moves from one spot to another without the transition being seen or the time measurable, Blake and Sam spanned a chasm between them. There was no way to put a caliper or a chronometer on their crossing. They would move through the remainder of their time on Earth with a limp, but it would not keep them from the race.

. . .

BLAKE REPORTED FOR duty at Bragg ready to complete the mission for which he had originally been called back to the teams. Only this time it was personal. This time his motivation had more blood running through it.

"Blake, it's good to see you," Bob Johnson said. "I know it's been bad for you. Are you all right?"

"I'm operational, sir. I appreciate your help and kindness though this. I'm ready to get back to work."

"Excellent, we have a lot on our plates."

The two men were sitting in Bob's office.

"Sir, may I assume the first course is to finish what we started in Beirut? As you can imagine, I'm highly motivated to capture or kill Abu al-Wafá."

"Of course I anticipated that, Blake, but I'm afraid we have had to shift our attention away from the Middle East for now, and I'm sure there's no way your target will be venturing out of that area any time soon. If we can get these new missions handled, we can perhaps pivot back to the leadership of the OIC. I should remind you that was our goal when we first went for Abu al-Wafá."

"Yes, sir, I understand, but—"

"Blake, I can imagine how you must feel and the drive you must feel to set things right, but the call is not yours. At this point, it's not mine. I think once you see what we face, you'll understand."

"Yes, sir." Blake tried to say it with conviction, but he had none to offer.

Blake's deflation was not lost on Colonel Johnson. He held out hope Blake could see past his personal issues and be the professional he'd always known.

"I don't need to go into detail on the background of the proliferation of Jihadists in America. That was covered pretty well in the briefing material you read before heading to Lebanon. What you don't know yet is how it's grown and the clear and present danger it currently poses."

The façade Blake presented was enough to keep Colonel Johnson moving on with the briefing.

"You also know we've been watching the Tri-Border area for decades. Where Brazil, Paraguay, and Argentina intersect has been a hot house for terrorists and their drug cartel friends, and our foreign policy has been feckless in making any difference. Their money laundering, gun running, and human trafficking operations continue and pose an even greater threat to the U.S.

"You may remember back about six years ago, Barack Obama and his socialist handlers opened our southern border to an unprecedented influx of illegals. By kneading the pliable sentiments of the ignorant and bludgeoning anyone with objections, the wave of humanity was advertised as poor helpless children fleeing violence in their home countries. It was a 'humanitarian crises.'

"It was that, but it was also manufactured. By not enforcing immigration law and illegally granting 'Dreamer' variance to it by executive fiat, the president threw open our border and effectively extended an invitation to flood our infrastructure. I'm not going to get into the discussion of his motive, but what we now know for sure is the children were a cover for the largest invasion of a foreign power onto American soil since the War of 1812. We also know, many of those children were radicalized and trained before being sent north. It might not have been from a single country or group, but they shared a motive; the overthrow of America."

"Colonel, you don't mean to imply the CIA and military will begin executing operations within our borders, do you?"

"That's a reasonable question, and one that's being bandied about on the Hill more every day. But, no, thankfully, we have no orders to execute martial law . . . yet."

"That's good news, sir."

"It is for now, Blake. We have been asked to formulate a few scenarios for how to deal with the terror and organized crime groups behind the insurgence. We're focusing on the Tri-Border area, but also addressing the newer Northern Triangle of Guatemala, El Salvador, and Honduras. They finally have a president in Brazil with the will to protect his people. That gives us access we haven't had down there for years. Unfortunately, he's the only one willing to help in that region.

"That's the easiest part at this point. The terrorists and drug cartels have managed to develop a pretty sophisticated self-defense grid in both areas, so it's going to take our best to carry out operations. They've even contracted with China for access to one of their spy satellites. The bad players are teaming up. While the suits in Washington have been scaling back on every area of national defense, the Islamists, Communists, and organized crime have been gathering strength and resources. We have to move now, or it won't matter what's happening in the Middle East."

"I see what you mean, but is it not still a high priority to go after the head of the snake? Would we not still greatly benefit from having someone high up in the terror network?"

"I know where you're going with that, Blake, but Abu al-Wafá, Ayman al-Zawahiri, and even the OIC are off the table for us right now, and on the plate of others. I have no doubt we'll be back to them, but for now our focus has been shifted. Are you going to be able to concentrate on this? I don't have time to be revisiting this argument. I need and want you with me, but you must be all in."

"I understand, sir, and I'm not willing to give you or our team less than my best. I just came here expecting something entirely different."

17

ABU YOUSSEF AND Omar landed at a small airstrip south east of Karachi, Pakistan, and were ushered into an SUV for the trip to the camp at which Ayman al-Zawahiri was currently located.

No one in the upper echelon of OIC operations stayed in any one place for more than a week. The infidels were always watching and listening by way of their satellites, towers, drones, and infiltrators. The drones were also capable of doing more than watch. Missiles fired from those mechanical demons killed many of their ranks. What the Americans pioneered, the Jews adopted and they were now using UAVs regularly to spy on and kill Islamists. Yet, good fortune always followed each murder. Those killed were enjoying the favor of Allah and the pleasures of jannah, the eternal paradise for Muslims, and there were always those ready to fill the vacated positions.

. . .

THE SMALL CAMP was at the edge of the Marho Kotri Wildlife Sanctuary on the Arabian Sea, which made possible multi-directional escape routes by land and water. Through this camp flowed aspiring Jihadists from all over the world. The course here had a very special focus, along with the normal small arms and explosive training. Graduates from this camp came with education in a variety of disciplines from teaching to architectural engineering. Their goal was to infiltrate the Great Satan, set up a "normal" life among the infidels and carry out civilization Jihad until the time came to finish its takedown by force.

The OIC knew they would only be able to get so far with penetration and deception. The Americans were unlike most of the rest of the world in that their love of freedom was deeply embedded in them, even though for many, it was just in the subconscious.

The Muslim Brotherhood—in alliance with what the Americans called "progressive politicians"—had, on at least one occasion, brought their government to the brink. They had nearly instituted the kind of fundamental change needed to replace their antiquated and Quran-damned system with sharia, only to be stopped by rebellion from the indigenous population. Thankfully, patience is a premiere Muslim virtue. With each setback came an incremental step of progress toward ultimate success. Continuing to flood American neighborhoods, schools, businesses, and government institutions with radicalized and trained Jihadists would inevitably tip the balance.

It was time for prayer when Abu Youssef and Omar arrived at the camp.

The meeting was held in what must have been the main living area of the leader's temporary quarters. After the worshippers rose from, and folded their prayer mats, tea was served. Then the room was cleared of all but the two men from Beirut and their hosts, Ayman and Muhammad al-Zawahiri. The unusual circumstance of having both brothers in the meeting was not lost on the men from Al-Asifa.

The elder Al-Zawahiri brother opened by saying he'd been told of the mission in Haifa and Abu al-Wafá's failure to kill the American and there was no need to revisit that subject.

Addressing Omar directly, he said, "I understand your desire to finish the job of killing this man who took your wife, and there will be time for that later. For now, we have much more important matters to deal with. Muhammad, please tell these men why we've brought them here."

"We have been blessed by Allah to have reclaimed the Caliphate lost in 1924, only this time it has been done properly and it will be ruled absolutely by Allah's will. The brutality and mass executions by our warriors in IS should convince those now under subjugation that we are not to be resisted. However, there is a nagging issue we must address. Our initial move into Syria was stopped when the renegades, Hassan Nasrallah and Hezbollah sided with the apostate ruler of that country. We finally defeated Al-Assad's regime and that has caused many Hezbollah fighters to regroup in the south of Syria to continue their work with Hamas against Israel while some have returned to Lebanon. We do not want them gaining more strength and influence in your homeland."

"We, of course, agree," Abu Youssef said. "Nasrallah has been a thorn in our side for far too long. We think he may be behind surreptitious attacks on our group, though he has managed to cover his tracks very well. He is smart enough to know he does not want to face us where he does not have a government to back him. But, we also have concern he may be making inroads to the Lebanese Army. We do not fear this army, but we will not benefit from defectors joining Hezbollah."

Abu Youssef paused for comment or question. After a moment of silence he continued. "We have two men working for us who have been close to Nasrallah for some time now. They converted to Sunni after our great successes in Libya and Iraq. They approached us about joining our ranks, but when we discovered their proximity to the Hezbollah leader we asked them to help us from within. They accepted, both because they came to see the true faith, and they were unhappy with their leader's thirst for personal power. Unfortunately, even they are not privy to every move Nasrallah makes."

"That is the main reason we have decided your group is best suited to the task before us," Muhammad said. "It is time to remove this rebel from among us and prevent him from accruing more power. Young men willing to die for Allah are our greatest asset and Nasrallah has been very successful in his recruiting efforts. We must stop him now and bring as many as possible to us from Hezbollah. We will accomplish many good things by this one death. You recently brought another one of these problems to us, Abu Youssef. Please repeat it now for the benefit of Abu al-Wafá."

"We received word from our brothers inside Nasrallah's camp that he has been talking to the Quds Force commander who was sent from Iran to assist in Hezbollah's resistance to our reclamation of Syria," Abu Youssef said. "The commander has been acting as liaison on behalf of Ali Khamenei about joining forces to take out the rulers of Saudi Arabia and the other oil rich lands on the Peninsula. We don't know yet exactly what shape that alliance may take or how they plan to execute it, but we can be assured they have the resources and personnel to do much damage."

Omar joined the conversation. "I had suspected as much. We know if the Shiites gain control of the great wealth under the feet of our Sunni brothers, it could tip the balance of power and disrupt our plans for the Caliphate. It would also embolden the Iranians in moving against our advances in galvanizing the Ummah. Perhaps the worst threat the Iranians pose is with their nuclear capabilities and desire to use them in their misguided push to pave the way for the Twelfth Imam. If they fail to take out the royal families and take over their nations, they could choose to send those weapons. The resulting global retribution could set us back decades."

"We also believe that removing Nasrallah will break the alliance he established between Hezbollah and Hamas in Gaza. We share our Palestinian brothers' desire to evict the occupiers of their land by killing as many as possible and subjugating the rest. But that is something we will do in good time, and in a way that will not result in the Jews turning the rest of our lands into a radioactive desert."

The older Al-Zawahiri brother knew better than anyone the geopolitical strategy needed to wage successful Jihad. He'd been one of the fathers of the Islamic resurgence starting in the eighties.

"By this, we will win back the full allegiance of Hamas and bring many of the warriors of Hezbollah with them," he said. "This is why we must have the blame for Nasrallah's death deposited at the door of the Jews. The OIC has lost ground in its efforts to isolate the occupiers from what little international sympathy remains. This method will not just detour attention attracted to us recently, it will refocus animus against the Little Satan."

"We see the wisdom in this assignment and we are honored to be chosen to be the sword of Allah in its execution," Abu Youssef bowed as he spoke.

As the men rose from the floor, Muhammad al-Zawahiri said, "We have full confidence you will be successful. You will be given any resource you need to carry out this mission, but it is critical that you insulate communications with us dealing with any part of this. The Jews are quite good at tracing electronic traffic, and there must be no links to us and Nasrallah's death."

"We understand and will obey. We will return home and devise a plan for your approval within days. We will get word to you through our ground channels."

When Abu Youssef and Omar exited, they were confronted with a caravan of vehicles lined up in front of the building. They were directed to the lead vehicle. As they passed the others, they noticed each was loaded with crates and luggage and two of them held women and children. They surmised the time spent in this location by the Al-Zawahiri brothers was over.

. . .

ON THE FLIGHT back to Lebanon, the conversation begun on the flight out was resumed.

"Abu Youssef, is there more you can tell me about who was behind the death of Abu Hamza?"

"As I told you before, we have reliable information that Hezbollah was involved, but we don't yet know how. Based on the power of the blast and the way it was probably delivered, it's likely they supplied the device. We have not been able to connect any individual to the delivery, but there was a produce truck parked briefly in the alley behind the café only minutes before the bomb went off. What I didn't mention earlier was that it is very curious there's been no talk of this around the local neighborhood. Boasting would be expected after the killing of such an important figure."

"There is also the fact someone knew we would be there at that time, or we were followed," Omar said. "Have you discovered anything to lead in one of these directions?"

"The way we think the bomb was delivered would play against the theory of you being followed. It's more likely someone supplied the information about your meeting. We think there is someone in our organization who is actively working against us, or it's possible someone could have simply been bought for this one thing. Which one matters not to me, this person must be found and he and his family must be destroyed. Disloyalty must be dealt with harshly."

"And I want to be the one to execute that judgment. Do you think this person could also be connected to the way the American pigs found my home?"

"I think that is logical. I will continue my investigation. You have other work to concentrate on for now."

"As you say, it will be done."

. . .

Omar's sister had just returned home with his sons after picking them up from school when a knock came on the door. Makkyiah grabbed the knob expecting to see the face of one of her neighbors. It startled her when she swung the door open to see Omar's associate, Cairo.

"Salam Alake, Makkyiah, I'm sorry to drop by unannounced. I was called to an unexpected errand nearby and when I finished, I was only a block from here. I know Omar has been gone quite a bit lately after the tragic death of Suzan, so I thought I could perhaps be a bit of encouragement to the boys."

"You surprised me, but it's alright," she said. "I was just expecting a neighbor, who often drops by during the day. I appreciate your interest in my nephews. They are good boys, but their lives have been difficult since losing their mother. Omar was here briefly a week ago, but he stays quite busy and his sons miss him."

"I know what it was like for me when I was Mohammad and Youssef's ages. If you don't mind, I won't have Mohammad out long, and then perhaps I can spend time with Youssef next week. I thought we could walk down the street for some frozen yogurt."

"I will see how much school work he has and if he'd like to go. Please wait a moment."

Several moments later, Mohammad, followed by his aunt, came to the door. Cairo took Mohammad around the shoulder and they walked toward the small market down the street.

"Mohammad, how are you doing?"

"I am okay I guess."

"I know how you must be feeling, that's why I've come by to see you."

"Yes, though I think Youssef is having a much harder time."

"I'm sure he is. You are both fortunate to have a loving aunt to watch over you. I will come by again soon to spend a little time with your brother."

"She is kind to us, but . . . "

"Yes, I know."

They arrived at the market and approached the small stand serving frozen yogurt and a few other treats. After making their selections, they sat at a table just off the sidewalk."

"Mohammad, you know we still pursue the man who took your mother and those who must have helped him while in our city."

"My father told me what happened on the ship, I can't understand why Allah would let that infidel slip through my father's grasp. My father is a fierce warrior."

"Indeed he is, which is why this American dog will be found and killed. It is only a matter of time. But, I wonder if you might like to help in this fatwa."

"I would do anything to take revenge on those who came to our home and murdered my mother. I don't think she would approve, but I'm learning a different way in Madrasah. Even if I had to die to kill the infidels, I would."

"You are truly becoming a man and slave of Allah. I swear to help you in this quest, though I must ask you not to trouble your father with this as he has much on his mind and important missions to carry out from which he must not be distracted. I also swear to protect you; you are of great value to our cause."

Thus was added to Cairo's plan that for which he'd previously only dared hope. Omar would be removed by the hand of his own son, Allah willing.

18

T HE OPERATIONAL PLAN for the assassination of Hassan Nasrallah and whoever might be close to him at the time was fully
Omar's to construct. While the search continued for the traitor among
them, Abu Youssef instructed him to keep the details isolated to the
two of them and to outsource the moving parts beyond Lebanon. This
was less of an issue than it would be normally, because the attack would
need to originate from Israel.

Abu Youssef got word to their agents within Hezbollah to arrange
a meeting. It would be critical to know the exact whereabouts of their
target and at least a reliable idea of how long he would be there. The
beauty of having more than one asset close to Nasrallah was the latitude
it offered in securing their covers and the increased width of information. In the meeting, a system was devised to make regular drops containing the most up-to-date location and duration-of-stay information
on their target and an emergency option for changes.

It took Omar only moments to devise a rough plan for killing the
Hezbollah leader and insuring the blame fell center-mass on Israel. The
first piece of the puzzle would be cut by arranging a meeting in Syria

with his old friend and compatriot, Rami, the PLO's top operative in Israel. Rami's help in Haifa was invaluable in supplying weapons and providing a means of escape. Years of knowing each other and cooperating on operations bound them by the kind of trust Omar shared with few others.

Omar carefully selected the site for their meeting to avoid attention and the risk of being seen by those who could compromise the mission before it ever began. He decided to employ a location near the Syrian side of the tunnel he had used when he first met Rami. His compatriot could cross the border without going through a checkpoint and Omar told no one except Abu Youssef where he would be and for how long.

The Israelis were on constant vigil for tunnels crossing into the country, but it was still impossible to cover every square inch of their borders. Hamas used the tunnels to penetrate their defenses and to rain thousands of rockets on population centers. Israel invaded Gaza in the summer of 2014 to destroy the tunnels, but many were back in operation months later.

The tunnel Omar chose was one of the oldest used exclusively by the PLO and Al-Asifa. The length and effectively-camouflaged openings made it almost impossible to see anyone entering or exiting from any angle except head on, and the two groups used it only for missions requiring minimal personnel. The opening on the Syrian side was inside the Ceasefire Corridor established between the two nations in 1974. They arrived at the shared safe house on the southwest side of Jubata Al Khashab within an hour of each other.

The men embraced. "Rami, my friend, thank you for coming," Omar said. "I hope your trip was uneventful."

"Abu al-Wafá, it is always a pleasure to see you, though it seems a little unusual to be with you again so soon. Surely, the target you missed in Haifa is not returning to this area. It would be very dangerous for you to try again with the Jews still looking for you."

"No, Rami, though I would take that risk if offered, I'm here to ask something very different of you."

"Then let me hear what you have in mind, though I must caution you that any operation inside the occupied territory will be more difficult than ever. Hamas has made things more complicated for us by their brazen and mostly futile attacks. They have lost many of their best-trained fighters and they've wasted millions of dollars on rockets that the Jews just slap from the sky. They have let their Hezbollah allies use them as a harassing tool to cover other operations more important to them."

"I think you may find the mission I'm tasked to carry out of interest to you and your group. We will kill Hassan Nasrallah."

Rami's facial expression showed a combination of disbelief and excitement. At first he did not reply, as if he was pondering a proper response. His words then were very deliberate and measured.

"That has been a desire of ours for some time, but there have been logistical and political reasons that have prevented us taking that action. I'm assuming this is sanctioned by the OIC, but why now?"

"Since the ouster of their soldiers from Syria, Hezbollah is weakened and scattered," Omar said, "but they have a revived incentive and backing. As you've no doubt been told, Nasrallah has become Iran's primary point of force in this part of the Middle East, and we believe they are conspiring on a much larger plan than the destruction of the Jews."

"We have similar information, but please go on."

For the next hour, Omar laid out the multiple reasons for the assassination and the benefits it would yield to all in the Sunni Sura.

"Yes, this confirms what our leadership has been seeing," Rami said. "I know they will give you full cooperation. Which brings us to your plan."

"The last goal of this mission is to have the Jews bear sole responsibility. This too will have several beneficial results which I know I need not explain to you." Omar paused for his words to sink in, hoping for a response from Rami. It came quickly.

"Of course, that is a wise plan indeed. How do we partner with you in this glorious endeavor?"

"We have the ability to know the location of Nasrallah and we already know the various locations he frequents. He obviously never follows any pattern, but that will be our part of this operation, along with supplying our people to coordinate the attack when that time comes."

"So what kind of attack do you propose?"

"Drone."

"Yes, that will be an effective way to reach the target inside Lebanon without attracting the radar attention of the Jews. And, if we can keep the distance to a minimum, it should evade the satellites of the Americans. That should eliminate any possibility of interception."

"One of Nasrallah's favorite safe houses is in Nabatieh," Omar said. "It also happens to be where he married his last wife from the Bade Aldeen tribe. Her youth and beauty usually keep him there a bit longer than his other hideouts. That puts him only about thirty-five kilometers from Karmiel, where I think you told me you have no camp or fixed assets, but the IDF has a station.

"Nasrallah moves through a series of tunnels and sleeps in bunkers so the missiles on the drone will need to be of the concrete piercing variety. Could you not launch from Karmiel under cover of darkness without being detected?"

"I believe we could, and I may know where to get the Israeli UAV and armament, but it will be very expensive," Rami said. "There are still some Jews who are primarily motivated by profit and, if we can offer the right price, I can get the drone, but the warheads will be a bit more difficult to obtain."

"Rami, you must find a way. Money is not an issue. If you have a greedy Jew who will get a drone for a price, then why not a warhead?"

"My old friend, my network here in Israel is small yet effective. Jews are hard to recruit. In reality, the man who will provide the drone is doing so because our people are holding his brother in Syria. The money only makes life easier for him to support the brother's family. But there is another Israeli who is very high in the Ordnance Corps of the IDF who I can contact regarding this matter."

"What is his motivation for being part of your network, Rami?"

"Yes, a good question. You actually know of this man because of his notoriety a couple of years ago. He was the IDF lieutenant colonel who crossed into south Lebanon with a patrol of IDF soldiers and was ambushed by Hezbollah. All were killed but him and he was wounded. He claimed one of his soldiers had been kidnapped at a roadblock in Northern Israel and he reacted immediately to recapture the man before Hezbollah could torture and kill him. He was called a courageous hero and showered with accolades for his actions. Actually, our people captured him in Lebanon. He was drunk and naked in an apartment with his Ukrainian girlfriend who was working in a UN compound near Tyre. His men thought he had been kidnapped and they crossed over looking for him. That's when they were ambushed and killed by our forces. The decision was made to send him back as a double agent rather than kill him. We had plenty of great photos that would ensure that he cooperated for a long time. He has been reliable so far. I think he is the man for this task too."

"Yes, yes, I remember him. His name was Avi . . . Avi Gul, I think. Good, then you can get the warhead?"

"Yes, and we will also need to execute the mission immediately after acquiring it, so the Jews will have no time to declare it missing or pursue it before the deed is done."

"We will transfer the funds to you immediately upon your request. As for the timing, we must do this as soon as possible. After you have confirmed the availability of the fully armed drone and the team to launch it, we will let you know the minute we are notified of Nasrallah's next arrival in Nabatieh. That will give us up to a week. I will have someone at the location verify his presence and to transmit GPS identification you can program into the device. We want it to dive into the building after it launches its missiles. The debris will be the best evidence that the Jews are responsible."

Omar elected to handle the Lebanese elements of his plan to kill the renegade Nasrallah personally.

· · ·

Now, THE HARD part would begin; waiting. Omar knew the game well but this was the part he most disliked. Furthermore, he was anxious to get this mission behind him so he could get back to the real passion in his life; killing the man who robbed him and his boys of the woman they loved. Finally the waiting was over.

The long month of waiting, putting all other things on hold, even his sons, as he awaited the message from their informant that the mosquito was lighting was finally over. The group used a dating Web site as one of many communication channels, hiding in plain sight. When it displayed the "smile" that told Simone/Omar there was a message to be delivered, the coded posting gave the time and place, one of several prearranged.

The only time electronic communications could be truly secure and trusted was in close proximity. Highly sensitive messages had to be relayed either in person, which carried its own hazards, or in a way that left no trail. As Omar walked past a trash can near the door of a restaurant in Chim, the application on his phone transmitted the proper algorithmic code to pick up the micro burst message emitted by the three-millimeter-wide dot stuck just under the lip of the opening. The transfer worked like a cut and paste function. Even if the dot was ever discovered and investigated, it was now void.

Seconds after touching the "decipher" icon with his right thumb, he saw the message displayed: YOUR SHIPMENT WILL ARRIVE AT THE REQUESTED LOCATION BETWEEN 1/18 AND 1/27.

Previous such messages contained vital information like the address and location of sleeping quarters for each of the locations Nasrallah frequented. Striking at night was the most common choice for finding someone where they were reported to be.

That gave Omar and Rami only two days to get the loaded UAV on site so they would be able to strike at the early end of the time Nasrallah was supposed to be in Nabatieh. A quick message sent on an e-commerce site told Rami it was time to set the plan in motion.

It took three days for Rami and his team of Israeli traitors to make their acquisition. The wait bore expectedly good results. They snatched one of six old X45B decommissioned stealth drones awaiting deconstruction. It was being replaced by the advanced D model which flew faster and higher and was less prone to malfunction. It carried two GBU-39 narrow diameter "bunker buster" bombs which could be fired with pin-point accuracy from as high as 40,000 feet. Avi Gul could only get one without risk of compromise, but that was all that was needed. Since the plan was to send the UAV into the building after firing the rockets, it would not exceed an altitude of 1,500 feet, so the crash of the UAV into the building would follow the rocket launch by no more than two minutes. The X45B would be sent into a power dive and guided into the target by its onboard GPS tracker. There would be no surviving the blast within a square block or an underground shelter shallower than fifty feet.

. . .

JANUARY 23, 2021, at three a.m., Omar was 400 meters from the target and six stories up. The Al-Asifa operative who accompanied Nasrallah to the location left his phone in his room above the bunker, fully charged and broadcasting its GPS location. At three-twenty-eight a.m. the neighborhood was rocked by a massive explosion. Nasrallah, his favorite wife, one child, and eight other family and staff instantly awoke in another dimension.

Smoke, fire, and debris were all that could be discerned as the darkness of a half-moon night was overtaken by the results of a deliberate assassination. Nasrallah was dead and Omar was pleased. Allah had surely shown him favor in this operation. Now the question was, would Allah show the same favor in the pursuit of the infidel who killed Suzan? *Insha'Allah!*

. . .

OMAR DROVE BACK to Beirut after verifying the blast had, in fact, turned Nasrallah's safe house into a crater. As usual, he would be able to count on the international media to let him know the details of who else died.

On the drive back, Omar's mind meandered through non-contiguous thoughts. Thinking about the fury of the blast in Nabatieh took him off to fleeting thoughts of the many bombs he'd planted over the years. That led him to think of the young woman forced to carry the bomb into the German night club, which brought him back to the new young wife of Nasrallah. *Was she as ignorant of her husband's actions as Suzan had been of mine?*

SUZAN, MY LOVE.
I have been part of so much death, so much loss, so much grief.

That thought took him back to carrying the corpse of his friend on his back after a mission gone wrong when he was still a teenager. They did what needed to be done, but the boy he swore to watch over paid for that success with this life.

· · ·

I TOLD HIS MOTHER *I would make sure he came back unharmed.*

Why, Allah, do you not protect those under your care? Why did you let my Suzan die? I was doing your work, I was serving you. WHY?

Abu Youssef cleared his throat which caused Omar to look up from his kabob. He then realized his superior had been speaking. Two members of Al Asifa were on station in front and at the rear of the café checking everything and everyone. News of the assassination of Nasrallah, just over a day old, was playing out in the media as they'd hoped. The Jews were disavowing anything to do with the attack, and the OIC talking heads from all over the world were calling them liars, condemning them, and making threats. The fuse was about to burn to the keg of gunpowder.

"Forgive me, Abu Youssef, I was thinking about the success of our mission and the work now to be done."

"I'm sure you were, but I sense something else, something different about you. You seem less focused. What happened in Nabatieh you have not told me?"

"Nothing. I am well. I assure you. Please go on. You were speaking of how to convince those in Hezbollah to realign with the OIC. Others may have to die."

Abu Youssef drew in a breath and opened his mouth to speak when he noticed Omar's eyes shift from his to over his left shoulder.

"What is it?"

"I think that is my son, Mohammad, who just came around from the end of the block."

He rose, waved, and called to his son, who was still more than fifty meters away. When his son looked his way, he froze in mid stride. Omar raised his hand again and pulled the air to him to assure his son it was okay to keep coming. Instead of continuing to walk forward, Mohammad suddenly spun to head back the way he came.

Omar stepped from behind the table to pursue Mohammad, when the figure of his first born was transformed into a ball of light and flame. Passersby and cars parked along the street absorbed most of the concussion wave and shrapnel, but it projected enough energy to knock Omar to the concrete and shatter the glass of the storefront.

Omar was back on his feet almost before he'd fully hit the ground. He took off in a dazed run.

Mohammad!

A block farther down the street, a sedan pulled from the curb and made a u-turn. Inside the car, barely audible curses flowed from Cairo.

"That damn kid! Another twenty meters. That's all I needed!"

19

"COLONEL JOHNSON, IT'S Blake," he said into the phone. "I'm still struggling with myself, but I don't think I can set what's happened in the last couple of months down yet. I know the missions you propose are important, and I'm inclined to simply comply, but I can't shake the need to make things right."

"By making things right, do you mean revenge?"

"That's part of my struggle, sir. I can't honestly deny what's in my heart, but I believe there's more, something more important. The images of Alia being shot and her cold body lying on that bed haunt me continually, and those thoughts almost always turn to me putting a bullet between Abu al-Wafa's eyes. Occasionally though, I'm left with something I can't describe even to myself. I feel the need to pursue this guy, but with a possible conclusion other than his death at my hands."

"Professionally, I don't think you are thinking clearly and I need you to get past your conflict, get your team together, and start planning your first mission in South America."

"I understand—"

"Let me finish, Blake."

"Sorry, sir."

"Personally, my opinion of you is unshaken, so I trust you'll make the decision you must whether I like it or not. However, you understand, I can't let you run autonomous operations with government assets. Blake, you are a fine man and a good soldier. You know you cannot decide what missions you want to run and which ones you want to reject. You love, and have risked your life repeatedly, for this Constitutional Republic. Where would we be if the military officer corps made those kinds of decisions? So, if you don't take these new orders, you'll have to resign your commission."

"Yes, sir, I expected that, and for the promotion to be rescinded. An honorable discharge is all I ask."

"You'll keep your rank and retire a lieutenant colonel with full benefits. That's the least this man's army owes you. But please, give this another few days before you make a final decision. Go see General Sam. He is such a wise and thoughtful mentor."

"Sir, my attitude is not going to change. I have had thirty days to think about this and I am more determined than you can understand. Regarding the retirement at my current rank, that's more than generous, sir, and I'll always be in your debt."

"Not at all, Blake. I think you're making a big mistake, but you've earned all you've received."

"Thank you, sir."

Well, that decision's made and executed, but where do I go from here?

* * *

TWO DAYS AFTER Blake resigned from the army, General Sam called.

"Hello, General Sam," Blake said. "How are things with you?"

"All is well around here, Blake. My farmhand and I have most of our fall chores done and we have just about enough wood chopped and stacked to get us through the winter. How are you and Sam doing?"

"Never better, sir, I think we have another Kingdom warrior on our hands. I don't think I've ever seen a kid have a grip on life and biblical truth like this one. I certainly didn't when I was his age. We hate getting up every morning and not having a wife and mom to greet us, but we're moving on. Maria has graciously agreed to keep Sam's schoolwork on track and to be available when I need her to stay with him."

"That's good, Blake. You and Alia have done a fine job with that boy, but as you know, God has no grandchildren. It's great to hear Sam is walking his own path in Christ. Did you talk with Colonel Johnson?"

"I did, and once again I'm grateful for your counsel. I'll be retiring as a lieutenant colonel effective immediately, though it will take a month or so for the paperwork to go through. I'm going to do some consulting on the southern operations they're planning before I officially leave."

"How do you feel now that you've pulled the trigger?"

"I believe that was the right move, but I'm no clearer on what to do next. I'm considering making contact with Mossad to see if they would take me on as a contractor to go after Abu al-Wafá. I know the right people over there and they know me well, so maybe we can work something out. They won't be pivoting their focus from the area any time soon."

"That's one plan I suppose, but are you sure this is God's will for you?"

"Am I sure? No, but the more I've thought and prayed about this, I feel an ever greater sense that this is in my path for a reason I won't discover until I get there."

"I can't argue that, Blake. I'll keep praying about this with you, but there may also be another way. I spoke with one of my oldest and most trusted friends the other day, I don't think you've met, but you'll be getting a call from an organization he works with."

"Roger that, sir, any friend of yours has my ear and automatic trust."

"Well, I've got more wood to chop. I can't go as long as I used to, so I have to attack this in stages. I should probably give it up all together, but there's something deeply satisfying about putting in that kind of work to produce your own heat in the winter."

"You never cease to amaze me, General, though I think had my dad lived, he'd probably still be chopping wood into his nineties as well. Have fun."

"Let me know if you get that call. Out here."

As usual, when General Sam said to expect something, Blake got the call early the next morning.

"This is Jacob."

"Mr. Hunter, this is Tosho Musashi with Global Reparations. I believe you were told I'd be calling."

"Yes, what can I do for you? Please call me Jacob."

"Thank you, I will. Jacob, you come highly recommended for a position we need to fill."

"What kind of position? My skill set is rather narrow."

"Why don't I start with who we are? Global Reparations is a non-profit organization that responds to disasters and emergencies anywhere on the planet. You may never have heard of us, we've only been in operation about a decade, and we don't care to attract attention because it just slows us down, and in some cases makes it hard to get where we need to be. We are primarily a team of medical and relief personnel, and we rarely stay in one place for very long. We see our job as going into situations when the need and risk are high. We do all we can to stabilize, then we make way for the larger organizations who have longer term mission strategies."

"That sounds great and must keep you all busy, but I'm not sure how I can be of help."

"Jacob, as I mentioned, we tend to go into dangerous areas and often when the meter is pegged. We've subcontracted our security since the beginning, but we think it's time we integrate that part of our organization. We would like you to consider joining us to head up that division."

"I appreciate the offer . . . I'm sorry, what is your name again?"

"Tosho Musashi, but please call me Tosh."

"Thanks, Tosh. I genuinely appreciate what you do and the offer, but the work I've done over my career has always been more proactive than reactive, and I'm sure those two don't work the same way."

"I can understand that, but the recommendation we received on you seemed clear you'd fit the job. Before we go further, may I ask a favor?"

"Sure."

"Come meet with us. Our VP of operations is in Washington for meetings and has time to see you tomorrow afternoon. I'm told you live a couple of hours south. Will that be a problem?"

"It shouldn't be, but I really don't want to waste your time."

"I can assure you, Jacob, not only will this not be a waste of our time, but I believe you will not think yours was wasted either. Will it be okay for me to text you the address and time for the meeting?"

"Sure. I'll let you know as soon as possible if anything changes the plan."

"We thank you, Jacob, and I look forward to seeing you tomorrow."

The meeting was set for two p.m. at the Global Reparations office on E Street NE, a couple of blocks from Union Station. Blake never liked being in a big city, and they didn't come much bigger or more congested than Washington, DC. He arrived at the address at one-fifty p.m. and was relieved to find a marked spot in front of the building as promised.

He wasn't sure what to expect, but he was a bit surprised to find the office located in a narrow "brownstone." A small bronze plaque next to the door was the only way to be sure he was in the right place. Blake pushed the intercom button and looked up into the security camera. Almost instantly a female voice came through the speaker. "Good afternoon, Colonel Hunter, we've been expecting you, please come in." The telltale buzz sounded and Blake pulled open the heavy oak and opaque leaded-glass door.

A trim and attractive woman, probably in her thirties, stepped from the room to Blake's left and greeted him with a winsome smile and solid handshake, "Welcome, I'm Jessie."

Her comportment and strength of grip caused him to ask, more as confirmation than query, "Thanks, in which branch did you serve?"

"I'm proud to say I still serve in the Guard. I was active duty for six years, 101st, Bastogne Regiment, medical. I made major a few months ago."

"Congratulations. What brought you here?"

"I think you're about to find that out for yourself. The boss wants me to bring you right back, follow me, if you will."

On their way to the back of the building, Blake noticed the offices were nicely squared away, but rather Spartan for an international organization. Then they entered what was clearly the executive office. It was a little better appointed than the others he passed, but still understated.

When Jessie stepped aside to introduce her boss, the sight of the man rising to his feet to move around his desk caused Blake's eyes to widen and his mouth to go slightly agape.

"Jacob Hunter," she said, "may I present—"

"General Garrison, sir, it's a great honor to meet you," Blake said, then thought, *Man, I hope I look half as good as this guy when I'm his age, he must be in his seventies.* "No one gets through Delta school without hearing about the legendary William F. Garrison. I've wanted to meet you ever since. I had no idea you were the 'old friend' General Sam was talking about in his call yesterday."

"Call me Bill," the general said. "I've been retired for quite a while and I fall well short of warranting the legendary label, I assure you. It's my pleasure to finally meet you, eh, Jacob. Our friend Sam has told me quite a bit about you." He then waved toward the corner of the room. "You met Tosh on the phone yesterday; he'll be sitting in with us. Have a seat." The two shook hands and took their seats. Garrison sat on the corner of his desk nearest Blake.

"Thanks, Jessie. Give me a buzz about fifteen minutes ahead of my next appointment, I think it's local and I may need to postpone."

"Of course, sir. Gentlemen, may I get you something to drink?" she asked. "I made some coffee right before you got here, Colonel Hunter. We also have soft drinks."

"Some ice water would be good if you don't mind," Blake said.

"I'll have some of that coffee, Jessie, thanks," the general said

"Nothing for me, Jess, thanks," said Tosho.

Blake and Garrison spent the time awaiting Jessie's return exchanging acquainting banter and discussing their common love for the venerated old general.

After Jessie brought the drinks, exited, and closed the door, Garrison wasted no time.

"Sam let me in on your secret, Blake, and it's safe here. At this point Tosh and I are the only ones in the organization with that knowledge. Sam knew if we were able to recruit you it would be important to start with no pretense, which is why I must also begin by asking your forgiveness."

"I can't imagine for what, sir, I trust General Sam with my life. I certainly trust him to know when and with whom he can share my true identity."

"Actually, Blake, I assumed that. I must ask your forgiveness for getting you here on quasi-false pretenses. Global Reparations is what Tosh told you, but I asked you here to talk about something quite different. But, before we begin, I must ask for your word in keeping what I'm about to tell you strictly confidential."

"You have it, sir."

20

" **G**LOBAL REPARATIONS IS a certified international relief organization we created in early 2009 and it functions as Tosh told you over the phone. What he couldn't tell you over an open line was GR acts as the public and benevolent face of another organization we started at the same time, The Sodality. You'll not be able to find us on any country's registry and a Google search will come up empty. I know I don't need to remind you of how the election of Barack Obama has resulted in a global crisis relative to the growth of radical Islam and the global Caliphate. I have never understood his reasons for supporting Islam and allowing them to humiliate America, including right here, within our own borders. His unwillingness to acknowledge they are a threat and stand up to them emboldened them. And his support for the likes of the Muslim Brotherhood with tax dollars from hard working Americans has heated a situation the new president has been unable to reverse.

"Like many Americans, we held out for decades thinking the people would snap out of their stupor and put a stop to the destruction of our Constitutional Republic. Unfortunately, that hope evaporated in

November of 2008 and it only took a few months to see our worst projections realized. I confess, I had to ask the forgiveness of a few of my colleagues who'd been pushing us to act since Carter." General Garrison hesitated a beat.

Blake picked up the cue. "I was still fairly young, but my dad told me he was encouraged when Carter was booted after one term and Reagan took the White House. Unfortunately, that renaissance didn't last long. Looking back it seems pretty clear the first Bush to become president wasn't exactly enamored with our Constitution. He seemed a bit too preoccupied with a new world order."

"America has been drifting from its principled moorings for a long time, but I know you don't need a history lesson and I need to get on with why we called you here," Garrison continued.

"A group of men, women, and their families have coalesced over the last thirty years or so who have worked in almost every sector of our society. We all share three core values: love of God, family, and country, in that order. We also recognize our common enemy is committed to but one value: self. We formed The Sodality for the preservation of the former and to repel the latter."

"You can certainly count me in on the former as well, Bill, but it's hard to imagine your group being very big considering how splintered America has become."

"Maybe now's a good time for me to jump in here," said Tosh. "Of course you're right, Blake, but it's a little like the old axiom about what brings a feuding family together; a common enemy. The people involved in The Sodality come from myriad backgrounds, life experiences, and even religious disciplines. What we share is the Bible and the willingness to maintain our differences while we focus our efforts on defeating those who want to create a world collective. For those of us in America, we have the added rallying points of The Declaration of Independence and Constitution—"

"Just a second. Sorry to stop you, Tosh, are you saying your organization includes foreign nationals?"

"We have representatives from many countries in the world involved in The Sodality, though we function day to day through a small board of leaders who came together in a process we can only explain as

Providential. We saw an amazing phenomenon along with the rise of the Tea Party in 2009. People from around the globe started speaking up about what made America special. They love their own countries, but they saw in our founding documents principles with no borders or boundaries. They could also speak with creditability about what happens to a people when those principles are overridden by human fiat." Garrison rose from his desk as he spoke and returned to his chair.

Before he could return to his explanation, Blake interrupted with a comment. "General, I'm a bit incredulous, if you will allow me to say so. I have been tracking terrorists for two decades now and have seen the intelligence on every terrorist group as well as every counterterrorist entity, and I have never seen this before? How could I not know about this? How could you keep something this big a secret? Is this the Illuminati that I have heard of all my life? Or is this some kind of One World Government you are setting up?"

"Sam told me you like getting to the point, maybe even more than the normal special operator. I was more that way a few years ago, but my grandkids have retrained me a bit. Nonetheless, you're right, it does seem incredible that we have kept this off the radar, but that is exactly what we have done." Garrison looked directly into Blake's eyes as his jaw tightened and his voice dropped a half octave. Blake was unsure whether he'd angered the old soldier but it really didn't matter much at that moment because Blake sensed his world was about to change drastically once more, depending on the decision he was about to make.

"Blake, this has been kept under the radar because it is the most serious thing any of us has ever been involved in and there is too much at stake to be careless. We intend to save the Western culture from an existential threat, period. Some of the wealthiest men in the world are involved, so there is no profit motive. And no, this is neither the Illuminati nor global government. We love our nations and our cultures too much to see them destroyed by radical Islam and weak western leaders, so we are simply helping reduce the threats to our futures."

Blake could sense the determination and sincerity in the voice of the man he only knew by reputation. "I hope you are not the only person in this coalition with the vision to go along with your courage and determination."

Garrison's countenance softened as he continued.

"As I alluded earlier, we are a coalition of men and women from three major sectors; military/law enforcement, business, and religion. Before you ask, within those groups there are those who have held public office, but one of the principles upon which we all agree is there should be no political class. So, to the point, we do what governments can't or won't because they have become a part of the problem. We have stations in fifteen countries from which we can conduct operations in every other, that's where Global Reparations is particularly helpful. We don't always work in tandem, but while GR is seeing to the humanitarian needs in, say, China for example, The Sodality is taking the fight to those who want to destroy freedom wherever it exists. That includes disrupting financial supply chains, cyber counter-warfare, search and rescue and other black ops, and targeting of leadership for capture or killing."

Blake did not flinch at the idea of killing terrorists. The general knew he wouldn't because General Sam assured him Blake was a man of steel nerves and resolve, operating on deeply held values and principles. They always make the best assassins. Blake spoke briefly, stating the obvious.

"Uh, sir, you must step on a lot of toes. Don't your operations overlap what other governments are doing?"

"Good question and one we addressed at our inception and included in our founding laws. We have two things working for us that have so far kept us from entanglements with our own and foreign governments. One, as I said earlier, our missions are those governments avoid or neglect. Second, thanks to our network and backing, we have better intel than any one government, including the U.S. What we came to realize very early on was the number of people ready, willing, and able to join us. They just needed the right group to join. I won't go into more detail on this for now. If you join us, you will be read into everything."

"I think I understand the basics of your organization and I certainly understand the motivation behind it. As I've watched empty suits ascend to positions of control over our country and the damage they've done, to our military in particular, I've wondered what could be done. This is a major paradigm shift though. It almost sounds like a shadow government."

"That thought is not unwarranted, in fact I'd have been a little concerned had you not brought it up, but no, and we will have nothing to do with replacing or overthrowing this or any other government. There are other groups and organizations in America working hard every day to push the federal genie back in the bottle and restore the limits of our founders' original intent. Our work is restricted to taking the fight to the bad guys who threaten the countries in our alliance."

"The fact you are involved and General Sam referred me is all the credibility I really need. Is the general directly involved?"

"If not for him, there probably wouldn't be a Sodality, and his knowledge of Russia has been priceless in our operations in that part of the world. His expertise in joint special operations not only created the Special Forces as we know it in America, it continues to shape how we function. And that brings us to why you're sitting here today. I had to stop leading missions a while back, and since then I've been responsible for planning and operational oversight. We have many skilled and reliable men and women on our teams, but it's come time to add a layer between me and the ground. It was bad enough when the major players were just looking out for themselves, now they're colluding. The job has grown exponentially over the last decade. We want you to take over the senior leadership role in our operations division. That means you plan all ground ops and lead the ones you choose."

"I'm honored, sir, and I can think of few other things I'd rather do than work for you. But, there is one thing I must do right now, and I have no idea how long it will take."

"Sam told me about your wife, Blake. You have my deepest sympathies. I know what you want to do. There's no doubt I'd be right where you are under similar circumstances. That's another reason we want you. We've been tracking Abu al-Wafá for some time and we know how close to the OIC leadership he is."

"If I may, sir, would this not have been a case where you and the U.S. military could have gotten cross threaded?"

"Not with Bob Johnson running the show over at Bragg."

"This goes a lot deeper than you've been letting on."

"Not everyone aligned with The Sodality works directly with us. We have colleagues who maintain positions in virtually all strata of the country. It wouldn't be possible for us to function as we do without help from within a great many offices and agencies. In other words, there are still many patriots in our government who want to help".

"Blake, if you join us, your first mission will be to complete the mission on which you were first sent when Bob called you back to the teams, capture or kill Abu al-Wafá. Now I know your preference is the latter, but as you know, our work to strike at the heart of the OIC would be accelerated with what's encased in that guy's head. Do you think you could keep your finger off the trigger if taking him alive works?"

"As you say, that's not what I had in mind. He is an evil man who has done more than just kill my wife. He needs to die and I have more reason than most to take him out. I honestly am not sure that I could resist if the opportunity to do so was there. I can only say I would try. But you know if I had him in the cross hairs, my instinct would be to kill, not capture.

"Fair enough, Blake, and I would feel the same but this is where you have to think beyond your own interests. He is far too valuable to make killing him the first option. His capture could deal a devastating blow to the global terror network."

"General, I've been following orders most of my life, though not with complete success. But, I've never passed this way before. When that moment comes and I have this animal on the other side of my reticle, I can't truthfully warrant my *no* will be *no*."

"That's the kind of answer I expect from a man of integrity. Sam told me to expect this from you. He's never let me down. Blake, I'm willing to take you at your word with the risk attached. I'm sure you will need a little time to sort things out, but we'll need your decision within forty-eight hours. Is that asking too much?"

"No, sir, I do need a little time to properly consider your offer and of course look at some arrangements I'd have to make, but I will honor your timeline."

"I appreciate that, Blake, I'm convinced you should join us, but I'll pray you see His will in this one way or the other."

The three men rose from their seats, shook hands, and Blake turned to leave.

21

B LAKE CALLED GENERAL Sam on his way back home from DC to see if he and younger Sam could spend the approaching Saturday with him on the farm.

"You know you are always welcome out here. You might want to bring a change of clothes though. I have a little work for you while you're here. We all have to earn our supper you know."

"I need a workout, and I know Sam will do anything for you. I wonder sometimes whether he might rather live with you. He loves you and your farm."

"And I love him, but there's never been a good substitute for a loving dad. You both need to wear boots you can get wet. I'll supply every-thing else."

"Whoa, this is actually starting to sound like work, but we'll be there around oh-eight-hundred, if that works for you."

"That's just right. See you boys then."

• • •

A RECENT STORM GENERATED straight-line winds through General Sam's land at upwards to sixty miles per hour. It was severe, but not like he'd seen before. This time several of his large trees lost branches, but none were uprooted. A couple of large branches came off the Eastern Hemlock near the pond and needed to be pulled out, cut, and stacked for seasoning.

General Sam mostly directed the operation, but he didn't hesitate to jump in when another pair of hands was needed. It was three o'clock in the afternoon by the time they were done. Blake and Sam were fairly covered in mud and ready for hot chocolate. They were grateful it wasn't mid-summer. Their feet and hands were numb, but the labor mostly insulated them from the cold weather.

About half way through the project, General Sam pulled young Sam aside for a short break. "Did your dad ever tell you about the time he was helping me chop some wood a few years back when he lost the axe?"

"No, sir, what happened? Did he lay it somewhere and forget where?"

"It was a little more dramatic than that . . . "

"Hey! We have work to do here. We don't have time for stories." It was obvious this was not a tale Blake wanted retold.

"You just keep working. Sam and I are talking here. As I was saying, it was a beautiful summer day, though a little warm. We'd just started and it was your dad's turn to chop while I stacked. I think he may have been trying to impress me and, as I said, it was in the upper eighties, as I recall. Anyway, his first backswing was so fast, the axe slipped out of his hands just as he got it past his head. The centrifugal force sent it flying behind him where it landed in the back of my Gator, containing the odorous results of cleaning out the horse stalls. He had to dig it out."

"My dad had to dig through horse poop to get the axe back?" As the image formed in his head, he started laughing uncontrollably, which made General Sam join him.

Blake was not as amused, but he enjoyed seeing his two favorite males laughing so hard they almost slipped off the tailgate of the general's truck.

Mrs. Murphy, General Sam's part-time housekeeper, prepared one of her signature meals of herb-roasted chicken, a potato and cauliflower gratin, grilled asparagus, and for dessert; pear cobbler and homemade vanilla ice cream. She was gone by the time they gathered at the table, so they were unable to lavish their praise on her. General Sam promised to relay their gratitude, though he assured them, she was not much of one for that sort of thing. She was the widow of a Marine who retired to the next tract over from General Sam. After the passing of their spouses, Mrs. Murphy offered to help out around the general's home a few days a week and on special occasions—to keep busy and make a little "mad money" as she called it. She retained much of her Irish humility.

All three ate to the bursting point and agreed it would probably be best to go back out and work off the calories, but clearer heads prevailed. Blake and Sam accepted with alacrity their host's offer to stay the night. After the day's work and huge dinner, driving even an hour held no appeal. They retired to the den where they played Scrabble. One game proved soporific for young Sam who almost fell asleep while brushing his teeth.

Blake returned to General Sam and they shared cigars and a dram of Irish whisky.

"I know you're beat and probably ready to join Sam in dreamville, but I'd like to hear about your meeting in DC and what you're thinking about the immediate future."

"You really blindsided me with who I'd be meeting. General Garrison certainly lives up to every expectation I've had before meeting him."

It took Blake about twenty minutes to retell the course of his introduction to The Sodality, even skipping details General Sam already knew about the organization.

"So, what do you think? And are you leaning toward a decision?"

"I've thought about the trajectory of America and its place in the world for a while, and I've always felt called to do my part to defend my country. The last decade or so, it seems we've given up the high ground in trying to retain our Republic and in protecting our people. I've ruminated on what could be done about it, and I even wondered if working within the system had any future at all. I guess now that I'm faced with a viable option in taking the fight to our enemies, I'm ambivalent. I'm as ready to strap it on as I've ever been, but I'm also really unsettled with the concept of doing it outside the government I've served for nearly twenty years. You have my unmitigated trust which is why I'm even entertaining this offer at all. I guess the OD Green has seeped into my skin over the years."

"I expected nothing less from you, Blake. The idea for The Sodality has been floating around me since just after World War Two. I was four square against it until the major moves were made to dismantle our Constitution, and in particular the separation of powers, at the time we were also seeing the greatest threat from without since Pearl Harbor. Left to the status quo, America might have already been pulled down to third world chaos. If you take their offer, you will find out what they've done in just a few years to buttress the wall around America. I see now there was no other way."

"I can see where this could require me to define my oath to support and defend the Constitution of the United States against all enemies, foreign and domestic and why that part of the oath comes before obeying the orders of the president. I've been blessed to work for men like you, General, whose honor I had never called into question. Most recently, however, working with Colonel Johnson and seeing the kind of people to whom he answers, I've wondered if I could stay that course. It's been a little murky for me of late, but I still believe in Providence."

"Ah, yes. Bob Johnson is a fine man and one of the best leaders the army has left. I'll let you in on a little secret. Bill told you about Bob's cooperation with The Sodality, but what he didn't tell you was what *Major* Johnson went through during the great leadership purge of the military in 2013 and 14. His sterling record along with a few strategic words from people like Bill Garrison kept him off the pink slip list, but it also took a lot of encouragement from a few of us to convince him not to quit. He is now one of the most important assets we have, but it takes incredible faith and patience on his part."

"It makes me wonder which takes more courage; running at the guns or standing at post answering to fools."

"Don't look now, but it sounds as though you're talking yourself into a decision. But before we go there, I want to be sure you know why I called Bill about you. First, he's known about you for some time and he's asked more than once about recruiting you. The main reason I've declined is because of the importance of the missions you were running and then because of Alia and you starting a family. Everything changed in Haifa and at CIA's Counter Terrorism Center which I knew would turn your life upside down. You going after Abu al-Wafá was a given, and I'd much rather see you do it with people who will have the resources to do it right. I think you can do some real good with The Sodality, but I want you to seriously consider your next move. I want what's best for you and Sam, Blake. You could be gone for some time hunting this guy and I don't think you could dig up more dangerous work."

"I know you're looking out for us," Blake said. "If I live to be a thousand, I'll never repay all you've meant to me and done for us. I know this is a bit of an odd segue, but you putting Sam's and my name together just then sparked a couple thoughts. Living in the two worlds of Blake Kershaw and Jacob Hunter is something to which I've never grown accustomed. I've never mentioned this to you before, but I find it remarkable you've never once even come close to using the wrong name with the wrong people. Alia had to take care to keep from having Sam hear her call me Blake and she ultimately had to give up the name all together . . . " After saying her name, the rest of the sentence tapered to a bare whisper as Blake fought the pressure seizing his throat.

The men sat in silence and stared into the fireplace blaze.

"Sorry, General . . . " Blake finally said. "The other thing is about my mom. I've thought about her almost as much as Alia lately. I don't regret the decision I made years ago regarding the faking of my death, but she is still my mom and now I miss her more than ever."

"Blake, you know you saved hundreds of thousands of Americans by stopping the Russian portable nuke from being detonated in Baltimore Harbor. It was a tremendous price for you to pay. We both knew it would be difficult to live the rest of your life without seeing your mother, but you saved so many lives by sacrificing a portion of your own. And the rules are there is no turning back once you commit. But now the situation has changed, and you are not playing by government rules if you take this job."

"General Sam, the truth is I really did not think I would survive that mission. I expected to die and I rationalized the decision by convincing myself she would be better off without me. She got my insurance you know. And I was still wandering aimlessly through life, feeling guilty for my dad's death, so maybe this was really about paying my dues to her?"

"Blake, your dad died by an Iraqi scud and not because of anything you did. I know you have yet to unload the guilt but that is a fact".

"Yeah, I know, but he was there because I burned down the tobacco barn with the year's income in it, and he had no choice but to volunteer for the Gulf War. But I am more rational about it now than I was then."

The old man read Blake's mind and knew exactly what he was pondering.

"If you take this job, Blake, you have to find full time care for Sam. I am pretty sure it has occurred to you that your mom would be the best choice.

"I know you've been thinking about this for some time, and I'm sure you've thought about how this will affect her. There are a number of good reasons to tell her now. I'm just concerned about the impact on her after all this time."

"As am I. Standing by Alia's grave that day with Sam, it was hard to parse where my grief weighed heaviest between losing her, Sam losing her, or the fact my mother's been left out of it all. I don't think I can move on to anything more in my life until I make things right with her."

"We should probably go through Colonel Johnson to let him know for the record. We would be breaching every tradecraft protocol in the book, but in this case, it is worth the risk. We should give her a secure device for getting in touch with us if there's ever a problem. Of course she'll have to maintain your cover outside her house. Do you think she can handle all that?"

"I've seen my mom go through things that have driven other people to all forms of destruction and she's kept her chin up and her hopefulness alive. I hate what I've done to her and I know this is going to be very difficult for us both, but I feel it to my bones, this is right. I also know there's risk involved, but the scales have dropped to the side of telling her. I want her to know everything and to have Sam in her life and her in his. Telling Sam he has a grandmother he's never met is going to be another hurdle, but I think he's old enough to handle it."

"Well, that answers the last question I had about you joining The Sodality. I know Maria has been a tremendous help to you, but you told me she has a life of her own as well. If your mom is up to keeping Sam when you're away, everyone wins. One last thing before I let you turn in. I think it would be best if you let me make the initial visit with your mom. Your altered appearance would probably make you knocking on her door and declaring who you really are problematic at best."

"I was hoping you'd say that. I'm further in your debt."

22

OMAR RAN THROUGH the debris thrown into the street by the blast and over the bodies of the few wounded and dead. When he reached the sidewalk corner on which he'd last seen his oldest son, what he found was more revolting than even his hardened sensibilities could handle. What remained of Mohammad was a scorched pool of blood and little else.

Omar collapsed on the still-hot concrete, emitting visceral screeches normally reserved for wounded animals.

When the police and EMTs arrived on the scene, it took six of them to move Omar from the corner to an ambulance to be examined. He managed to wrest himself free of the men restraining him with the help of Abu Youssef's assurances he'd take care of this friend. It also helped to have the two hulking Al Asifa guards get between their charges and the local constabulary.

Abu Youssef walked Omar to the car parked a couple doors down from the café. The four men climbed in and left the area. Omar remained folded onto himself for the drive back to the mosque. Only the sound of his exaggerated breathing could be heard. The other three

kept as still and silent as possible, not wanting to be caught in the violence they might otherwise ignite.

Allah, you have once again failed me, Omar thought. *Why do I serve
you? You only bring death and destruction to me. You are not merciful, you
are not just, you care nothing for me or those I love. If I am wrong, speak
to me. Speak to me as the Christian God speaks to His people. Speak to
me as Suzan's God spoke to her. I have been your slave and done as you've
commanded. I've killed your enemies and have always been willing to die
for you. Tell me why you have allowed the death of my son, my wife, Abu
Hamza, Sameer. TELL ME . . . SPEAK! Your yoke of slavery is upon me
and you've stripped my life from every love I once thought you had given me.
You are a murderer and thief and deceiving liar!*

*The Christians are united, the Jews are united, they do not kill each
other. Why do your slaves kill each other? Why is there no peace in you? In
my home with Suzan there was peace, there was unconditional love. Everything with you must be earned, and still there is no peace, no acceptance,
only strife and hatred. You say we fight Satan when we kill Christians and
Jews. I saw goodness in my Suzan and I see evil in your slaves. Are you God
or Satan? TALK TO ME YOU IDOL OF STONE!*

* * *

WITH AN ASHEN face and slack posture, Omar shuffled into Abu
Youssef's office after washing and donning fresh clothing. During the
rote process, he wondered why he bothered. *Why be clean? Why wear
these robes? Why kneel and pray?* Everything he'd ever learned and was
ingrained in his life was shaking, a veneer was separating from his reality
and he wasn't sure he wanted to see what lay behind.

"Abu al-Wafá, I grieve with you, but I must ask you to listen to me.
You must clear your mind enough to hear my words, for they are about
what I think has led to the death of your eldest."

Omar's gaze rose from the floor between his feet to meet Abu
Youssef's eyes and his countenance transformed from reflecting desola-
tion to concentrated interest.

Needing no further prompt, Abu Youssef steeled himself and said, "I
was unable to tell you at the café what I wish I'd been able to tell you

long before today. Our pursuit for who has been behind the attacks on you has led us to Cairo."

The air in the room suddenly turned dank and thick. Abu Youssef was ready for a savage eruption, but after nearly a minute it hadn't come. What he did see was Omar's expression change again. The pallid color is his face shaded to crimson, his eyelids narrowed, and his mouth compressed as to almost disappear.

"He dies *now!*" On the last word, Omar clasped the chair arms to rise.

"Abu al-Wafá, wait a moment. You will not find him. He has gone into hiding, which is how I was unaware of his plan to use your son to kill you and me. Our people have been unable to locate him since we uncovered the last damning piece of evidence about his activities. We tracked down the Shi'a dog he employed to plant the bomb that killed Abu Hamza and almost you. The whimpering coward told us who gave him the task under just the threat of torture. We left him for you to finish as you wish, he has nowhere to go. His imam was not so weak, but he must have been able to signal Cairo before we got to him. It took hours and much blood, but he told us Cairo was controlling the plot and then we ended his worthless life. We extracted some vengeance for you. The imam also revealed Cairo's alliance with Hezbollah. We went looking for Cairo, but we have been unable to locate him. He may not even be in Lebanon. We think he may be getting help from outside the country as well; Syria or perhaps Iran. We know he has thrown in with the Shiites, but we don't yet know to what extent."

"There are no borders or barriers able to keep me from finding him and slowly extracting his life from him," Omar said. "I will send him to Hell one piece at a time."

"I will put the full weight of our assets behind you."

"If he wants me dead, perhaps we should help that along."

"I do not understand."

"I will become the lamb put at stake to attract the lion. Let us prepare a mission for me in Jordan. The struggle between our sects rages there and I will not be insulated as I am here or in Syria. I will go alone under the guise of gathering intelligence. But, how do we get this information to Cairo in a way he will not be suspicious?"

"You can leave that to me, what we've uncovered in our pursuit of Cairo will be applied to trap him in Jordan. The operative loyal to us who remains in Hezbollah is actively seeking information about Cairo's whereabouts. However, care must be taken not to compromise his work for us on other matters, but I believe he will be the help we need to draw the lion to slaughter."

. . .

OIC OPERATIONS WAS notified of the plan to send Omar into Jordan to gather intelligence on the incursion of Shiite militias and to meet with Brigadier General Mostafa Al Nawasrah, head of Jordan's Joint Special Operations Command. The general was instrumental in preventing Hezbollah from spreading into his country. Jordan falling into the hands of the Iranian and Russian-backed Shiites would give them a strategic platform from which to attack the Arabian Peninsula. Omar's mission with the general was to coordinate attacks on the weakened Hezbollah and the wayward leadership of Hamas.

The Al-Asifa agents within Hezbollah would once again be used to channel information, this time into their organization. The agent who was with Nasrallah when he was assassinated was presumed dead and would be used as the main conduit between the two rival groups. Information regarding the OIC mission in Jordan would be disseminated through the remaining leadership of Hezbollah. The mission and Omar's presence would be irresistible to Cairo and the Shiite Sura.

During the month of preparation for the trip to Amman, Omar relocated his son, Youssef, to live with Suzan's parents in Borj Hammoud. He wanted him removed as far from danger as possible without being too far from his reach. Suzan's parents had many questions that Omar either deflected or answered with lies. They wanted the boy and Omar wanted him where he'd be loved and protected, which overruled curiosity and debate. Omar acquiesced to Youssef being placed in the Armenian Evangelical Shamlian Tatigian Secondary School without a hint of protest.

Youssef's reaction to hearing about the death of his brother tore at Omar's soul. After his initial reaction of shock, he became morose and taciturn to the point it was difficult to pry more than monosyllabic responses from him. Omar felt hope and a strange calm about entrusting the last of his family to these Christian people. If he didn't die in Jordan, the life he'd lived since a boy was nonetheless destined to end.

. . .

Omar's thoughts were back with his oldest son when Cairo entered the hotel lobby. His position behind the glass partition of the restaurant and reflected light of the large chandelier obscured him from being seen from the lobby. Cairo strode to the reception desk. He carried a valise and a soft briefcase. As Cairo executed the routine of check in, Omar carefully scanned the lobby and outside the glass entrance for security Cairo may have had in tow. The message he received from Abu Youssef about Cairo's arrival was well within the variance to be allowed for any travel.

Omar, with the help of the general, arranged with the hotel to give him access to the room in which Cairo would be staying. He waited in the restaurant twenty minutes after Cairo headed to the bank of elevators. No one followed him and no one entered the hotel who looked even remotely like Hezbollah. The plan, fed to the Shiite Sura, was to put Cairo onto Omar the next day.

Cairo would never try to kill me himself, he thought. *Where are his assassins?*

Convinced he was alone, but no less wary, Omar headed to the stairwell.

Stopping at each floor landing, Omar peered through the small square window of the door and then slowly opened the door to look down the hall both ways. On the second and fifth floors there were a few people coming and going from their rooms, but none posed a threat.

Omar continued his reconnaissance up to the eighth floor, then returned to the sixth. Cairo was in room 606, a corner suite. The hotel management was instructed to leave four rooms on either side of room 606 vacant.

Omar crept to the door and silently passed the card over the lock sensor. Knowing the beep, though not loud, could alert Cairo, he was ready to burst through the door the second the green light flashed.

Cairo sat on the couch facing the door about four meters inside the room. He looked up wearing a malevolent smirk.

Omar sighted down the slide of his silenced pistol, placing the top of the centered foresight squarely between the eyes of the man he planned to put to the most painful end he could concoct.

"Ah, my old friend Omar," Cairo said. "I expected you sooner. I was beginning to wonder if you'd become fearful and thought better of coming for me."

Betrayal!

From the adjoining rooms on either side of the living area came two men armed with sub-machine pistols.

"Lower your weapon, old friend, or you will die right here, right now."

"Only after I have put a bullet into that tiny brain of yours."

"You may want to give your last thought to your son, Youssef, before you pull the trigger, because he and the infidels he's with will pay the price of your revenge. Haven't you killed enough of your family?"

Without a word, Omar removed his left hand from the support grip on his pistol and slowly started lowering it with his right.

"Your arrogance has not only put your wife and son in the ground, it has brought you to your own demise. You've thought yourself so valuable, you've let trust blind you. I bought Abu Youssef months ago when his wife was dying of cancer and he had no way of getting her the medical attention she needed to survive. How do you think we knew you and Abu Hamza would be at that café? Did you actually think the Americans were clever enough to find you on their own? You are a fool and you can ponder your stupidity on your way down six stories to your death."

Glancing to the man to his right, Cairo said, "Take him out to the balcony and toss him off."

As the two men flanking him moved in, from behind his back, Omar slowly lifted a grenade. At shoulder height his thumb forced off the protective cap then compressed the arming button. An M-85C multi-function grenade could be used in several variations of shoulder-fired and modular launchers or it could be hand thrown. Roughly the dimensions of a full-sized pistol grip it held enough syn-comp explosive to shred everything in a fifteen meter radius. Cairo's face lost its mirth and his men froze in place. Even a drop from that height to carpet would be enough to detonate it.

"As you say, Cairo, I have less reason to live than ever, but killing you will fulfill my last useful purpose on Earth."

Time slowed to half speed as Omar tossed the grenade toward the glass table before Cairo. The two gunmen spun in a hopeless effort to dive into the rooms from whence they came. The arc of the lethal device was tracked by Cairo's bulging eyes, which was the only bodily function terror left him. Outside his conscious thought, something about the grenade seemed odd.

Time instantaneously accelerated the split second the grenade made contact with the table and the room expanded.

23

General Sam stepped out of his farmhand, Ben's, truck and thanked him again for driving him into town. The general maintained his driver's license and drove around the mostly rural area where he lived, but he preferred to have others behind the wheel for longer trips and especially in the city. Richmond's population and resultant traffic exploded after the southern border incursion of 2014 and much of the city budget was diverted to "humanitarian" needs. The infrastructure was one of the losers of the supplanted tax revenue, which of course had to keep rising at the expense of long time residents. Being driven around in a four by four also made maneuvering crumbling roads less hazardous.

Ben had errands of his own to run and would be ready for the general's call for retrieval.

General Sam paused before pushing the doorbell button, bowed his head, and silently sent up another confident request for wisdom from the only proven Provider.

Katy Griffin opened the door and greeted General Sam. Dr. Griffin stood behind her and extended his hand. They invited the general in and to a seat in the living room.

"It's good to see you both. How have you been?"

"All is well here," the doctor said. "I'm in semi-retirement, so Katy and I have had a little extra time to travel and have some fun."

"It has been wonderful to have him around more and to see a bit more of our country. We just got back from a turn through the West. Believe it or not, I'd never been to the Grand Canyon or Yellowstone before; they are magnificent. But, don't worry. We're not going to bore you with home movies."

"I haven't heard that term in many years, the General said. It brings back a lot of great memories. I would actually love to see some pictures of your trip if you'd like to show them."

He might have been stalling or perhaps a wiser tack was in play, but for the next hour, the three viewed brilliant images displayed on a wall-mounted video panel and talked about some of America's signature landmarks. General Sam seasoned the conversation with his seemingly inexhaustible knowledge of history. He was particularly loquacious when the tour finally arrived at Mount Rushmore. The sacrifices made by Washington and his family to win the independence of the colonies received special dramatic treatment.

"It was an absolutely wonderful trip, but we were more than ready to come home. We're not exactly kids anymore, are we, Vance?" Katy said. "Well, that's more than enough about what we've been doing. Tell us, Sam, how are things with you and what's been keeping you busy?"

"There's always something to be done on the farm, and I stay in touch with the folks I've worked with over the years who, on occasion, need help with a problem or just need to talk. I'm not sure how much help I render, but it's good to stay engaged. I wish I could say my experience was not so much in demand, but the world's problems keep piling up. More and more I wonder how close we might be to the Last Days."

"We feel the same way," Vance said. "We experienced a few of the problems you might be talking about, which is why we were anxious to get home even though we were having such a great time. Traveling around America was not like this when I was a young man. I can still remember walking out on the tarmac to board an airplane after stopping only long enough to hand my ticket to the attendant. It took us two hours from the time we arrived at the airport to board the plane, and the indignities of being literally passed through the hands of the TSA, makes me wonder if I ever want to fly again. I'd have been sued into oblivion had I ever handled a patient like that. I understand the need for caution in our time, but I'm not sure that's the intent of some of the policies the federal government has implemented in the last twenty years."

"You probably don't want to get me started on that subject, Vance. I'll just say bureaucrats make lousy soldiers and lawmen. Anymore, I question what useful function if any they serve."

"I know exactly what you mean. They make lousy doctors, too. Getting out of the healthcare system, which has become an oxymoron, was the greatest relief of my long career. The administrators from the White House to the hospital business offices have turned the healing arts into a broken vending machine . . . uh, sorry. You almost got *me* started there. Anyway, I'm happy to be back making a few house calls on people I've treated for years. The Lord has amply supplied our finances, so now I barter for my services."

"Those were the days . . . Uh, Katy and Vance, I always appreciate you letting me drop by occasionally to catch up, but on this occasion I have something special to talk with you about. I've prayed about this a number of times before getting here today, so I'm just going to jump in and trust His presence."

General Sam paused long enough to gauge their initial reaction and when they remained silent; he took a deep breath and said, "Katy, Blake is alive."

Katy did not respond to Sam's words. Her blank stare said it all. Her son was dead, yet a man she loved and trusted was telling her differently. She was not prepared for this news from Sam because it could not be true. She just stared into his eyes, hoping that something in his countenance would give her a clue as to what was happening. It did not.

"What?"

"It's a very long story and you will hear it, but I needed to start with what's most important. Blake's death was faked and he's been working for the government ever since. He lives not far from here and he wants to come see you when you're ready."

Katy turned pale as her hands and body began to tremble, her mind racing and processing. Alive? *My Blake is alive. How? Faked? How could that be? What is happening here? Am I dreaming?* Katy was wobbly and about to lose her balance when Vance took her arm and guided her gently to a large recliner.

"Sam, I am so confused," she said. "Are you saying my Blake did not die? That he is alive and well? How? What is this about? Where is he right now? Can I see him? Do you have a photo? Please, Sam, tell me all you can!" The tears began to drip from her cheeks as the reality of what she was just told settled into her mind. Her son was alive.

Thank you, Dear God. Now I realize why I never really believed he was dead.

"You said when I'm ready? What does that mean, Sam? I must see him now. When can I see him?" Katy paused suddenly, a strange look on her face and then more tears. "Oh my Lord, Sam," she sobbed. "He has been in a coma all these years. It doesn't matter, I must see him now."

The old general's wide grin brought Katy immediate relief and he replied, "No, Katy, he is healthier than any of us. He is fine."

"Then why isn't he here right now to see me in person?"

"Well, that's part of the long story, but you should know, he wanted to do that as well, but I talked him into letting me visit you first. Back in 2010, Blake was recruited by the CIA to take the place of a guy who converted to Islam in prison. It was part of a very important operation being conducted here and overseas. It was so important, in fact, that Blake had to be removed from all public records so his disappearance wouldn't attract attention. The only way to do that was to fake his death. The only way he could replace the guy from prison was to have extensive plastic surgery. We thought having Blake show up at your door wearing a face you've never seen might have been harder on you than me telling you first."

"Please tell me his mission was a success, Sam."

"Katy, the nuclear device that exploded out on the Chesapeake Bay would have exploded in the Baltimore Harbor except for Blake's courage and sacrifice. And when the entire Supreme Council in Iran was killed by a mysterious explosion, saving Israel from a nuclear holocaust, that was also your son. His actions have probably saved several million lives, and an entire nation of God's chosen people."

Katy sat silently for a moment trying to grasp all that had been said in the last five minutes. The initial shock and disbelief produced in her by General Sam's opening words and subsequent revelations converted to other much deeper emotions as he explained why Blake was not there. By the time he finished, she was softly weeping into her hands as her husband wrapped her tightly in his arms.

"I think it's best I say no more about this and let Blake tell you the rest. However, if you could indulge me for just a bit longer, I need to ask something of you and tell you one more thing."

Without lifting her face from her hands, Katy nodded.

"Please forgive me for my part in causing you such pain. I was part of the recruitment process that brought Blake into all this. Under the same circumstances, I'd do it all again, but I am deeply sorry for your suffering. I pray the days ahead will bring you healing and even joy. That last part should give a jump start when I tell you the last thing you need to know before Blake arrives."

Katy raised her head and looked into General Sam's eyes.

"He'll be bringing your grandson with him."

24

WHEN HIS STUNNED senses started to come back on line, Cairo could not be sure where he was or whether he was alive or dead. His ears rang as though he was standing inside a struck bell and his burning eyes couldn't penetrate the haze when he managed to force his lids open a few millimeters. Suddenly, reality coalesced.

That was not a fragmentation grenade . . . Omar!

He pushed his fists into the seat of the couch to stand and that's when sharp pain shot up from his legs and feet.

"Hassan, Hafiz, where are you?"

"I am here." The voice came from Cairo's right. "Over here," from his left.

"Hassan, go after Omar. Hafiz, come help me. I am injured."

The air conditioning was helping to clear the room of tear gas and, since Cairo's men were on the floor when the grenade went off, their eyes were recovering quickly. Hassan headed to the door as Hafiz stumbled over the chair next to the couch, trying to reach his boss.

The combination of the grenade impacting the glass top of the coffee table and its detonation sent shards of glass into Cairo but not with enough velocity to cause more than superficial damage.

A beam of light intermittently penetrated the smoke as if searching for something. "Is everyone okay?" It was the voice of the hotel security manager. He was followed by a rather large man with an old Colt AR-15. Cairo was not worried about this rapid response to the grenade blast; after all, these guys were on the payroll too. He greased their palms as well since he expected there was going to be some local police interest in a dead man on the sidewalk outside the hotel. Although he had not anticipated the grenade, Cairo knew the security manager would be a key figure in keeping the police at bay.

Hassan returned to the room twenty minutes after being ordered out.

"You could not find him?"

"No, I ran down the stairwell and searched through the rear service areas and out the back. I searched the perimeter and came back through the front. There are, of course, many rooms he could be hiding in, but I don't think he is still in the building; I wouldn't be if I was him. I asked a few people if they saw him, but I found no help. We should go. The police were arriving as I entered the elevator to return."

Cairo went to the room containing his bags, pulled out and put on a fresh pair of pants and stuffed the bloodied pair in the bag. Removing his pants dislodged most of the larger pieces of glass from this legs, the rest would have to wait. The DNA he inevitably left behind would be of no consequence since he'd already abandoned his life in Beirut and was headed out of the Middle East. He and his men moved to the elevator and left the building as though they were oblivious to anything out of the ordinary.

It would have been far more satisfying for Cairo to have Omar splattered on the hotel's rear parking lot, but he was nonetheless out of his way. He was effectively squeezed out of his place in Al Asifa, his family, and now his home. Omar was rendered a man without.

. . .

By the time Cairo and his men were recovering from the stun grenade, Omar was walking out the front door of the hotel and flagging down a taxi. To the casual observer, he appeared calm, a hair's width beneath his surface raged a volcanic mass. Only his years of training and practice allowed him to contain the fury, confusion, and grief threatening to drive him mad long enough to get clear of the immediate menace.

He folded himself into the back seat of the taxi, closed the door, and looked back into the hotel just in time to see one of Cairo's men exit the stairwell. Omar watched him turn to his left without even glancing in his direction, obviously headed toward the back of the hotel. For just a flash, Omar entertained the desire to go around back and kill the dog as he would surely exit through the rear service door.

Wait behind the door, come from behind, grab his chin in both hands, put my right knee in his back, pull with both hands, push with my knee and snap his neck as I ride his body to the ground.

"Where do you want to go?" The driver was asking with unfettered irritation.

Where can I go? I can trust no one. I must get to Youssef as soon as possible . . . but how?

"Sir, I've turned on the meter. I must know where you want to go."

"Take me to the nearest shopping mall."

Once he was dropped off at the main entrance to the City Mall, Omar proceeded to the café and bistro area and found a place to sit where he could keep an eye on foot traffic as he waited for the last glow of daylight to fade. When full dark came, he rose and headed to the parking lot.

It took him only a few minutes to find an unlocked car not under video surveillance where it was obvious employees parked. He drove from the parking lot ten minutes later headed west toward Al Zarqa, assuming all routes north would get the most attention from those who might be looking for him.

By staying off highways and taking a circuitous route, Omar stretched what would normally be a four hour drive into seven, which included driving north of Beirut to Jounieh. Every minute was consumed with thought, planning, and what could be interpreted as prayer.

Allah, you have finally proven me a fool. I am a fool to have ever believed or trusted in you. You are the destroyer. I have wasted my life and my family serving your evil ways. I will waste not another thought or word on you.

Of course, to leave Islam was to be branded an apostate and to move to the receiving end of Jihad, which meant he was setting a timer for his death at the hands of his own people. He could not go to his sister, mother, extended family or former comrades for help. They would consider it an act of worship to their devil-god to kill him and his son as written by Mohammad. If there was to be any chance of life for Youssef, Omar would have to look to his lifelong enemies. At least he could offer the Americans and Jews something they valued in exchange for their help to get him and his son out of the belly of the beast. This in itself would require careful planning and circumstantial favor he had no reason to expect. Perhaps Suzan's God would grant him favor for young Youssef's sake.

With that thought, the conflagration of hatred and lust for vengeance consuming his soul was slowly replaced by an easing, a calm assurance he'd never felt before and had no means to understand.

He chose Jounieh because he'd rarely been there, so the chances of being seen by anyone who knew him were low. He checked into a small motel using cash and went straight for the stationary.

Dear Mr. Nassoor,

I am writing to explain why I have taken Youssef from you. I placed you and your family in danger when I brought my son to you, and I'm hoping the danger will be removed with him. I cannot tell you why this has all happened or what will happen with me and your grandson now. I can tell you Youssef will only be safe with me and those looking for us should leave you be. If anyone comes to you, show them this letter and tell them about Youssef not returning from school.

I hope one day to be able to return to you in person to tell you the complete truth about me, and to seek your forgiveness for all the evil I have visited on your daughter and your family. Suzan showed me love I'd never known and I repaid her with death. I wish to cause you no further harm.

As I am able, I will let you know how Youssef is doing, but I will be unable to give you any details of our location. Please save his possessions until I can get them back for him.

Thank you for taking Youssef in, even for such a short time. I swear to do everything in my power to secure his life and happiness.

Omar al Qobani

On his way to pick Youssef up at his school, Omar stopped a block from the Nassoor home and gave a boy on a bicycle a 5,000 pound banknote to deliver the letter. He followed him.

When Youssef was two blocks from the school, Omar pulled up alongside him at the curb.

"Youssef, please get in the car quickly."

"Father, what are you doing here? I thought you were to be gone for some time."

"Please, my son, get in the car and I will explain."

Youssef opened the back door of the small sedan and threw his backpack on the seat and then got in next to his father.

"Does Grandfather know you are here, are we going there now?"

"No Youssef, I'm afraid you will not be returning to their home for now, but I have let them know I have you. I'm taking you now to get all you will need for the next several weeks. I'm sorry for a great many things and now for taking you so suddenly from your grandparents."

"But what if I don't want to leave? What if I want to stay here with them and go to this school?"

"We have no choice now, Youssef. All the people I have trusted have betrayed me and threatened your life. I cannot risk losing you. You are all I have left and I swear to give you a chance at a life you deserve, a life away from the devils I have served since I was your age."

"Where will we go?"

"For now, we will leave Beirut and stay where we will not be found until I can make arrangements to get you out of their reach."

"Me? But will we not be together?"

"My desire is to be with you, Youssef, and I will be, but that may not be possible at first. What I must do now, you cannot. Where I must go, you cannot follow. I must get you to safety before I do the things that must be done to sever old bonds and build new ones. When my work is done, we will be together from then on."

When Youssef said nothing, Omar looked over to see him slumped in his seat with his chin on his chest. Omar pulled into the parking lot of a general store and took a spot farthest from the entrance.

"Youssef, I know this is hard and I don't blame you for being confused and angry with me . . . "

Youssef raised and turned his head to face his father. His eyes coruscated from the pools of tears welled to overflowing. When he drew in a breath to speak, a corpulent tear rolled down his left cheek.

"When Mohammad died, I blamed you, I even hated you. I was also very angry at God for letting you live and for taking Mohammad and my mother. Grandfather helped me remember what Mother always taught us about grace and the Gospel. He reminded me of where God's people go when they leave their bodies here. My mother waits for me in eternity. Mohammad was very confused and angry, but the last time we talked, hours before he died, he told me he still believed in the forgiveness of Jesus. Grandfather told me it was you who needed love and prayer before it was too late. I've prayed for you every day since. I love you Father. I miss my mother, Mohammed, and *you*. No one is left but you and me and I am scared of losing you too."

25

"HI, MOM." THE voice was of someone who was not sure what reaction to expect, almost timid.

The man standing on Katy's front porch was a stranger but for two things, his voice and his eyes. Plastic surgery and ten years could not break the bond a mother forms with a creation from her body.

"Blake!" Katy wrapped her arms around his neck and held him with the portent of never letting go.

A movie would never have a scene like this because screen time is so expensive and audiences have very little patience. Blake held the little woman with slightly less pressure than would crack a rib. The embrace reclaimed in moments what had been lost in years. They held each other in silence as halcyon images flowed through their memories. From the precipitation falling on the concrete, one might think it came from a micro weather system in the porch ceiling above them.

"Mom, I am so sorry. Can you forgive me?"

"I forgave you the moment General Sam told me you were coming here. I know you would never hurt me by choice."

Finally, she opened her eyes and noticed the two trucks parked at her curb. General Sam passed Blake and Katy just after she opened her door and he headed to his farmhand's four by four to sit with young Sam.

"Is my grandson out there?"

"He is, and he can't wait to meet you. He doesn't know the story behind all this either, but he wants to know you."

"And I need to know him, get him in here!"

The back door on Ben's King Cab truck flew open before Blake closed half the distance to it. Sam jumped out and ran to take his dad's hand. Blake never did well doing things not covered in a manual. *How do I introduce my nine-year-old son to his grandmother he never knew he had until now?* As Ben and General Sam pulled away, once again, a woman came to Blake's rescue.

Katy spoke as soon as Blake and Sam stepped up onto the porch. "Hi, Sam, I'm your Grandmother Katy, would you mind a hug?"

"No, ma'am."

Katy only had to bend slightly to enfold Sam in a warm and gentle hug. She had to restrain herself for fear of making their first meeting uncomfortable for him, so she released him after just a few seconds.

"You boys come in and let's have some lunch."

Over sandwiches and Katy's bean soup, they caught up on the most current circumstances in their lives. Blake told them Alia passed away, and that he'd explain with the rest of their story later. Katy was captivated by Sam's conversational skills and vocabulary. When she asked about his school, Blake and Sam tag-teamed to talk about Alia's disdain for government schools; between that, and her love for teaching and learning, she had been led to home school her son. Sam consistently tested three to six grades higher than his peer group ensconced in what Alia referred to as "indoctrination centers" passing themselves off as public schools. This third grader read at a so-called ninth grade level and he was already learning beginning calculus.

When Katy and Dr. Griffin returned from moving the lunch dishes to the kitchen, they all relocated to the living room. Vance showed great patience and love for his wife as he continued to sit, attentively listening. Only a couple of times did he interject questions to keep him engaged in the context of the narrative.

"I think it's time you heard what's brought us to this day," Blake said.

"I told Sam before we got here a little about you and why he shouldn't be surprised when you call me Blake, but I've waited to get here to fill in the blanks."

"Mom and Dr. Griffin, you remember back in 2010 when the ship containing a nuclear bomb detonated about a mile outside Chesapeake Bay east of Norfolk?"

"Yes, Blake, General Sam told us about the mission that required your changed identity and faked death. And please, call me Vance," the doctor said. "Sam, I'd be honored if you'd call me granddad or something like that."

Blake looked at Sam then back to Vance and said, "Yes, sir, we will, thank you."

"Vance, before I tell you more about our lives, I want to thank you with all I have for loving and caring for my mother as you have. I don't think I could have taken that assignment if you hadn't been in the picture. I will always be in your debt."

"I appreciate that, Blake, but there's no debt accrued. I've been blessed beyond all I could ever deserve to have your mom as my wife and best friend. And I wouldn't have met her had I not patched you up after your deployment to Afghanistan. Please, go on with your story."

"To infiltrate the terrorist organization we suspected had acquired nuclear weapons, I had to take the identity of a man named Grant Reinbolt," Blake said. "He converted and was radicalized in prison where he was also recruited to receive one of the devices in North Carolina. We managed to stop that ship before it got to America.

"I'm sure General Sam told you this is all classified, and because of that, I can't tell you many more details. I hope you don't mind, but we did thorough background checks and cleared you both for this and the bit more I'm going to tell you."

Katy glanced over at her husband who smiled. "Of course we don't mind, Blake, we know very little about the world you've been living in, but we understand the need to keep secrets. I'm anxious to hear about Sam's mom."

"Then now's the perfect time," Blake said. "When I woke up from the operation that changed my face, a woman was there at my bedside who'd been assigned to teach me everything I'd need to know about the man I'd be replacing. We call it a "legend" in the business. She converted to Christianity from Islam, so she was able to help me with the language and culture of the group I penetrated. My head was bandaged crown to neck, so I didn't see her for the first ten days or so I knew her. I know now I'd already fallen for her before I ever saw her. When the bandages came off and Alia was standing there, it was all over but the 'I dos.'

"General Sam probably also told you a bit about the operation in Iran, so I won't get into the details, but you should know Alia saved my life at the end of that one. Had she not gone around protocol and pushed some sensitive buttons, I'd probably be dead or in an Iranian prison. We married as soon as I was able to stand on my own."

"Oh, Blake, she sounds absolutely wonderful," Katy said. "I know we would have loved each other. What happened to her?"

The lightness in the room shifted as Blake's countenance lost its reflection of cherished memories. When he looked into his mother's eyes, they each knew exactly what the other was feeling. Unlike Blake's, her loss was decades in the past. The raw wound created by the sting of death heals over time, but the scar never fades. In their shared gaze, they also recognized the hope only eternally-minded people can grasp.

Blake wrapped his arm around his son and held him close as he told the story of the cruise and what happened at its conclusion in Haifa. Mostly for Sam's sake, he told them about the terrorist, but not about the operation in Beirut.

"So, the last thing my Alia did on Earth was to take the bullet meant for me. I can't know yet why the Lord let it happen this way, but I do know, had there been a decision to be made, she would not have hesitated. She is the most courageous and selfless woman I've ever known. She was indeed cut from the same bolt of cloth as you, Mom."

The foursome had piled nearly half a box of used tissues on the coffee table by the end of the story. They rose to share hugs all round. The doctor couldn't stand to see the biohazard linger a second longer. He gathered and discarded the pile, chemically cleaned the table, and washed his hands.

When everyone returned from visiting the bathroom, Blake said, "While we're talking about hard things, I need to tell you about what I'll be doing next and how it might affect all of you."

Katy's smile returned. "Unless you plan to change identities again, I think I can handle whatever you have to tell us."

"No, thanks be to God. There're no plans for another deep cover job. I've accepted an offer from one of the legends of the Special Forces community to continue doing the work of fighting radical Islam. I can't go into any detail about the organization or exactly what we'll be doing, but it's a little like the security contractors the government's been using for years."

"Are you going to have to move?" Katy asked. "That would be very unwelcome news."

"No, I can operate from here, but it does mean I'll be going on assignment regularly and that will mean being gone for blocks of time. Sam and I have talked about this some already. We aren't happy about being apart, but Sam understands the work I have to do."

"I'm not sure I understand, Blake," Katy said. "You've given so much for your country already. You've nearly died several times, not to mention playing dead for a decade, haven't you given enough?"

"General Sam and I have run around that tree a few times recently, but we end up where we started every time," Blake said. "The world is more dangerous today than ever. I don't want to add alarm to everything else I've put you through today, but America is on the brink of being overthrown and there aren't that many standing in the gap anymore."

"Your mother and I attend a Bible study that started in our church but has grown into having weekly meetings in several neighborhoods," Vance said. "In the beginning, it was an introductory course on Christian citizenship, but it's matured into much more. We study the Bible, but we also engage the culture and government by making our voices heard in town hall meetings, circulating petitions and voter guides, and holding our politicians accountable. Lately, our Bible studies have gravitated to eschatology. I don't mean to start preaching, Blake, that's certainly not one of my skills, but all this to say, I think we know what you're talking about. I confess, when I was full-time in my practice, I spent very little time keeping up with news and world events. Like many Christians, I was more concerned about doing my life than truly following Christ. By the time I got my head in the game, so to speak, I was ashamed and almost fearful."

"The work you and your group does is every bit as important as that being done by patriots all over this country and, as I'm learning, around the world. "It's going to take us all to stand for His Kingdom and defeat the darkness. It has been my calling to fight physically, and I'm more confident than ever that calling has not been revoked."

"It was always a problem getting your mind changed once it was set," Katy said. "But when you say it's a calling from God, I have no other response than to say, my love and prayers will be with you wherever this calling takes you."

"Thanks, Mom," Blake said. "I've never doubted that about you. I have one more thing to ask."

Before Blake could continue, Katy smiled and said, "We would love to look after Sam as much as you need and he wants."

26

BASHAAR IMMEDIATELY RECOGNIZED the man who'd just entered his shop. He could see his hands were empty and he was wearing simple clothing, under which not much could be hidden. The main possibility of him having a weapon would be in his belt behind his back. He nodded at him and slowly moved behind the sales counter. There were a couple of the neighborhood boys looking around the shop, admiring the new model of trail bike the owner just brought to the sales floor.

Omar turned to look at a shelf stacked with tire tubes which gave Bashaar a good look at his backside.

No weapons, no bomb vest, what's this guy up to?

In spite of the increased terrorist activity in Beirut over the previous several months and the recommendations from Jerusalem to think about closing up shop, Bashaar insisted he could still be of use where he was.

He came close to reconsidering when the head of Hezbollah was assassinated with an Israeli UAV. The death of Hassan Nasrallah was just the excuse Hamas, Hezbollah, and the other Jew-haters in the region needed to launch attacks from every direction. Egypt no longer proactively suppressed terrorists on their northeast border, which kept weapons and bodies flowing into Gaza. Now Jordan was showing signs of dropping their treaty with Israel and America. If that happened, World War III would be launched on the tip of a Jericho missile.

All the while, the Caliphate continued to expand and Lebanon was part of the land being reclaimed by the Islamic State. It was a matter of time before Bashaar would be forced to retreat. The writing was appearing on the wall and this would be the only way it would finish. He would return to the land of his fathers to join their last stand.

Since the Americans raided the home of the man now standing in his shop, Bashaar had raised his caution level and his sensitivity to rumor. Perhaps he'd missed something or overstayed better judgment. He tapped the screen of his point-of-purchase computer with his left hand while keeping a grip on the pistol in the holster mounted under the counter.

Fire three rounds on my way to the emergency exit.

The boys exhausted their lust for the new bicycle on the reality of their financial station and ambled out the door after thanking Bashaar for the cokes.

Here we go, he thought.

"You won't be needing that weapon unless you have directives of which I'm unaware," Omar said.

"Weapon, directives?" Bashaar replied. "I'm afraid I don't know what you mean. May I interest you in the new Bianchi Super Record? It has been redesigned for this year but the price has not gone up. Or perhaps you'd prefer something for leisure rides?"

"Bashaar, I know who and what you are, so we can dispense with the games," Omar said. "I'm not here to hurt you or capture you. However, if I know about you, you can be sure others do as well. You might want to think about relocating. I can help you keep your life to spy another day, but you must help me first."

"And I know who and what you are," Bashaar replied. "Trusting you is not my first instinct . . . for that matter it's probably not my last either."

"It should be apparent to you I've come unarmed and I'm sure you've checked your cameras by now so you know I'm alone. We have suspected you to be a Jewish spy for some time now, but watching the comings and goings from here has proven valuable enough to keep you here and alive, so far. Those days may be ending soon. I wanted to kill you after I was told the Americans were here before they came to my home, but my superiors stayed my hand and I had more important issues to address."

Bashaar released the safety on the Tanfoglio .40 Compact and eased it from the holster. "You should know I sincerely regret my part in the death of your wife. I never rejoice over the deaths of innocents and I understand your wife was a Christian."

"She was and, as I said, you won't need that gun for me. I no longer seek retribution for my wife's death. I'm seeking something much different."

As he slid the pistol back into place, Bashaar said, "You might also want to know the man who pulled the trigger hated himself for it." He released his grip on the stock, but he kept his hand nearby. "After what you did in Haifa, you should understand my caution."

"I have regrets of my own, but that is not what I came here to discuss."

"Very well . . . what do you want to talk about?"

"To prove my life and agenda have changed, I will offer something very important to you and your people. I am prepared to give you the names of the Israelis who have supported our operations. They helped us obtain the drone that killed Nasrallah and they helped me in Haifa. I only know the names of the top three but with the sophistication of your investigative elements, it should be easy enough to uncover the majority of the network operating inside your borders."

"You know who ran that operation with the drone?"

"Yes, because I ran the operation. I was there to verify impact and results. I can give you information about the organization that planned and carried it out. The rest is up to your government to decide what to do with what I can provide you."

"As you are aware, the information you offer would be most important to my government. We have known for years that insurgents were inside our government but, except for a couple of low-level operatives, we have had no success in discovering who these spies are. I will need details to run through my people for verification. If this checks out, I will be in a position to return the favor. You should probably tell me now what you want in return, it may not be possible."

"What I need from you is small but of great importance to me. I need your help in contacting the Americans and giving them your assurance of my act of good faith toward your people. I want them to secure my safe passage out of the Middle East and help in getting my son to England. I have walked the wrong path for far too long and I want a different life for my son."

"Getting your son into England is not something I can promise, though, with the Americans help, the odds are good. Will you not want to reside there as well?"

"My plans must remain mine for now, but I can tell you I have a relative in London who can sponsor my son and see to his education there. I am in need of your help, but that does not mean I trust you or that I will remain unarmed should you try to turn my plans against me."

"Then we understand each other. I will contact you tomorrow with the answer from my government but I think I can assure you now that we have an agreement. Please be prepared to provide those names to me early tomorrow. "

Bashaar moved to lock the door to his shop and flip the "open" sign. He ushered Omar to his workshop where he recorded the details of the operation that had most nations of the world at Israel's throat. He even tried to get Omar to give him the names but, as he expected, Omar would not budge until he had an official agreement. At the end of their meeting, Omar put one final deal point on the table which left Bashaar with raised eyebrows.

Omar saw to two final details after returning to his apartment in Jounieh. He first placed a call to Oxford, England.

Suzan's brother, Joseph, moved to the UK in 2010 to finish an advanced degree in theology and religion. He ascended to headmaster of Oxford Christian School in 2016. Joseph and his English wife of eighteen years remained childless and jumped at the chance to take Youssef in, even for a short time. Youssef was not anxious to be separated from his father again, but he loved his Uncle Joseph and Aunt Renee and he looked forward to getting back into school.

His second call was to a number in Haifa. Rami answered on the third ring with his normal cheerful greeting.

"Rami," Omar said, "please do not ask me any questions nor say my name. Just listen. Get out and do it now. Leave everything behind and be out tonight. Rami, do as I tell you or your world will collapse around you."

27

BLAKE COULD NOT resist the invitation from his mom and step-father to spend a couple of nights with them, and neither could Sam. They wanted to do a more thorough job of catching up on what they'd missed during their decade of separation. Sam took to being a grandson as though cast for the role. Katy, on the other hand, found grandparenting a joy she'd never expected to know. In two days she managed to establish herself as Sam's benefactor and ally. Blake was both delighted and chagrined.

The reunion with his mother was not exactly what he anticipated. Blake felt more than a little concern that the decade of separation and the circumstances surrounding his disappearance would create an irrep-arable strain on his relationship with his mother. After all, how do you allow your mother to believe you are dead for so many years and then just walk back into her life as if nothing happened? Blake was prepared for anger and resentment from the woman he loved the most now that Alia was gone. But it simply was not that way with his mother, and he should have known this. After the initial awkward greetings, his mother was just as he remembered: loving, nurturing, and upbeat. She wept as he told her about Alia, as if she'd known her all her life. Then it occurred to Blake he'd worried for nothing. His mother was an extraordinary woman who was always forgiving and consoling. That was exactly how his Alia was and now Sam would have a grandmother with the same character as his mother. *Thank You, Lord, for Your grace.*

• • •

Maria came for lunch on day three to meet Blake's folks and to get Sam caught up on his schoolwork. Although she lived two hours away, she was very committed to Blake and Sam because she was Alia's best friend. Maria never asked questions about their personal lives because she knew they were involved in things beyond her understanding. She truly loved little Sam and wanted the best for him. A broad overview of Blake's past and new present was all Maria needed to know. She didn't know a background check was also conducted on her, but she was told to leave Blake Kershaw in the grave. She also volunteered to come twice a week to the Griffins to help Sam with the subjects giving him a bit of trouble and to administer the exams he needed on occasion. Katy had no anxiety about Sam's homeschooling routine, but they all agreed he'd benefit from the continuity.

• • •

When Blake called Bill Garrison to accept the position, he was told he'd have to fly to the Czech Republic to get oriented to The Sodality's operations procedures and prepare for his first mission. He was expected to be away from CONUS for at least a month depending on how quickly he could get up to speed and complete mission one.

Maria and Blake left at the same time late in the afternoon. Any residual concerns Blake had about leaving Sam with people the boy had only known for about forty-eight hours evaporated when Sam could hardly be bothered to give him a hug before heading to his truck. He and Grams, as he'd taken to calling her, were in the middle of a project. The satellite phone he left with the Griffins would allow them to stay in touch no matter where he was in the world. A three- digit code would alert The Sodality's security division to trouble, and agents would track the phone and respond in under an hour. The tracker was linked to Katy's and Vance's cell phones and both their vehicles.

Blake boarded an aging Global Reparations Airbus A320 making a routine supply run to their European headquarters in Brno, Czech Republic. It was clear extravagance was not a flaw in this organization. The aircraft was solid and the accommodations were about what he'd known in the army; designed for capacity, not comfort. The flight from Dulles took ten hours, including a brief refueling stop in Lisbon, Portugal.

The Global Reparations building was located on the Brno-Turany Airport grounds and had about 100,000 square feet under roof. All European and West Asian emergency response from GR was initiated from this location. Václav Havel was the president when Brno was picked for the international headquarters for both entities. He was a long time friend of General Garrison and an early opponent of radical Islam for good reason. Havel was born three years before the Nazi invasion of Poland and the start of World War II and he spent his creative and political life battling Communist totalitarianism. After leaving politics in 2011, he continued to be an important member of The Sodality council, though this fact was never recorded in any Czech public files. The Czech government continued to work toward status among the larger members of the EU, and having a highly regarded humanitarian organization located on their soil was a nice addition to their national résumé.

. . .

TOSHO MUSASHI GREETED Blake when he exited the aircraft and escorted him to an SUV for the short ride to Global Reparations.

Blake was led through the front entrance and back into the main warehouse. Half way to the rear, they took a left turn and came to a door marked, MECHANICAL. The inside was exactly as you'd expect until they came to another wide door marked, UTILITIES. Tosh pressed his hand to the knob side of the wall, which produced a distinct click and behind the door was an elevator.

No visible sensor panel. I guess the money they save on airplane seats they spend on security.

The pair entered the large lift and Tosh pressed the metallic circle next to SL-3.

Why do they always put spec ops underground?

The elevator door opened to a small room containing a reception/security desk. At the elevator door and the door exiting the room stood two well-equipped and conditioned troops, one male, one female. Blake was issued a packet of materials containing his new credentials, security passes, and resource access numbers. After his biometrics were collected, Tosh, led him through the door into a much larger room filled with cubicles.

"Your tour begins here," Tosh said with a sweep of his hand. "This is our communications center. There is, of course, redundancy, but this is the main hub for all incoming and outgoing transmissions within The Sodality. Everything from your real-time mission comms to resource requests comes through here. You have executive level one authority, so this room circumvents the red tape you may have become accustomed to in the army."

"That's a novel idea, but what about oversight?"

"We've purposefully kept our command authority structure small and tight. General Garrison oversees all operations, but since we've never been infected by the cancer of political correctness, the people he selects are profiled all the way to a preference for chunky or smooth peanut butter. Of course there's no such thing as zero defects, but when your organization is dominated by people with the right stuff, it polices itself very well."

"How many people work here?"

"At this location, we have about three-hundred, not counting the field personnel. When you get a better handle on the scope of what we do, you'll see how motivated our people tend to be. The world has devolved considerably into antipathy and lethargy, but there remains a large number of highly skilled and determined men and women who value freedom and know it's not cheap. We have the Obama administration to thank for many of our best people. His purge of believers from the military, intelligence, and technology sectors in the eight years he lived in

DC public housing gave us a rich labor pool from which to choose. Our three-hundred people like to say they think they could do the necessary work done in the Pentagon by the twenty thousand still there."

"That word 'necessary' is very important."

"Indeed it is. Okay, Blake, let's keep moving. You've got a lot to see and people to meet before I hand you off to the boss."

Blake was impressed with the camaraderie and efficiency he found in every office and department. Everyone he met was expecting him and gave him a warm reception. Tosh saved the best for last; the command center. The room probably measured fifty by fifty feet and every square inch was in use. Rows of work stations with every kind of electronic equipment imaginable were surrounded by huge video panels displaying images and messages from all over the world. Where the first division Blake visited handled all communications, this one clearly handled all intelligence and operations data collections, command and control. Blake was most amazed that the room did not create a din of ambient noise. They'd somehow figured out how to isolate voices and speakers to confined spaces.

"Whoa! Now I know for sure where you guys spend your money."

Bill Garrison rose from a work station arrayed with six video panels and took Blake's hand in what felt like the coils of a python. "Welcome to the central nervous system of our little endeavor, Blake."

"From what I've seen already, it might be small in scale, but not lacking in potency. I think I've found a home."

"We certainly hope so, Blake, we have a lot of work to do."

Tosh patted Blake on the back and shook his hand. "I'm very glad you're here, Blake, maybe now the boss will lighten up on me a bit."

Before Tosh could turn to leave, General Garrison said, "Like hell. We're raising the heat on these fascist bastards. Here's your chance to prove what you're always saying about Asian superiority."

"I've always reserved those comments for certain Caucasians who seem to need help with their humility on occasion."

"Yeah, yeah. Don't you have something to do instead of standing around here?"

"Yes I do, sir, and I'm off to see it." Bill and Blake could see the grin on Tosh's face even when he wheeled and headed out of the room.

"That guy's a pain in the ass, but he sure comes in handy. You could probably tell we've been working together for quite a while."

"Yes, sir, I've seen that kind of loyalty and commitment a few times. It only comes with mileage."

"WELL SAID. NOW BACK to business. You'll have a few days to process how things work here and what we expect of you, but let me just say this for now. I take my leadership cues from George Washington who said, 'Discipline is the soul of an army. It makes small numbers formidable; procures success to the weak, and esteem to all.' You and I know General Washington meant not only discipline in the techniques of warfare, but in personal honor. Everyone in The Sodality has signed on to the same strict moral code you did before you left to come here. I knew you would have no trouble signing on, Blake, but I want to emphasize how important it is for you to lead in that example. You can come to me with anything at any time, but know the standard we set is intractable."

"Yes, sir, I understand. I'm honored to join a group going in the morally opposite direction of the larger culture and, I hate to say, even our military. I also welcome the oversight."

"Good man. Let's get busy. We got some new intel on your first target before you left the states and it was confirmed while you were in the air. Abu al-Wafá wants to defect."

Blake stood in stunned silence for a few seconds.

"That's out of left field, what's the story?"

"I'm told you know a Mossad agent in Beirut named Bashaar."

"Yes, sir, he helped us when we went after Abu al-Wafá last year."

"Well, our terrorist approached him and convinced him he wanted out and was willing to pay to prove his sincerity. He was the one who assassinated Hassan Nasrallah and he's given the Israelis what they need to get the world off their backs over that killing. Needless to say, this is huge for Israel and will be a significant blow to the OIC."

"That it will, but how did we come by this information? Does Mossad have an arrangement with us as well?"

"Not officially, of course, but there are key figures throughout the Israeli defense structure who work with us. However, in this case, it

came through the normal U.S. State and military channels and ultimately made it to Bob Johnson. His response up line was thanks, but
no thanks. That will keep the weasels in State out of the loop. We have
already back channeled our reception and acceptance to our people in
Israel. I've set it up for you to coordinate directly with Bashaar."

"It would seem the 'capture or kill' options have been reduced by
one. Under these circumstances, do you think it's best for me to be
on scene? Is there any concern it could make the plan go sideways?
My desire to go after him has not diminished, but as always, I want to
minimize risk."

"That was my first thought as well, but that option has also been
removed. Abu al-Wafá made your involvement requisite to the deal.
This is one of those bizarre twists that defy human logic. Considering
the history between you two, one would think he's either crazy or up to
no good. His message through Bashaar was he would only leave if you
led the extraction team. He says his own people have directly or indi-
rectly tried to kill him four times and he trusts only you to get him. We
won't know all the details of why he's defecting or what he has to offer
until we get him in, but we already know he's a window into the upper
echelon of the OIC."

"Left field somehow got my coordinates and is firing for effect. This
could mean a few things, none of which bode well, but I don't see how
we can pass this up."

"That's why I've already proposed the extraction happen on Cyprus.
That will put it a bit more on our turf and should be a good test of his
intentions. We should have his response within twenty-four hours."

"That doesn't give me much time to assemble and train a team."

"So true, which is why I've taken the liberty of making offers to a
few of your old colleagues. Aaron Page, Sergeant Major Randall, and
Daniel Steele have all accepted and are due here tomorrow. They are all
in retired status now and anxious to strap it on with you again. None
of them have the whole picture of our organization, but Bob Johnson
asked them to just trust you and me on this and they have agreed to
do so. As far as they are concerned, this is a covert U.S. government
operation. I know you and Harry Chee have the longest standing relationship, but he decided to replace you with Colonel Johnson, he likes

being closer to home. I've also selected two other of my best to round out your team. You will have some backup on Cyprus, but not much. You okay with all that?"

"Yes, sir, I'd feel a lot better with Harry's voice coming through my earpiece, but the other guys are top shelf and anyone you pick will suit me fine. How long will we have to train?"

"Evidently, things are very hot for Abu al-Wafá, so he wants this done right away. I've proposed two weeks from today. I expect that answer along with the one about location."

"Then I'd better get to planning."

"There's a station set up for you right over there."

28

B LAKE'S TEAM, CALL sign "Chili Pepper," was given the green light to execute operation "Solstice" after receiving the message from Bashaar confirming arrangements to extract the renamed Omar from a safe house outside Larnaca, Cyprus. In the message, Abu al-Wafá asked that all future reference to him be by his real name.

. . .

I T WAS TO be Bashaar's last transmission from Lebanon. When customers and friends came to the shop as usual the next day, they would find it closed. It would be a couple of days before the locals would realize the shop would not reopen and Bashaar was gone without a trace.

. . .

O MAR LEFT THE apartment in Jounieh at dusk carrying a small piece of luggage. The taxi dropped him off at the Port of Jounieh where

JERRY BOYKIN AND KAMAL SALEEM

he boarded a forty-foot deep sea fishing boat chartered to take him to Larnaca.

The first mate threw off the bow and stern lines and jumped aboard. The captain began to ease out of the harbor as the first mate coiled the bow line, then went to the back to do the same at the stern. Out of earshot at the back of the boat, the first mate pulled his phone, and tapped a contact icon.

"Hi, my sweet, I just wanted to let you know everything is okay and the package you ordered is on the way." There was no response from the other end, just a few seconds pause before the connection was severed.

• • •

THE SIX-MAN SODALITY team trained for their mission in sub-level four of the Global Reparations headquarters in an area that looked like a huge movie set. Building facades and room modules made it easy to replicate the Larnaca safe house and the buildings on either side and across the street. The two operators added to the team blended with the rest of Blake's team like veteran session musicians.

Guido, a former SEAL, specialized in urban and close-quarters combat. He was awarded the Navy Cross after dropping into Iraq in 2014 to extract a group of Christians from a monastery on a hillside after they were chased from their homes in Mosul by the Islamic State. The terrorists continued to pursue the families into the hills in their lust to purge Iraq of anyone who did not bow to their rule. Three of Guido's twelve-man team were killed and the other nine received various wounds keeping themselves between the Jihadists and the innocents as they moved them out of harm's way. Guido showed uncommon valor in leading his team out of what would otherwise have been a failed mission.

He left the military when the Pentagon forced the integration of women into the teams, which led to the lowering of fitness standards. Their work was hard enough without dulling the edge of their skills and conditioning. Also, Guido came from a very poor Italian neighborhood in New York where his Godly mom taught him to respect and protect all women. That value would have been deeply compromised when women were thrown in with his guys. He joined the Navy after working his way through Patrick Henry College in Virginia, where he graduated at the top of his class with a degree in government. His hobby was keeping up with the governmental structures of nations around the world.

The second addition to Blake's team from the existing Sodality troops was Neil, who spent ten years in British Special Operations, the last five years in the Special Reconnaissance Regiment, where he led an insurgence team gathering intelligence in some of the most dangerous hot spots in the Middle East. His skills included signals intel and HUMINT gathering, languages, and all types of transport. He could fly most small aircraft, pilot powered and sail boats, and drive cars like a Hollywood stuntman. The only problem with him being on this op was his being black, of South African ancestry.

Black people were not common in Cyprus and he would stand out a bit, but Blake was willing to take the risk because Neil was so good at so many things.

The Chili Peppers took a week to design, practice, and refine operation "Solstice." It took another week to gather the latest intel from Cyprus and Beirut, and set up logistics for infil, exfil, and contingences. Even though this was to be a "permissive" extraction, Blake's normal caution and Omar's history as Abu al-Wafá dictated that the team be prepared for multiple contingencies. In reality, Blake did not trust this man in the least. In fact, he was not even sure he would be able to resist the urge to kill Omar as soon as he saw him. He'd made a pledge not to but he knew his hatred of the man could ultimately prevail.

Chili Pepper arrived in Larnaca the day after Omar was ensconced in the Israeli Mossad safe house on Kosti Palama in a quiet residential area, about half a klik from the coast. The plan was to deploy to the location, set up, and then execute the extraction at midnight.

As usual, Blake would lead the frontal approach and he would be accompanied by Daniel, who was once again the team medic. Aaron and Neil found an overlook perch atop a two-story office building across the street. Neil monitored the data and comms feedback from Brno, spotted for Aaron, and acted as ground backup for the rest of the team as needed. ReeRee and Guido would each take a side of the small residence and converge on the back before Blake and Daniel knocked on the front door.

Before deploying to their positions, Blake assembled his team in one of the vans for a requisite of every mission launched by Sodality agents; prayer. The mandate had been implemented by General Garrison in the original operations manual and was not optional. Though many variations of Christian and Jewish faith, and some with none, were represented on the teams, no one ever voiced even a minor complaint. Blake thought it was the best tactical procedure he'd ever read in a manual.

"Father in Heaven," Blake prayed. "Thank You for our lives and this opportunity to serve You in the fight against evil. Please sharpen our minds and bodies to perform with excellence and honor. We seek Your protection from harm and provision of success according to Your perfect will. Our thanks go to You now in the name of the living Christ. Amen"

Blake pulled a phone from his tactical vest and tapped a preset number to the safe house keeper to deliver the code alerting him to their imminent approach.

"This is Pizza Hut, verifying delivery."

"Yes, we've been waiting."

With the proper code transferred, the safe house keeper rose from his chair in the kitchen to notify Omar. When he entered the hall and glanced back toward the rear of the house as was his habit, he caught a shadow of movement through the window.

Must be part of the team, he thought.

At 2359, everyone was in place and the ground assault team was ready to move, when Neil's calm but urgent British accent came over the transceivers in their ears. "Chili One, this is Three, hostiles armed with small arms are moving on the location from the rear. I count eight, four approaching from either side of the house behind. The closest of the four moving to the rear looks to be about six meters from the back door."

Crap! Can't we ever catch a break? Blake thought. *There's no time to consult operations.*

"Chili One to all Chili elements, execute option alpha, shields up."

The back door of the safe house exploded twelve meters from Omar. He was in the front living area awaiting the arrival of the Americans. Unfortunately for the safe house keeper, his hand was within an inch of the back doorknob when the charge ignited. He was shattered and his mangled body was thrown back into the hall. At the sound of the blast, Omar reacted immediately by bolting to his feet.

Two men armed with AK-47s came through the hole where the rear door once was. The one in the lead had his weapon up and ready when Omar crossed the hall opening headed to the stairs. The three-round burst from the assault rifle was two-thirds on target. One round passed clean through Omar's right side just above his waist, the other through his right deltoid. The third missed high and left.

Outside, Aaron dropped the two gunmen coming up the right side of the house as ReeRee and Guido double-tapped the two coming from the left. They continued down the left side to the rear.

Omar managed to get halfway up the stairs when the front door burst open and Blake came through, followed closely by Daniel. As soon as they were over the threshold, Blake moved quickly to his right and Daniel moved left to the base of the staircase. Those moves cleared them from the six rounds headed their way from the two gunmen coming past the kitchen. A hand motion from Blake to Daniel sent him low as Blake swung back around the corner of the hall aiming head high. Precise bursts from their HK MP7A1 bullpups stopped the threats before they could fire another round or take another step. Now two more lay in pools of blood as a result of the superior accuracy of men who had done this many times. Blake had no time to check to see if all three men were dead. He had more pressing things requiring his attention.

Just as Blake was about to pursue whoever dashed up the stairway, he remembered Neil saying there were eight bad guys. In the pause after his arresting thoughts, a metallic clatter came down the hall.

"Grenade!" he shouted.

Blake dove into the corner closest to the interior wall of the room as Daniel dropped to the base of the first stair. Fortunately the grenade didn't quite make it into the room before it detonated. Blake was safe within the right triangle shielded from the shrapnel by the hallway wall. Daniel felt something punch his right boot.

Blake sat up and slid with his back against the wall to prepare a fire zone that would remove Daniel from the crossfire when the grenade-tosser appeared. Daniel flipped around and stuck his rifle around the bottom baluster. Their firing angles turned out to be perfect.

Blake jumped up and he and Daniel checked to be sure four bad guy corpses lay in the hall. He could tell at a glance that the Mossad safe-house keeper was dead.

"This is Chili One, SITREP."

The team confirmed all threats were neutralized and all team members were unhurt.

Blake turned and headed up the stairs; he was not in a good mood.

That sorry bastard set me up again! If he is in this building, he is a dead man.

Climbing the stairs behind Blake, Daniel glanced down to discover the tip of his right boot was gone. Grenade shrapnel clipped the ends of two toes but did little damage.

Blake, with Daniel on his six, moved through the two rooms at the top of the stairs and found them empty. That left the bathroom at the end of the hall. They moved to either side of the closed door with their backs against the narrow walls. Blake gave Daniel the sign and he quietly stepped in front of the door and thrust his tip-less right boot at the door beside the knob. He swung back against the wall as Blake wheeled to enter the room.

Omar was sitting on the toilet holding a towel against his right side which dropped when he raised his left hand in surrender.

Blake's view was mostly restricted by his weapon's Mini Tactical Reflex sight. He could see only Omar's head. "You used up your last chance to get me, you son-of-a-bitch." His voice was level and just below conversational volume. At the end of the sentence, only an eighth of pound of pressure to the trigger on Blake's rifle remained to be applied to end Omar's life.

Movement . . .

It was first a ruffling of the curtain on the bathtub then a hand over the side. A boy stood and slowly stepped from the tub holding his arms up. His face was red and moist from crying and displayed a combination of terror and pleading. He trembled from finger tips to knees, all of which caused his Arabic to come out in a quaver. "P . . . P . . . Please do not shoot my father."

This is not the way it all should unfold, Blake thought. *This is between the two of us, Omar and me. There is no reason for a child to be involved.*

Blake lowered his rifle and took a step back. He suddenly saw young Sam standing before him instead of the boy who stepped from the tub. His anger was gone that quickly and was replaced with a much stronger sense of compassion.

In passable English, Omar said, "I swear, those men were here to kill me as perhaps you can tell from the holes in me. I did not betray you."

Blake paused momentarily as his mind raced. *Wait a minute . . . here is my chance, now is the time for revenge against the man who killed my Alia. Why should I believe you? Shoot now and be done with it. Now, shoot and kill the devil. He deserves it.*

Blake raised the sub-machine gun a second time. Omar glanced at his son as if to say farewell. Now Blake would pay this man back for taking the person he loved most in the world. But his heart and his head were at odds. His head won out or perhaps it was the other way around. He lowered his weapon a second time. The boy was the game changer.

"Then we'd better get you both out of here in case they have more coming," he said. "Daniel, field dress his wounds and let's get out of here. All Chili elements, execute exfil alpha."

Blake knelt to look Youssef in the eyes and said in Arabic, "You are safe now. No one's going to hurt you or your father. Stay between me and my friend here until we get you both out of the house."

Blake then turned to Omar. "Leave your bag here and take your son's."

29

TWO UNMARKED VANS carried Blake's team and their charges to the Larnaca airport and a private terminal, where they boarded a Saab 340C turbo prop. They landed on Malta three hours later.

Daniel was able to stabilize Omar's condition on the aircraft with his medical kit and the supplies onboard. Both gunshot wounds were through and through, the bleeding was arrested and Daniel assessed that additional treatment could wait until they got to Malta.

During the flight, Blake kept thinking about how different things were when the U.S. government didn't run the operation. Things were just simpler, and Blake liked it that way. The only disadvantage was they had to use civilian medical facilities whereas they would have gone straight into the U.S. Naval hospital in Sigonela, Sicily, if this had been a military operation.

Oh well, you have to take the good with the bad.

The meds for pain caused Omar to sleep for the entire flight and Youssef sat next to him at the rear of the cabin without saying or doing much. The flight attendant, another Sodality agent, took great care to see to their comfort.

In transit, Neil received transmissions from Brno after filing their after-action report. The Sodality's contact with Cyprus law enforcement was funneling information collected by the officers at the scene of the extraction. They had nine confirmed kills—eight Lebanese and one undetermined—due to extensive damage. The identities of the terrorists were still being researched, but the two they already had in hand confirmed they were Hezbollah.

Hezbollah . . . Shiites . . . after Omar? Interesting.

None of them carried identification of any kind, which seemed to track with other parts of the investigation, showing they'd come somehow surreptitiously by water and not through any normal points of entry. Two Zodiac boats were found on a stretch of private beach inside the breakwater where Dhekelia Road comes within eighty meters of the water. That meant they were dropped off by another larger boat somewhere in the Med. They found a travel bag on site but had not yet determined to whom it belonged.

The local counter-terrorism team was trying to find those who had to have worked in support of the terrorist incursion team. They tracked down the boat captain who brought Omar and Youssef to Cyprus. He was in the cabin of his boat still docked at Larnaca Marina, his throat was cut, and there were indications of torture. There was no sign of the first mate.

The team assembled at the front of the airplane and spoke in hushed tones. Neil briefed only Blake on the reports from Brno.

"Good job back there everyone," Blake said. "That was perfect execution of a simple job gone sideways, especially considering we weren't expecting a kid to be there."

"All except for my boot and a couple toenails," Daniel said as he looked down at his right foot. "But I guess it could have been worse."

All the guys offered the expected chuckle, to which Aaron added, "The only way less damage could have been done was for you to be hit in the head. I will buy you a new pair of boots if you will just stop with the whining."

Everyone enjoyed that one but Daniel.

Blake grabbed Daniel by the shoulder. "It has been worse, Daniel, and you've come through it. We're grateful to have you back on the team." A grin spread across his face as he continued. "But, unfortunately, there's no budget to pay for your replacement boots, since you failed to properly care for them."

In mock dejection, Daniel lowered his chin to his chest. "Roger that, Boss."

"Okay, here's the plan," Blake said. As instructed before we left our base, we say nothing of who we are or where we're from around our captives until our people on Malta have time to vet Omar. He assumes we are American military and that's all he needs to think at this point. He also knows who I am, but again that's too much already. They will be treated well, but as possible hostiles until they are cleared. Any questions on that?"

A moment and a few head shakes later Blake continued. "We will deliver him to Malta to recover from his wounds while he goes through interrogation. The medical team that will work on him is unwitting to the full extent of our operations and the key personalities of our group just as a couple of you are. This is where we operate on trust. You must trust me and the medical team must trust all of us. But none of us will trust Omar for now. We know he says he wants to separate from radical Islam, and he's put a good foot forward by helping the Israelis out with their latest bad rap and the international ill will it's generated. That's important, but it could just as well be a Trojan Horse he's riding in to get behind our gates. So, what we don't know is what he intends to do from here. I'm told we have the personnel and equipment on Malta to get us a long way toward figuring this out. Our hope is he can deliver some of the top leadership of OIC."

Aaron spoke up. "Gutting this group would be good for the world, but this guy is as bad as they come, and I trust him about as far as I can bowl him. How can we ever be sure he's switched sides?"

"I guess only time will bear that out. Aaron, you and I know there have been others who have come out of radical Islam and proved their transformations by joining the other side of the fight. I see no reason to think he's made that kind of decision, so we'll just keep him and his son on a very short leash."

The meeting broke up, but no one slept on the flight except Omar and Youssef.

. . .

ALL BUT BLAKE boarded another aircraft headed back to the Czech Republic as soon as they deplaned at the Malta International Airport. Neil and Guido would be assigned to other missions after a couple days to decompress and debrief.

In addition to debrief and rest for Page, Steele, and Randall, General Garrison would personally introduce them to The Sodality. From the moment they were initially contacted to join Blake's team, every part and time in their lives was sifted by Sodality Intelligence. Their service records were sterling and two of the three had clean civilian records. The exception was Randall, who was once arrested in his hometown of Cut & Shoot, Texas for assault. The charges were dropped when the local DA got the facts. ReeRee put a guy—who had him by three inches and fifty pounds—in the hospital when he came out of a bar late one night and happened upon his victim punching a woman.

After being presented with The Sodality, all three special operators were enthusiastic about its purpose and structure. Only Page declined joining full-time. He wanted to stay near his home in Virginia under no standing obligation to deploy for indefinite periods of time. He took the Cyprus mission because it was Blake and short term, and he was willing to take the occasional Sodality contract in the future. He had a lot of family where he lived and he wanted to be there if the very real danger of a violent Islamic uprising launched on U.S. soil. He led a group of his family and his church in preparing to survive what they perceived as the inevitable meltdown coming as the result of governmental corruption, monetary and market stupidity, and the Islamic invasion. They formed and trained a "Minute Men" styled militia which had several members of law enforcement in their ranks.

Of the three, only Aaron Page was a professing and practicing Christian, but the other two said they believed in God, and they both obviously conducted themselves honorably. General Garrison loved running an operation with no restrictions on proselytizing. When he met separately with the two men who accepted the offer to join the full-time ranks, he made two things crystal clear: he and the organization would be fully committed to them and he expected the same in return, and the code of morality and conduct they signed was inflexible. They took each point with sobriety and reaffirmed their resolve.

. . .

THE SAFE HOUSE on Malta was more like a safe office. The unit was located in a complex housing a medical clinic and other outpatient services. The passive security system was complimented with armed guards doubling as office staff. A QRF was stationed under two kliks away at the Malta International Airport. It was composed of Gurkas, obviously recruited by the British members of the Sodality. Gurkas were known to be the most loyal and courageous soldiers in Europe, if not in the entire world. Clearly, no intruder would get very far into this safe house.

Omar and Youssef were settled into a small apartment with one of the two bedrooms equipped as well as any hospital.

Waiting for them in the apartment was a woman named Loren. She directed the two men handling the gurney to deposit Omar in the hospital bed and check his vitals.

"Hello, Youssef," she said, in perfect Arabic. "My name is Loren. I'm here to take care of your father's wounds. We'll take good care of you both. Are you well? Are you hungry or thirsty?"

"I just want to be with my father. He is going to get well isn't he? You must promise me you will not take me from him. Please."

"I will not separate you and your father. Yes, he will recover just fine. A full report of his condition was sent to me while you were flying here. I have to work on him a little, but he's going to be as good as new very soon. Let's go see him together right now."

"Mr. Hunter," she said. "If you don't mind staying a while, I need to get Omar fixed up, but I'd like to speak with you as soon as I finish. It shouldn't take much longer than an hour, I just need to clean out his wounds and stitch them up."

"I need to be here anyway while things get settled," Blake said. "But I would appreciate it if one of your guys could stay in the apartment long enough for me to step outside and make a phone call."

"No problem," Loren said, then turned to the boy. "Come with me, Youssef, they should be done taking your father's temperature by now."

Blake watched as Loren ushered Youssef into the next room and he caught himself lingering a bit longer than decorum dictated on her long brunette hair and shapely form.

Blake shook his head like clearing it from a blow. *What the heck was that?*

The sat-phone rang six times before his mom's voice came on. "Blake? Is that you?"

"Hi, Mom, I know it's getting late there. I'm just calling to check in."

"Oh, good! Sam was just asking if we'd hear from you soon. I know I can't ask where you are or what you've been doing, but is everything okay?"

"That's the main reason I'm calling. We had a little difficulty earlier, but it all worked out well. I'll be on this job for at least another month. I'm sorry about that. Is everything well there? Wait just a sec, did you say Sam was *just* asking, is he still up?"

"We finished watching a movie a few minutes ago and he's getting ready for bed. Don't worry, I'm not letting him stay up late every night. He's such a good boy, Blake, and he's doing so well with his studies. It's hard to say no when he asks for something special on rare occasions."

"Mom, worrying about Sam being with you rates right up there with worrying whether God's going to take a leave of absence. I miss you all and I'll get back there as soon as possible."

"I know you will, son . . . Hey, Sam just came out of the bathroom." Then Katy's slightly distant voice said, "Hey, Sam, your dad is on the phone, would you like to say hi?"

"Would I?" Though Sam's voice came from a few feet away from the phone, it was received with ample volume.

"I love you, son, be safe," Katy said. "We're anxious to have you back. Vance sends his regards and says he's praying for you every day. We all are."

"I love you, Mom . . . "

In a flash, Sam was on the line. "Dad, hi! I miss you and I wish you were back. It's great here!"

Blake hit the END icon on the sat-phone panel after twenty minutes of listening to his exuberant son go on about how great his new grandparents were and his latest educational discoveries.

30

"HOW ARE THEY doing today?"

Blake was making his daily visit to check on Omar and Youssef and, more every day, he looked forward to seeing Loren. He was deeply conflicted about his growing attraction to his female colleague. His nights continued to be filled with thoughts and dreams of Alia which kept his grief alive and maintained an underlayment of guilt whenever he was in Loren's presence. His struggle made it difficult for him to balance his personal feelings with his professional responsibilities when they were together. The pull was strong to keep his distance for the sake of Alia and his work. However, this strained against his need to develop a good working relationship with a colleague to whom he was gravitationally attracted.

He was drawn to her simple, unadorned beauty, but it was more her character he found appealing. She was incredibly skilled in medicine, and was as warm and caring as anyone he'd known. She was also intelligent and without guile, which manifested as unvarnished toughness. In addition to seeing to Omar's quick and comfortable recovery from two gunshot wounds and making Youssef feel secure and safe, she was conducting tests and interrogations on both as the first level vetting of the defecting Islamists.

With Youssef she used refined conversational techniques to assess his truthfulness and what was important to him. It was much more complicated with Omar. Their interlocution as she treated him was combined with sophisticated monitoring equipment, drugs, and questioning to coalesce a psychological profile, and as clear a picture as possible of his veracity. Omar willfully submitted in writing to the entire process. The Sodality had no concern for domestic or international prosecutorial protocol and, under hostile conditions, they would pursue a much more aggressive program of information extraction. In Omar's case, since he was in their custody voluntarily, he was granted commensurate respect.

· · ·

"I'M READY TO sign his release," Loren said. "He's physically fit to travel and I see no danger in taking him to the next level of processing in Brno. I'm ninety percent positive he's not working a plan to infiltrate our ranks to do us harm. The ten percent variance I withhold because of his ongoing concern about doing harm to a few of his ex-compatriots for whom he still cares, and he is in a faith void. He is rejecting the religion upon which his entire life was built, but that's a tenacious grip from which to wrest free. I have no reserves about Youssef. He is a bright and sincere boy who has suffered repeated significant trauma in the last year. As we were told, his mother, Suzan, was a believer and she did the Lord's work in her boys. Youssef's faith in Christ is apparent and his own. It's also clear Omar has been influenced by his wife's faith."

At Loren's last statement, Blake bowed his head.

"I'm sorry, Blake, I didn't mean to revive sadness for you. This is important though, because Youssef told me he knows you are the one who killed his mother. It shows remarkable depth of faith that he holds no hate or anger toward you."

"Thanks for that, Loren, I wasn't sure he knew, and I haven't wanted to interfere in your work, but I would like to speak with both of them about her death now that I know, and your work is done. It's remarkable that in the time I've spent with Youssef these last two weeks; I couldn't discern he knew. He is quite a kid and in a number of ways he reminds me of my Sam."

"You beat me to it, Blake. I'm not your counselor and in a way it's none of my business, but I was going to suggest that very thing. I think those conversations will do you all good and if I may wax a bit cold, they will also contribute to our assessment of Omar."

"I find it hard to conceive of you having any coldness . . . " The phrase crossed his lips before he realized the thought was formed and he was instantly embarrassed at his all too personal comment.

Loren noticed the slight blush to Blake's countenance and jumped to his rescue. "Oh, trust me, I'm as flawed as the next gal, but I appreciate the vote of confidence."

He's cute, smart, and tough. I wonder . . .

Though not quite recovered, Blake said, "You're welcome . . . uh . . . maybe I should go ahead and see if Omar's up to a talk."

"You do that. I'll finish my paperwork and make arrangements with Brno for their transfer. You should be able to leave tomorrow."

"Thanks for everything Loren, you've been a great help. This organization really does know how to pick 'em."

"Right back at ya'. I'll be praying this all works out to His glory."

"Amen." Blake rose from the chair in the dining area and headed to Omar's room.

● ● ●

"How are you feeling?"

"Better than I expected to in this short time. Loren is quite good at her work."

"I agree. I need to speak with you about something personal. Can we do that and would you prefer English or Arabic?"

"Of course, I would like that as well. I think more practice in English would be good."

"Very well . . . ah . . . I'm not quite sure how to start, though I've had lots of time to think and pray about it." Blake paused a few seconds to form his words, never taking his gaze from Omar's eyes. "I need your forgiveness for killing your wife. From the moment I discovered what I'd done, my spirit has been stained with remorse. It was an accident. Now that I've gotten to know your son, my suspicions about Suzan have been confirmed. She must have been a wonderful woman."

Omar sat silently. When Blake said his wife's name, Omar turned his eyes to focus on some point out into the galaxy as his pupils began to glisten and the reservoirs of his lower eyelids filled beyond capacity.

Just as thoughts of rejection started to materialize in Blake's mind, Omar looked back at him and said, "Mister Hunter, I'm not sure I understand what you say about your spirit and forgiveness as you request. It is an unfamiliar concept for me, but I no longer hold you responsible for the death of my dear Suzan. She was a truly beautiful and loving woman and she followed the Jesus you Christians have built your religion on. If there really is the Heaven your religion teaches, I have no doubt my Suzan is there and holds you blameless. I can only now give her what she always deserved from me; an honest attempt to understand.

"Now, I must tell you of my deep regret for ending the life of your wife. I cannot be excused, but this has had much to do with why I am here today. I now see that the hatred that took me to Haifa and caused her death I can no longer endure. It has driven my entire life and all but destroyed everything I love. It has turned long trusted comrades into my executioners. This hatred must be exterminated and I want it to start here, and with us."

Blake was now in a state of mental exhaustion and conflicting sentiments. He'd done what he knew he needed to do in seeking forgiveness for killing Omar's wife. But was it because he was truly remorseful or because he simply wanted to clear his conscience? And now the man he had apologized to was doing the same thing, apologizing for taking Blake's wife's life. This is not the way Blake ever expected things to unfold. It could have all been over at the safe house in Larnaca except for a young Arab boy stepping out of a tub. Blake knew it was all Providential and that God had a plan for all this. Blake was not sure what that plan included, but he was willing at this point to allow God to lead him through it. And he was beginning to wonder whether it might include Loren.

Stop that kind of thinking, it is wrong! Alia was the only woman I will ever love.

Blake returned to his discussion with Omar.

"Omar, I forgive you. May I also speak with your son about this? I need his forgiveness as well."

Omar extended his hand which Blake took in a firm grasp while being mindful of the pain just extending it had to be causing him. "You may speak with my son, and I thank you for it. I also hope to have the opportunity to speak with your . . . Sam is it?"

. . .

OMAR, YOUSSEF, AND Blake arrived in Brno where Omar went through a final battery of tests and interviews. From the intelligence traffic coming out of Lebanon, the story concocted and disseminated about the deaths of nine terrorists in an apparent sectarian clash on Cyprus was holding up. Omar was officially dead and gone. One of the immediate rewards of leaving Omar's bag containing his personal effects and identification to be attributed to the dead Israeli was Omar's uninterrupted access to the Intranet through which all OIC communications traveled. There were questions about the missing boy, but no interest in pursuit.

Omar was given provisional certification by the security and intelligence departments of The Sodality to be made operational upon his physical recovery.

. . .

BILL GARRISON AND Jacob Hunter met with Omar to present him with who they really were and what they had in mind for him. They were somewhat surprised when Omar told them he was relieved to hear the American government was not in control of their organization. He'd helped with the gross infiltration of The Muslim Brotherhood into every level of America's political, military, law enforcement, and administrative infrastructure by channeling money and people through Al Asifa into the unsuspecting country. Working with this government would be inherently dangerous for him, which is why he wanted his son sent away.

. . .

Putting Youssef on the airplane for England proved to be more difficult for Omar than he ever imagined. His son clung to him and begged through the fits and starts of crying not to be separated from him again. Omar's tears could not be restrained, though he wanted to show his son resolve and strength. He finally realized he was trying to convince himself. Omar reached down and lifted Youssef into the deepest and longest hug they'd ever shared.

"My beloved son," he said. "We must part for now if we are to ever have a good life together. You are still so young and it is not right what you have been through. I must do what I can now to be the father you should have had all along. Please help me by being strong. Obey your aunt and uncle and work hard on your studies. I will call you every chance I get and I swear to come for you as soon as possible. I love you. Now, say no more. Go get on the airplane, I will speak with you tonight."

A Sodality agent was provided to be sure Youssef arrived safely in Oxford.

. . .

Omar outlined the leadership structure of OIC operations and his ability to access them without going into every detail. His information intersected at several points with intel gathered by the U.S. and The Sodality, and the blanks he filled in had the missions planning sector vibrating. It would take weeks to develop a master plan to deconstruct OIC, who were the most execrable fascists since the demons who came up with the death camps in Eastern Europe during the mid-twentieth century. From there they could begin to prioritize missions and ascribe assets.

Omar committed to supply direction, key contacts, and even to go on select missions. He conditioned moving forward on being able to find and kill Cairo.

31

"WHY IS THIS guy so important? The list we've gone over with you has many more names positioned higher in the network. Why do we need to go after Cairo first?" Blake was given full leave to execute the first mission of their coalition with Omar.

"He is the main reason I am here working with you now," Omar replied. "You remember, I told you hatred turned my comrades into my enemies. I discovered not long ago that Cairo has been behind several attempts on my life. His hatred for me and my blindness have taken my mentor, my wife, and my first born son. As long as he lives, any work we do in the Middle East risks compromise if he discovers I'm not dead. He is also connected by Iran to the network operations in America, Canada, and South America."

"Are you sure this is not just about revenge? I can say without hypocrisy I'm qualified to ask that question and deal with the answer."

"I cannot deny my heart burns with the need to put an end to this foul pig. It just happens that his death also serves a larger purpose. But, make no mistake; I would be pursuing him with or without your help. In any case, Cairo must be eliminated before I can help you."

"So, how are we going to find this guy?"

"I've given this much thought and I think I know how we can isolate him where he'll least expect to be attacked. I've not spoken of this in a very long time, and never to anyone other than Cairo, but it must also be one of the reasons he went to a great deal of trouble to kill me. He is a *manuke*, a homosexual. According to Islam's laws, homosexual men must be killed and lesbians stoned to death; that is why in sharia law-led nations they have no open homosexuals."

"Well, that's disgusting, but I don't see how that helps us find him."

"You will see when I tell you the story. There was a young boy in our neighborhood who is older than Cairo and who never fit in with the rest of us. We discovered later it was because he is a homosexual. He was from a family closely tied to a leading imam, so he was untouchable. Years later, I saw him and Cairo come out of the theater together. In our culture, you do not associate with any undesirable person, so it made no sense to me to see these two together. I confronted Cairo and he flew into a rage and swore to ruin me with our Sura if I ever spoke such an outrageous accusation. I see now it was a mistake, but I chose to keep that secret to this day."

"A short time after our confrontation, I heard that the man I saw Cairo with moved to Damascus to take a job offer. After he moved, Cairo took the regular assignment of communications transfers between Damascus and Beirut. I remember thinking at the time how strange that was. Cairo never wanted to do routine work for our network. He said to me once when we were boys he thought that kind of work should be left to women and the retarded. His responsibilities grew in Syria as the war there accelerated along with the conflict within OIC caused by Hezbollah. Omar never lacked for reasons to go to Damascus and to be with Yahya Tarboosh. If your people can find this Kurd, we will find Cairo."

"I think we can do that."

. . .

IT TOOK THE intelligence division twenty-four hours to identify and sift three positive hits on the combination of name, age bracket, and location. The employment possibilities included an engineer at an architectural firm, a graphic designer at a women's clothier, and a janitor. The strong suspicions they had about the second option was confirmed by an agent on the ground. Electronic and video surveillance was erected and after three days, a ninety-eight percent confidence report was delivered to Brno. Now they'd have to set up on site and wait for Cairo.

Blake assembled his team in a ready room and mapped out the plan for the operation in Damascus. As with most plans, the goal was simple; wait for the target to enter the watched site, then go in and put him down. In this case, the unusual variable was they'd be taking an outsider on the mission.

The team that went to Cyprus was reassembled with the exception of Aaron Page. The difference between the marksmanship skills of Aaron and Guido was a sixteenth of an inch in a three-round group at 1,000 yards, so Guido took on the sniper role.

Research on Cairo turned up bits and pieces of information that indicated he was in some way working with the Shiites, particularly in Syria. The growing evidence that the entire team of assassins sent to kill Omar in Cyprus were Hezbollah furthered the theory. The Sodality's work concentrated on the more powerful and well-funded Sunni factions, while chasing leads on the less powerful sects when they presented themselves. Cairo was looking to be as strong a lead as they'd had in over a year. That was going to complicate things. Blake was issued a new directive.

. . .

BLAKE AND OMAR connected over dinner in the Sodality dining hall.

"Omar, we need to talk about the mission to get Cairo."

"Yes, what is it?" Omar lowered his fork and gave Blake his attention.

"We've been issued new orders; Cairo is to be captured not killed."

Omar's features darkened and he took the news with silence.

"Look," Blake said, "I know what we agreed and I'm not one to break a commitment without good reason. Our research has revealed some evidence Cairo has been living a dual existence. As you say, he officially works for the Sunni Sura and Al Asifa specifically. However, we've uncovered contacts he's made with Hezbollah in Lebanon and Shi'a rebels in Syria. We think he could help us unlock some of the strategies coming out of Iran."

"I know of his complicity with the Shiites," Omar said, "but letting him live does not suit me and I believe you will regret it as well."

"I, of all people, can understand how you feel. I had this same conversation before I came after you in Cyprus. I know Cairo is not you and he's not going to willingly cooperate, but the people facilitating this mission want him alive and I'm bound to comply. You can still go with us, or you can be left here."

"I will go. If it is information you seek, get Cairo's briefcase. It is of well-worn brown leather and he is never without it. We all carried vital information and codes on us at all times, but I think what Cairo carries in that case may be just what you seek."

Omar pushed his unfinished plate of food toward the center of the table, rose and left without another word spoken.

• • •

CHILI PEPPER ARRIVED in the Golan Heights in a Twin Otter with the help of Mossad, who lit the primitive runway which was little more than a stretch of road. A UN marked van was ready to take them to Damascus.

The intel awaiting their arrival was a bit of a shock to the team. Surveillance indicated seeing a man emerge from the apartment building, indentified as the home of Tarboosh, while they were in the air. He matched the description of Cairo. Evidently, they had been awaiting the arrival of their target, who was already there. The team deployed.

• • •

THE APARTMENT BUILDING was on a block lined on both sides with similar four-story "walk-ups." A few had shops on the first floor and only a few had garages. It was not exactly an optimum environment for snatching a bad guy. Guido found a roof spot across the street and two doors south where he could set up his over watch on top of the entrance to the roof. In this position, he couldn't be seen from any angle but above. He got there by scaling the exposed plumbing running up the back of the building.

"Chili Three is in place and standing by. The show has not begun."

"Copy, Three, check back when the curtain goes up."

Blake, Omar, ReeRee, Daniel, and Neil sat in the UN marked van one block over from the target building. The plan was to wait in the cramped space until Guido reported Cairo and Yahya leaving. Local intel assets hacked into Yahya's phone and found a calendar entry for that evening for the theater and will-call reservations for two.

At eighteen-fifty: "Chili Three to One, the overture is being played. Images coming . . . now."

"Copy, Chili Three, stand by."

Neil brought up three photos taken through Guido's scope on his flex-slate video panel which he turned to show Omar.

"Is that Cairo?"

"It is that *ibn haram*."

Blake placed his hand on Omar's shoulder and looked him in the eye. "Omar, I know this is not how you wanted this to go down and I don't blame you. But, I must ask you to stay here with Neil while Daniel and I go get Cairo. I have Bill Garrison's word that once we've extracted from him what we need, he will be yours to do with as you please. Can you handle that?"

"It is as you say. This does not please me, but I don't see where I have options."

"We'll be right back with the trash."

Blake, Daniel, and ReeRee exited the van. The entire team was dressed and equipped as Free Syrian Army soldiers so they could move around the city without attracting attention.

"Chili One to all elements, curtain up in ten."

The incursion team entered the apartment building through the front door. ReeRee proceeded to and through the back door while Blake and Daniel headed up the stairs to the third floor.

Daniel was able to open the apartment door and disable the simple security alarm in under a minute.

Blake and Daniel divided the apartment, each taking half to search for Cairo's briefcase and any other potentially valuable intelligence items.

Thirty minutes later: "Chili One to Six, we've got nothing, any suggestions?"

Omar, unaccustomed to call signs, had to be nudged by Neil to respond to Blake's transmission, "Check out the dry room, the storage room over the bathroom"

"Did you just say what I thought you said?"

"Yes, there should be a door or a panel."

"Roger that, stand by."

Seemingly endless turmoil and war produced a culture in the Middle East where everyone kept survival stock to see them through the weeks when outside sources went off line. In many urban apartments where space was at a premium, the bathroom ceiling would be lowered to allow the addition of a storage area most commonly called a "dry room." As Omar suggested, that was precisely where Blake found Cairo's worn leather briefcase, tucked in a fifty pound sack of rice. Quickly checking inside, he found several thumb-drives, a ten-terabyte hard drive, a tablet, a 7.62 x 25 Tokarev, and about $50,000 in several currencies.

Bingo!

"Good call, Six. Standing by for curtain call."

This was the part of missions operators hated most; waiting.

At twenty-two-oh-six, Guido said, "Chili Three to One, the curtain's coming down."

"Copy."

Blake and Daniel had two minutes to get into position. Blake stood with his back to the wall where he'd be unseen when the front door was opened, Daniel stood in the shadows of the living room where he had a straight line of sight to the front door. He was armed with the same kind of dart gun he didn't get to use in Beirut, only this time the drug it delivered was much more powerful.

The front door opened and Cairo entered first. From there it seemed several things happened simultaneously. Yahya cleared the threshold, but before he could turn to close the door, Blake slammed it shut. As that happened, Daniel landed a perfect dart hit to Cairo's chest just above his heart. In that same instant, Yahya reached to the small of his back as Daniel's second dart pierced the breast pocket of his jacket, but he didn't go down.

BEFORE DANIEL COULD GET off another shot, Yahya had cleared his Makarov PM. He got it raised forty-five degrees toward Daniel, then he dropped as if he'd stepped into a hole. Standing two meters behind him, Blake lowered his suppressed 1911.

Damn.

"Chili One to all Chili elements. Time to take the limo."

Blake and Daniel gathered up Cairo and his briefcase. When they removed the dart from the dead Kurd's chest, they found it had struck him in his wallet. They headed to the street where the van would be waiting.

32

STRESS TENDS TO bring the real person within us forward. Cairo's essential cowardice surfaced the moment he awoke on the aircraft headed to Brno in The Czech Republic. Daniel went back to the front of the cabin to rejoin the rest of the team after administering the drug to arouse their captive. The first image to concenter before Cairo was the face of Omar Qobani.

He recoiled in his seat, almost putting his head through the closed window shade. Cacophonous Arabic erupted from his terrified face, "No! This cannot be! You are dead! You must be dead! I made sure you were dead! You bastard!"

His wide-eyed, dilated gaze moved to the man in the next seat up from Omar. "Who are you? Why am I here? Why . . . am I bound... there is pain in my side...did you shoot me? Where is Yahya?"

Blake looked to Omar and said, "This is the bad guy who's brought so much misery to you? I expected a man, not a scared child." Omar translated for Cairo, who spoke rudimentary English, but Omar wanted to be sure Blake's sarcasm wasn't lost on him.

"*Ya ibn asharmoota!*"

"You're in a very bad position to be insulting my mother. We haven't shot you *yet*. We just cut out the GPS chip our guy detected on you before we left. We found a goat to put it in; your guys are going to have fun chasing you down."

The situation started to settle into Cairo's brain. He sat up as best he could, looked Blake in the eye, and said in a much calmer, but still stressed, voice, "If you let me live, I have information you will find useful." He refused to look back at Omar, which was probably in his best interest.

• • •

WITHIN HOURS OF being in Sodality custody, Cairo's mouth was flowing like a breached dam. The credibility of the intel he gushed was verified by instruments, drugs, and established records.

Blake, Bill, and Omar assembled to pore over the collated information provided by Cairo. The light he shed on the Shi'a side of the OIC and their divergent agenda gave Blake and his operations division another prong of strategy. They would be able to work up through both sides of this two-headed beast to lop off both, leaving no one to take their places . . . at least for some time.

Bill and Blake noticed Omar fell silent during the last five minutes of the discussion prioritizing the target list.

Blake waved his hand before Omar's unfocused stare and said, "Omar, are you okay? Have we missed something here?"

"I don't think you've missed anything regarding the information provided by Cairo, but I have a suggestion you will probably not like."

Bill stood to stretch his legs. "Don't hold back, Omar, your trust factor around here is on a vertical ascent after the way you handled Damascus."

"If you really want to strike a blow that will cripple the entire Jihadi network and make going after the other players less difficult, you should kill America's Special Envoy to the OIC."

Bill fell heavily back into his chair and Blake's eyes widened.

"You must know he does not work in America's interests. He is one of the OIC's most prized infiltrators. Your people think because he was raised in your country since he turned five years old and was educated in your best schools that he is one of you. You could not even see past his public statements in support of Radical Islam because they were thinly cloaked by words like "moderate" and "tolerant." As with all of our infiltrators, you must read what they say in Arabic, not just what they are saying in English. He is the primary conduit between the OIC and the Jihadists on your soil; ISIL has been in your country for many years. Killing him would be to the global Islamic network what severing an artery is to the human body."

Silence prevailed as Blake and Bill considered the ramifications of Omar's proposal.

Before either could make the first objection, Omar, who was concentrating on one of the video panels mounted on the wall over Bill's shoulder, raised his hand in the universal sign of "hold up a minute."

Blake looked to his left and Bill swiveled in his chair one-hundred-eighty degrees to face the screen. The room's six panels arrayed on four walls displayed two fixed Intranet feeds and the others could display any video content desired, including every cable channel in the world. When they first entered the room, Omar put two Al Jazeera channels, Arabic and American, on panels where he could see them.

"The current discussion may be of no consequence . . . they are about to launch an attack on your capital. I'm afraid what I gave the Jews to buy my way here could prove to be their downfall. And, the thirty pieces of silver your Al Gore took from the Al Jazeera owners in Qatar when he brought their network to America may be yours."

Blake turned from watching Al Jazeera America to Omar. "Whoa, wait a minute, what are you talking about and how do you know?"

"Did you see the banner scrolling across the bottom of the Al Jazeera America screen a few seconds ago? That was the third time in the last ten minutes. Did you see the words "Pentagon," "Congress," and "Cattle?"

"I saw that crawler. It was a story about congressional funding for supplying beef to the military."

"Perhaps, but the Jihadists in America know what those carefully chosen words mean when combined with the other words in the sentence, that was a launch code and according to the rest of the message, you only have forty-eight hours to do something about it."

Bill was back to facing Omar. "Okay, what kind of attack; where and how?"

"You both know that several countries in the Middle East have been developing chemical and biological WMDs for some time now," Omar said. "While Pakistan, North Korea, and Iran have kept most of the world distracted with their nuclear programs, Iraq, Lebanon, Syria, and a few others have been working on lethal agents and ways to deliver them. About three years ago a scientist in South Lebanon refined a strain of anthrax for which there can be no inoculation or treatment."

"Plans were formulated two years ago to smuggle several hundred pounds of these spores through America's open Mexican and Canadian borders. The delivery devices are simple and innocuous using CO_2 canisters to aerosolize up to five pounds of the almost smoke-fine particles. Just one would be enough to kill more than a thousand people if released outdoors. Released indoors, that same device would kill everyone in a building the size of Harrods of London and render it uninhabitable indefinitely.

"This particular plan has a number of their embedded people in the Pentagon and U.S. Capital going to work in two days, each carrying one of these devices in their briefcases, backpacks, and the like. We have kept mostly quiet in America for the last five years and your guard has lowered, so these trusted people will not be searched. Mid-morning, the day after tomorrow, they will trigger their devices in unison. It will effectively decapitate your federal government, taking them off the world stage.

"What we gathered from Cairo puts the final piece in place. Most think Iran will attack Israel, and they will at some point, but this operation will allow Iran to send a downpour of nuclear and conventionally tipped rockets and missiles on Riyadh and Mecca with no concern of reprisal from the U.S. They will kill their rivals and seize their oil, but most important to them, it will ignite the chaos they believe will set the stage for the entrance of the Twelfth Imam and the end of Western civilization."

A few expletives filled the air before Bill said, "That puts us in a hell of a mess."

"How so, Boss? This is a gold mine and a chance to save thousands of Americans." Blake began to see young Sam and his mom in the recesses of his consciousness. "How could there be any question about what to do next?"

"Blake, this is where we must think strategically."

"I don't get it. Sorry." Blake glanced at Omar who was clearly on the same wavelength as Bill from the look on his face.

"We're facing what Churchill faced, in what we now know as the Coventry Blitz, during World War Two. They cracked Germany's most secret code, *Ultra*, and got their plans for bombing the English industrial town. He had to decide whether to reveal their possession of the code by foiling their plans, or let them bomb in hopes of using the code to ultimately defeat the Axis Powers." He paused to let that register then continued. "Do we reveal The Sodality and Omar by presenting this to the U.S. government, which may or may not believe us, or do we keep our secret status in hopes of totally crushing the global Jihadi network?"

CHARACTER LIST

ABU YOUSSEF: Abu Hamza's second in command

ALIA HUNTER: Blake's wife

ASAM: CIA driver in Beirut

AYMAN AL-ZAWAHIRI: The head of OIC operations

BASHAAR: Israeli agent/bike shop owner

BEN: General Sam's farmhand

LT. GEN. BILL GARRISON: Among the top leadership of The Sodality

BLAKE KERSHAW / JACOB HUNTER: Virginia born soldier – lead protagonist

LT. COL. BOB JOHNSON: Blake's former unit commander and new Delta commander

CAIRO: A member of Omar's terror cell

CECIL KERSHAW: Blake's father

CECIL SAM HUNTER: Blake's and Alia's son

DANIEL STEELE: Medic and interrogator on Blake's team

HARRY CHEE: comms and surveillance and one of Blake's best friends

HASSAN NASRALLAH: the leader of Hezbollah

SERGEANT MAJOR JAMES "REEREE" RANDALL: technology and intel analyst on Blake's team

JOE GUTHRIE: Kershaw neighbor and family friend

KATY KERSHAW GRIFFIN: Blake's mother

LOREN: Sodality operative and nurse

MAKKYIAH: Omar's favorite sister

MARIA: Sam's nanny

MOHAMMAD: Omar's older son

MUNA AL QOBANI: Omar's mother

NASSOOR: Suzan's family name

OMAR AL QOBANI / ABU AL-WAFÁ: Lebanese born terrorist – lead antagonist

GEN. SAM WILSON: Blake's college professor and mentor

SUZAN AL QOBANI: Omar's wife

TOSHO MUSASHI: Deputy Director of Operations for The Sodality

DR. VANCE GRIFFIN: Blake's surgeon and his Mom's new husband

YOUSSEF: Omar's younger son

GLOSSARY

Abu: Father of . . .

Al-Asifa: The Storm, Omar's terrorist group

BOLO: Be On the Look Out

EW: Electronic warfare

HUMINT: Human intelligence

IC: Intelligence Community

Imam: A Muslim cleric

Jannah: The Muslim equivalent of heaven

Jizya: Penalty tax as a penance for not being Muslim

JSOC: Joint Special Operations Command

Keffiyeh: Traditional Arab headdress

Klik: kilometer

QRF: Quick Reaction Force

SCI: Sensitive Compartmented Information

Sharia law: Strict Islamic rules for all areas of life

Shytan: Arabic for Satan

SIGINT: Signals Intelligence

SVTC: Secure Video Tele-conference

Ummah: The Islamic community

ABOUT THE AUTHORS

JERRY BOYKIN

In real life, Blake Kershaw is known as retired LTG of the United States Army, William "Jerry" Boykin. What makes the novel you've just read feel so authentic is found in the experiences of its authors. Thirty-six years of Jerry's life was spent fighting terrorists all over the world. He now fights them by speaking and writing, but his reach has not shortened and his effect has not been blunted.

The Coalition is a novel, but the fabrications and facts are hard to parse. That's on purpose.

Jerry wrote his memoirs back in 2008, and the book continues to sell very well. *Never Surrender: A Soldier's Journey to the Crossroads of Faith and Freedom* can be acquired most anywhere books are sold, where you'll also find his other books:

Danger Close: A Novel (2010)

Kiloton Threat: A Novel (2011)

The Warrior's Soul: 5 Powerful Principles to Make You a Stringer Man of God (Jan. 6, 2015)

KAMAL SALEEM

The story you've just read is based on the lives of two real and living people. The terrorist, Omar, goes by the name Kamal Saleem in everyday life. He was born and raised, just as The Coalition says, in Beirut, Lebanon. His childhood was bathed in the Muslim religion and at the age of seven, he was recruited into the Muslim Brotherhood.

Though much of *The Coalition* is fabricated, it is spun from the whole cloth of fact and extrapolation. Exposing the existential threat of radical Islam around the world and especially within America is Kamal's life mission, and no one is better equipped.

To understand who this man is and what makes him qualified to speak with such authority, get and read his book, *The Blood of Lambs: A Former Terrorist's Memoir of Death and Redemption.*

Available at: Koome Ministries

Koome Ministries (http://koomeministries.com/store/index. php?route=product/product&product_id=50)